VIRAGO
CLASSIC NON-FICTION

Angela Carter

Angela Carter (1940–1992) was born in Eastbourne and brought up in south Yorkshire. One of Britain's most original and disturbing writers, she read English at Bristol University and wrote her first novel, *Shadow Dance*, in 1965. *The Magic Toyshop* won the John Llewellyn Rhys Prize in 1969 and *Several Perceptions* won the Somerset Maugham Prize in 1968. More novels followed and in 1974 her translation of the fairy tales of Charles Perrault was published, and in the early nineties she edited the *Virago Book of Fairy Tales* (2 vols). Her journalism appeared in almost every major publication; a collection of the best of these are published by Virago in *Nothing Sacred* (1982). She also wrote poetry and a film script together with Neil Jordan of her story 'The Company of Wolves'. Her last novel, *Wise Children*, was published to widespread acclaim in 1991. Angela Carter's death at age fifty-one in February 1992 'robbed the English literary scene of one of its most vivacious and compelling voices' (*Independent*).

By Angela Carter

Fiction
Shadow Dance
The Magic Toyshop
Several Perceptions
Heroes and Villains
Love
The Infernal Desire Machines of Doctor Hoffman
Fireworks
The Passion of New Eve
The Bloody Chamber
Nights at the Circus
Black Venus
Wise Children
American Ghosts And Old World Wonders

Non-fiction
The Sadeian Woman: an Exercise in Cultural History
Nothing Sacred
The Virago Book of Fairytales (editor)
Expletives Deleted

NOTHING SACRED

Selected Writings

Angela Carter

A *Virago* Book

Published by Virago Press 2000

First published by Virago Press Limited 1982
Reprinted 1985, 1987, 1992, 1993

Copyright © Angela Carter 1967, 1970, 1971, 1972, 1974,
1975, 1976, 1977, 1978, 1979, 1980, 1981, 1982,
1983, 1989, 1990

This selection and all introductory matter
Copyright © Angela Carter 1982 and 1992

The 1992 revised edition included five new pieces:
'The Recession Style', 'Frida Kahlo', 'Louise Brooks',
'Love in a Cold Climate' and 'Alison's Giggle'

A CIP catalogue record for this book
is available from the British Library

ISBN 0 86068 269 2

Printed and bound in Great Britain by
Clays Ltd, St Ives plc

Virago
A Division of
Little, Brown and Company (UK)
Brettenham House
Lancaster Place
London WC2E 7EN

CONTENTS

Acknowledgements

All the following pieces were originally published in New Society, with the exception of these: 'The Mother Lode', which first appeared in the New Review; 'The Belle as Businesswoman', which first appeared in the Observer; the review of Anthony Alpers' biography of Katherine Mansfield, which first appeared in the Guardian; and the study of Colette, and the book review of Louise Brooks which originally appeared in the London Review of Books; 'Alison's Giggle' was first published in The Left and The Erotic, Lawrence and Wishart, 1983; 'Frida Kahlo' was first published by Redstone Press, 1989; 'Love in a Cold Climate' was given as a paper at a conference on the Language of Passion, University of Pisa, 1990.

I would like to thank both Paul Barker, and also Tony Gould, of New Society, who, over a period of fifteen years or so, never batted an eyelid and always corrected my spelling. Thank you.

Illustrations

The photograph on page 1 is of Angela Carter with her mother in 1944; the illustration on page 27 is a drawing from a Japanese comic; on page 59 is a photograph of Angela Carter in 1967 taken by Gil Chambers; on page 83 an advertisement from a Frederick's of Hollywood catalogue; on page 129 Louise Brooks, Lulu in G.W. Pabst's film Pandora's Box; on page 163 D.H. Lawrence as a baby.

1

FAMILY
ROMANCES

The Mother Lode

The first house in which I remember living gives a false impression of our circumstances. This house was part of the archaeology of my mother's mother's life and gran dug it up again and dived back within it when the times became precarious, that is, in 1940, and she took me with her, for safety's sake, with this result: that I always feel secure in South Yorkshire.

This first house of my memory was a living fossil, a two-up, two-down, red-brick, slate-tiled, terraced miners' cottage architecturally antique by the nineteenth-century standards of the rest of the village. There was a lavatory at the end of the garden beyond a scraggy clump of Michaelmas daisies that never looked well in themselves, always sere, never blooming, the perennial ghosts of themselves, as if ill-nourished by an exhausted soil. This garden was not attached to the cottage; the back door opened on to a paved yard, with a coal-hole beside the back gate that my grandmother topped up with a bit of judicious thieving for, unlike the other coal-holes along the terrace, ours was not entitled to the free hand-out from the pits for miners' families. Nor did we need one. We were perfectly well-off. But gran couldn't resist knocking off a lump or two. She called this activity: 'snawking', either a dialect or a self-invented word, I don't know which.

There was an access lane between the gate of the yard and the gate of the garden, so it was a very long trip out to the lavatory, especially in winter. We used chamber-pots a good deal – 'jerries' – cause of much hilarity due to the hostilities. My mother had a pastel-coloured, Victorian indelicacy which she loved to repeat: 'When did the queen reign over China?' This whimsical and harmless scatological pun was my first introduction to the wonderful world of verbal transformations, and also a first perception that a joke need not be funny to give pleasure.

Beyond the brick-built lavatory, to which we used to light our way after dark with a candle lantern, was a red-brick, time-stained, soot-dulled wall that bounded an unkempt field; this field was divided by a lugubrious canal, in which old mattresses and pieces of bicycle used to float. The canal was fringed with willows, cruelly lopped, and their branches were always hung with rags tied in knots. I don't know why. It was a witchy, unpremeditated sight. Among the tips where we kids used to play were strange pools of oleaginous, clay-streaked water. A neighbour's child drowned in one of them.

The elements of desolation in the landscape give no clue to the Mediterranean extraversion and loquacity of the inhabitants. Similarly, all this grass-roots, working-class stuff, the miners' cottage and the bog at the end of the garden and all, is true, but not strictly accurate. The processes of social mobility had got under way long before I had ever been thought of, although my mother always assured me I had never been thought of as such, had simply arrived and, as I will make plain, somewhat inconveniently, too.

We took this trip back, not to my mother's but to *her* mother's roots because of the War. My grandmother had not lived in her native village herself since she was a girl and now she was an old woman, squat, fierce and black-clad like the granny in the Giles' cartoons in the *Sunday Express*; because she, an old woman, took me back to her childhood, I think I became the child she had been, in a sense, for the first five years of my life. She reared me as a tough, arrogant and pragmatic Yorkshire child and my mother was powerless to prevent it.

My mother learned she was carrying me at about the time the Second World War was declared; with the family talent for magic realism, she once told me she had been to the doctor's on the very day. It must have been a distressing and agitated pregnancy. Shortly after she began to assemble all the birthing bric-à-brac, the entire child population of our part of South London was removed to the South Coast, away from the bombs, or so it was thought. My brother, then eleven, was sent away with them but my mother followed him because my father quickly rented a flat in a prosperous, shingle-beached resort. Which is why I was born in East-bourne, not a place I'd have chosen, although my mother said that if Debussy had composed *La Mer* whilst sitting on Beachy Head, I should not turn my nose up at the place.

So off they all went, my mother and my embryonic self, my brother and my maternal grandmother went with them, to look after them all, while my father, in a reserved occupation, and who, besides, had served the whole term of the First World War, stayed behind in London to work but he came down whenever he could manage it and that was very often because he and my mother were very attached to each other.

My mother went into labour in Eastbourne but when she came out of it we were on the front line because Dunkirk fell while I was shouldering my way into the world; my grandmother said there was *one* place in the world the Germans would not dare to bomb so we all shifted ourselves to a cottage that my father now rented for us next door to the one in which my great-aunt, Sophia, my grandmother's sister, and her brother, my great-uncle, Sydney, lived. And though the Germans bombed hell out of the South Coast and also bombed the heart out of Sheffield, twenty odd miles away from where we had removed, not one bomb fell on us, just as she had predicted.

Uncle Syd worked down Manvers Main Colliery. He was a tall, gaunt man of a beautiful, shy dignity, who had, I understand, originally wanted to be a bookie but whose mother had not let him. I remember him all pigeon-coloured, soft greys touched with beige, the colour of the clothes he was wearing when I last saw him, when he came down south for my gran's funeral. And a pearl tie-pin. And a gold watch-chain, across his camel-coloured waist-coat.

Sophie was a teacher. She had no formal qualifications at all, I think, had simply never left school but stayed on to teach the babies the three R's and did so until she retired in the 1950s, quali-fied eventually by experience, natural aptitude and, probably, strength of character. Besides, by then she had taught several generations of the village to read and write, probably taught most of the education committee to read and write. She, too, had a great deal of formal dignity; I remember how, unlike my grandmother, who had lived in London most of her life, Syd and Sophie both had very soft voices, country voices. Though we could hear Syd's cough through the wall, the dreadful, choking cough that all the men over forty in the village had.

The South Yorkshire coalfields are not half as ugly as they may seem at first glance. Rather like the potteries, they are somehow time-locked, still almost a half-rural society as it must have been in the early days of the Industrial Revolution. The wounded and despoiled countryside remains lush and green around the workings; sheep graze right up to the pit-heads, although the sheep I saw when I was a child were all black with soot, and Doncaster Market is far richer in local agricultural produce than the pretend-markets in Devon. There is a quite un-English pre-occupation with food; the pig is dealt with in a bewildering and delicious variety of ways but butter and cheese are good, too, and so is bread, the perfume of next morning's loaves nightly flavouring the air around the corner bakery.

The streets of the red-brick villages are laid out in grid-like parallels, cheapest of housing for working families, yet they manage to fold into the landscape with a certain, gritty reticence although it is one of gentle hills; there is none of the scenic drama of West Yorkshire, instead, a bizarre sense of mucky pastoral. The colliers were often famous poachers in their spare time. My granny taught me songs that celebrated the wily fox, the poacher's comrade, and his depredations of bourgeois farmyards:

Old Mother Flipperty-flop jumped out of bed,
Out of the window she stuck 'er 'ead –
'John, John, the grey goose is gone
And the fox is off to his den, oh!'

It is almost the landscape of D.H. Lawrence, almost that of the Chatterleys, Mellors was as tough on the poachers as only a true class-traitor could be. Lawrence ratted on it all, of course, Lawrence, the great, guilty chronicler of English social mobility, the classic, seedy Brit full of queasy, self-justificatory class shame and that is why they identify with him so much in British universities, I tell you. I know the *truth*. Him and his la-did-dah mother.

But I read *The Rainbow* a little while ago, searching for some of the flavour of the lives of my grandmother and her family eighty years ago, ninety years ago, in a village not unlike Eastwood, only a little more gritty, and there was Sophie, teaching school like Ursula Brangwen but making a much better job of it, I'm happy to say, perhaps since nobody sent her to Sheffield High School and taught her to give herself airs. At that, I hear my grandmother speaking in my head.

But Sophie *did* trek all the way to Leeds to go to art classes. Ruskin was a strong influence in these parts. To my knowledge, Sophie never drew or painted for pleasure when she was grown-up but she taught me the rudiments of perspective, and most of the alphabet, before I was five. Her father, my great-grandfather, had he owned a pub? At this point, they vanish into mist; there is a brewery in Sheffield with their family name, but it is a common enough name in South Yorkshire. Some connection was supposed to have been the cock-fighting king of the entire country but all this is irretrievable, now. I do not even know if they had seen better days, but I doubt it.

All the same, there was a beautiful parlour-organ in Sophie's pocket-handkerchief-sized front room and a grandfather clock so old it is now in the museum in Barnsley and a glass-fronted cabinet full of ancient blue-and-white china that must have been very fine because my mother always lusted after it but never managed to get her hands on it, in the end, because Sophie outlived her, to Sophie's grief. At night, the kitchen was lit by the dim, greenish, moth-like light of gas mantles; we took candles up the steep wooden stairs to bed. There was a coal range, that Sophie blacked; no hot water; a tin bath filled with kettles in which Syd washed off his pit dirt. There were no pit-head baths at Manvers Main until 1947, when the mines were nationalised.

Smelling of sweat and the sharp, mineral odour of coal dust, the miners came off the shift blacked up as for a minstrel show, their eyeballs and teeth gleaming, in their ragged jackets, braces, overalls, and I remember gangs of them exhaustedly swaggering home, so huge, so genial and so proudly filthy they seemed almost superhuman. I'm a sucker for the worker hero, you bet. I think most of them thought that nationalisation would mean workers' control and were justifiably pissed off when they found out it didn't, sold down the river by the Labour Party again, the old story.

Death was part of daily life, also; scarcely a family had not its fatality, its mutilated, its grey-faced old man coughing his lungs out in the chair by the range. And everybody was, of course, very poor. It wasn't until the 1960s that miners were earning anything like a reasonable living wage and by then Sophie had electricity, and a bathroom, and a gas-stove, benefits she accepted from the Coal Board without gratitude, for they were no more than her due.

Of course I romanticise it. Why the hell not. I cry with pure anger when I pass the pits beside the railway-line from Sheffield to Leeds; the workings, grand and heartless monuments to the anonymous dead.

We are not a close-knit but nevertheless an obsessive family, sustained, as must be obvious, by a subjectively rich if objectively commonplace folk-lore. And claustrophobic as a Jewish family, to which we have many similarities, even if we do not see one another often. I cannot escape them, nor do I wish to do so. They are the inhabitants of my heart, and the rhetoric and sentimentality of such a phrase is also built into me by the rich Highland sentimentality of my father's people that always made my mother embarrassed.

Since they were a matriarchal clan, my mother's side of the family bulked first and largest, if not finally most significantly.

My maternal grandmother seemed to my infant self a woman of such physical and spiritual heaviness she might have been born with a greater degree of gravity than most people. She came from a community where women rule the roost and she effortlessly imparted a sense of my sex's ascendancy in the scheme of things, every word and gesture of hers displayed a natural dominance, a native savagery, and I am very grateful for all that, now, although the core of steel was a bit inconvenient when I was looking for boyfriends in the South in the late fifties, when girls were supposed to be as soft and as pink as a nursuree.

Gran was ninety when she died ten years ago and wandering in her mind, so she'd talk about the miners' strikes of her girlhood, how they'd march in their pit dirt and rags with banners and music, they would play harmonicas, and she leaned out of the attics of the house where she worked as a chambermaid to watch. She would have made a bloody awful chambermaid, unnaturally servile until something inside her snapped.

My maternal grandfather, who died before I was born, originally hailed from East Anglia. There was no work on the farms so he joined the army and I think his regiment must have been sent to South Yorkshire to put down the strikes. Nobody ever told me this in so many words, but I can think of no other reason why he should have arrived there in time to meet my grandmother in the late 1880s or early nineties. He met her; they were engaged; and he was sent to India.

When we were clearing out my grandmother's effects, we found a little stack of certificates for exams my grandfather had passed in the army. In Baluchistan, in the Punjab, in Simla, he had become astoundingly literate and numerate. He must also have learned to argue like hell. Furthermore, he became radicalised, unless the seeds had already been sewn in the seething radicalism of the coalfields. He wrote to my grandmother once a week for seven years. Characteristically unsentimental, she threw away their letters, with their extraordinary fund of information about an NCO coming to consciousness through the contradictions inherent in the Raj, but she kept the stamps. What stamp albums my uncles had.

Of all the dead in my family, this unknown grandfather is the one I would most like to have talked to. He had the widest experience and perhaps the greatest capacity for interpreting it. There are things about him that give me great pleasure; for example, as a hobby, later in life, he enjoyed, though only in a modest, yet a not entirely unsuccessful way, playing the Stock Exchange, as if to prove to himself the childish simplicity with which the capitalist system operated. My grandmother thwarted this flair, she never trusted banks, she kept his money in mattresses, no really, in biscuit tins, on her person, in her big, black, leather bag.

When my mother's father came home, he married gran and joined the ILP and went to live in London, first Southwark, then Battersea, four children in a two-bedroom rabbit hutch. A yard, no garden. No bath. To the end of her life, my dotty aunt, who lived with gran, washed at the public slipper bath.

They were magnificently unbowed. There was a piano for the children, who played it; and did amateur dramatics; and went to see Shakespeare and Ibsen and Sybil Thorndyke in *Saint Joan* at the Old Vic. He was a clerk in the War Department; he used his literacy to be shot of manual labour, first rung up the ladder of social mobility, then worked in one of the first of the clerical trades unions. (Which may have been down a snake.) He got out of the slums, feet first, in his coffin; gran stuck it out until the street was demolished in 1956. Before the First World War, he chaired a meeting at which Lenin spoke. He shook Lenin by the hand and he led my eldest uncle, then a small boy, up to shake Lenin's hand, also. This uncle, however, grew up to adopt a political stance somewhat, as the Americans say, to the right of Attila the Hun.

My maternal grandfather died of cirrhosis. A life-long teeto-taller, the years in India had wrecked his liver. My grandmother's house was full of relics of the Empire, an ebony elephant, spears, a carved coconut shell representing the Hindu cosmogeny, beautiful shells from tropical seas, some with pierced messages: A Present From The Andaman Islands. Also enormous quantities of souvenir china, mugs, teapots and sugar basins commemorating every coronation from that of Edward VII to that of Elizabeth II; there was even a brace of scarlet enamelled tin trays from Victoria's Diamond Jubilee. Contradictions of English socialism. And enormous quantities of books, of course, some very strange: Foxe's *Books of Martyrs*, not one but three copies; Macchiavelli; *Twenty – Thousand Leagues Under The Sea*.

Their children were indefatigable self-educators, examination passers and prize-winners; those shelves were crammed with prizes for good conduct, for aptitude, for general excellence, for overall progress, though my gran fucked it all up for my mother. An intolerably bright girl, my mother won a scholarship to a ladies' grammar school, a big deal, in those days, from a Battersea elementary school. My gran attended prize-days to watch my mother score her loot with a huge Votes For Women badge pinned to her lapel and my mother, my poor mother, was ashamed because my gran was zapping the option her daughter had been given to be a lady just by standing up for her own rights not to be. (My mother used to sing The Internationale to me but only because she liked the tune.)

Perhaps my mother was ashamed of gran, as well, because gran talked broad Yorkshire until the day she died, all 'sithee' and 'thyssen' and ' 'e were runnin' like buggery'. When she gracelessly shoved a plate of food in front of you, she'd growl: 'Get it down thee,' with a dreadful menace. She taught me how to whistle. She hated tears and whining to no purpose; 'don't be soft,' she'd say. Though she was often wrong, she was never silly. When I or anyone else was silly, she would wither me: 'Tha bloody fool,' making a broken dipthong out of the long 'o'. How to transcribe it: half-way between 'foo-ill' and 'foyle'.

When I was eighteen, I went to visit her rigged out in all the atrocious sartorial splendour of the underground high-style of the late fifties, black-mesh stockings, spike-heeled shoes, bum-hugging skirt, jacket with a black fox collar. She laughed so much she wet herself. 'You wait a few years and you'll be old and ugly, just like me,' she cackled. She herself dressed in dark dresses of heavy rayon crêpe, with grey Lisle stockings bound under the knee with two loops of knotted elastic.

Her personality had an architectonic quality; I think of her when I see some of the great London railway termini, especially St Pancras, with its soot and turrets, and she overshadowed her own daughters, whom she did not understand – my mother, who liked things to be nice; my dotty aunt. But my mother had not the strength to put even much physical distance between them, let alone keep the old monster at an emotional arm's length. Although gran only actually lived with us in Yorkshire, and went back to her own house, five miles away, when we all went back to London at ceasefire, I remember her as always and ineradicably *there* until I was ten or eleven, by which time she was growing physically debilitated. I would have said, 'frail', but that is quite the wrong word.

But my grandmother's toughness was a limitation of its own. There was to be no struggle for my mother, who married herself young to an adoring husband who indulged her, who was subject to ill-health, who spoke standard south London English, who continued to wear fancy clothes long after she was both wife and mother. My grandmother could have known of no qualities in herself she could usefully transmit to this girl who must have seemed a stranger to her. So, instead, she nagged her daughter's apparent weaknesses.

With the insight of hindsight, I'd have liked to have been able to protect my mother from the domineering old harridan, with her rough tongue and primitive sense of justice, but I did not see it like that, then. I did not see there was a drama between mother and daughter.

At my wedding, my grandmother spread brown sugar on her smoked salmon and ate it with relish. She did not approve of the man whom I married because he wore a belt to keep his trousers up instead of braces. She wore her hair in a bun on the very top of her head and secured it with giant, tortoiseshell pins.

When I lived in Japan, I learned to admire their tolerant acceptance of the involuntary nature of family life. Love in the sense of passionate attachment has nothing to do with it; the Japanese even have a different verb to define the arbitrary affection that grows among these chance juxtapositions of intimate strangers. There is also the genetic and environmental snare, of course; they are they and you are you but, nevertheless, alike. I would have defended my mother with my grandmother's weapons.

I also admire the Russian use of patronymics, although matronymics would do just as well. Aeneas carried his aged father on his back from the ruins of Troy and so do we all, whether we like it or not, perhaps even if we have never known them. But my own father recently resigned the post to go and live with his own brother and father, moving smartly out of our family back into his own, reverting, in his seventh decade, to the youthful role of sib. At an age when most parents become their children's children, he redefined himself as the equal of his son and daughter. He can cope with the ruins of Troy very well under his own steam. He will carry *me* out of them, I dare say.

When my father attached a plastic paraqueet he'd bought at Woolworth's, his favourite shop, to a disused gas fitting on the ceiling of our kitchen in south London, my mother said to him in a voice of weary petulance: 'Age cannot wither nor accustom stale your infinite variety.' They had then been married for thirty-five years.

My father has lined the walls of his own new home with pictures of my mother when she was young and beautiful; and beautiful she certainly was, with a broad, Slavonic jaw and high cheekbones like Anna Karenina, she took a striking photograph and had the talent for histrionics her pictures imply. They used to row dreadfully and pelt one another with household utensils, whilst shrieking with rage. Then my mother would finally break down and cry, possibly tears of sheer frustration that he was bigger than she, and my father, in an ecstasy of remorse – we've always been very good at remorse and its manifestations in action, emotional blackmail and irrational guilt – my father would go out and buy her chocolates.

The gift wiped away all resentment, as it happened, because he often bought her chocolates when they had not rowed at all. He really loved to buy her things. She herself liked Harrods, especially the sale, and sometimes Harvey Nichols; he could never see the difference between these places and Woolworth's except the restaurants but, since they very much enjoyed eating lunch out, he was happy to go with her, happy to carry the packages.

A morning's shopping was a major trip and they could indulge their taste for this diversion freely because my father worked from three o'clock in the afternoon until midnight most days. My mother was sometimes sorry for herself, to spend all her evenings alone, but he would come back in the middle of the night with the next day's newspapers and make her tea and bring her biscuits and they would chatter away for hours in the early morning. If I was awake, I could hear them through the wall.

Their life together was one of daytime treats and midnight

feasts when I was usually at school or in bed. They spent more time alone with one another than do those parents who use children as an excuse for not talking to one another, and at times of the day when they were both rested and refreshed. No wonder they got on one another's nerves, sometimes. Then the storms were amazing. One could never rely on tranquillity, or not for long. But the rows were never conducted in hushed whispers – not of that 'pas devant les enfants' rubbish and were never about anything important, like money. Or me. At least, not yet. They were about nothing at all, a blocked-up lavatory, a blunt carving knife, my father's enthusiastic but not terribly scrupulous washing up. ('He'd like to wash up before we sat down to dinner.' 'He thinks we're going to want mustard all week.') Their rowing was the noisy music of compatibility.

It was a household in which midnight was early and breakfast merged imperceptibly into lunch. I can remember no rules, no punishments and I was expected to answer back. Once you were inside the door, a curious kind of dream-time operated; life passed at a languorous pace, everything was gently untidy, and none of the clocks ever told the right time, although they ticked away busily. We relied on the radio for the right time.

I went to look at this second house in which I lived last Christmas, the time for sentimental journeys. It was a good deal nicer than I had remembered it; a largish, even imposing Edwardian terrace house with a bay at the front and a little garden at the back, abutting on the Victoria-Brighton line. I had remembered it as smaller, poky, even. The entire street looked brighter and fresher than in the past; there were a few chocolate brown doors and the glimpse of a Japanese paper lantern in some front-rooms. Hardly any net curtains, now. The whole area is clearly on the up, again, but my father sold the house five years ago, sold it for peanuts, glad to be shot of it now she was gone, and went off.

My father and mother had settled down, as I've said, only a few miles away from her own family if 500 miles away from his, in Balham, then, in the mid-twenties, a solid, middle-class suburb, lace curtains, privet hedges and so on. They planted roses in the arid soil of the back garden and, unfairly enough, for my father only entered the garden to brutally prune them, they bloomed lavishly every June. They furnished the house with mahogany sideboard, leather settee, oak Welsh-dresser – handsome furniture; I wouldn't mind some of it, now, only my father abandoned most of it there. He has no affection for possessions, unless they have only sentimental value. He keeps my wedding dress. Perhaps in case I need it again. No, he'd want to buy me a new one. But my mother loved nice things and said, when I told her I was leaving my husband, to be sure to take with me some silver-plated tea-spoons she had recently given me. I did not and have often regretted it.

Here, when we came back from Yorkshire at the end of the War to a street that had had the residue of respectability bombed out of it, we settled into a curious kind of deviant middle-class life, all little luxuries and no small comforts, no refrigerator, no washing-machine, no consumer durables at all, but cream with puddings and terribly expensive soap and everything went to the laundry. And we were too messy for genuine discomfort. But our household became increasingly anachronistic as the neighbourhood turned into a twilight zone. A social-realist family life for those first seminal five years, that I remember so well because the experience was finite; but the next ten years have a far more elusive flavour, it was as though we were stranded, somehow. A self-contained family unit with a curious, self-crafted life-style, almost but not quite an arty one, a very unself-conscious one, that flourished on its own terms but was increasingly at variance with the changes going on around it. My mother's passion for respectability in itself became a source of deviance; she actively encouraged me to wear black woollen stockings at a time when they were a positive sign of depravity. She forbade me lipstick in the days when only female beatniks did not wear lipstick. It was all very strange.

Since my father returned to his granite village beside its granite sea, returned not only to his native land – Scotland – but to the very house in which he grew up, triumphantly accomplishing the dearest dream of every migrant worker, I understand better how it was we were always somehow askew. I felt like a foreigner because my mother had married a foreigner, although neither she nor he himself ever realised it. Being a Scot, he never fully comprehended the English class system, nor did he realise he might have been socially upwardly mobile within it; he only thought he had not done badly, which is a different perspective upon it. He had seen what Dr Johnson, one of my mother's favourites, called the finest thing a Scotsman can see, the high road to England, and he took it; did well enough; married happily; ushered into the world two satisfactory children. And then he went home, a symmetric life. He was a journalist until he retired and, of course, journalists have a curious marginality of their own, a professional detachment. If he had pretensions, they would have been to style as such, I think. He remains something of a dandy. He has always enjoyed walking sticks, bow ties, selects a different form of headgear for different hours of the day.

So we did not quite fit in, thank goodness; alienated is the only way to be, after all. After the War, my mother was always trying to persuade him to move to a posher neighbourhood, as if she thought *that* was the problem, and a house big enough to have my gran live with us, as though the presence of my gran would not have cancelled the whole thing out. Mum fancied Streatham; she had her eye on one house after another and sometimes we were so near to moving that she would pack all the books up in cardboard boxes, but, when it came to the point, my father wouldn't budge.

He entered into the fantasy of the thing wholeheartedly, of course; estate agent after estate agent was led up the garden path by him, but, when the crunch came, he could not do it. I don't think it was the idea of living with gran that put him off; they recognised that, in their ways, they were a match for one another and treated one another with deference. But he was himself utterly oblivious of the way the neighbourhood was growing seedy, the way the house was falling down. 'Nothing wrong with the old shack,' he'd say, as the woodworm gnawed the rafters and the defective wiring ignited small conflagrations hither and thither. 'Nothing wrong with the old shack.' Not defensively – rather, with the air of a man startled that anyone might think otherwise.

No. He hated the idea of a big mortgage. He liked to have the odd bob in his pocket, for chocolates, for ice-cream, for lunches out, for nice things for my mother, for his own modest dandyism, for occasional taxis that turned into taxis everywhere after my mother grew ill. Also, he particularly enjoyed travelling first-class on the railways – oh, those exquisite night-trains to Scotland! We could not afford a nicer house and all those luxuries besides; he did elaborate sums on the backs of envelopes to regretfully prove it – and then would climb back happily to the little eyrie he'd made for himself in the attic, where he would lie on his bed listening to obscure continental stations on his radio, smoking his pipe. 'What are you *doing*?' she'd shout from the bottom of the stairs. 'Contemplating the futility of it all,' he'd say. 'Contemplating the futility of it all, you old trout.'

When she told him how much she hated being called an old trout, he'd riposte: 'The trout is the most beautiful of fish.'

Charm is our curse.

So they stayed put. After he retired from work, maybe the only move he really wanted to make was back to Scotland but she would not hear of that, to put herself at the tender mercies of his kin and of the deathly climate. After I left home, they turned increasingly in on themselves; a good deal of the joy evaporated from their lives with my mother's illness and there was her own mother's death, a great blow since the umbilical cord had been ill-severed. But that was later, when I was no longer a child.

My mother and father were well on in their marriage when I was born, so there is a great deal about them I do not know and I do not remember them when they were young. My father was older when I was born than I am now. But he loved to take snaps in those unknown-to-me days and there are dozens of albums of pictures of my mother. My mother in wonderfully snappy clothes with my brother in his photogenic babyhood; with a black and white dog they had; in an open tourer my father subsequently crashed; on beaches; in fields among cornstooks; at the piano; playing at typing on my father's typewriter, every inch the dimpled twenties child-bride. My mother would often say what a lovely time she and my dad had before the War and there is the proof of it, trapped in the amber of the perpetual summer of the amateur photographer, redolent of a modest yet authentic period glamour.

I was not in any way part of that life, which had ended with the War; and the War ended with the onset of their middle-age. After the War, everything became drab and drabness, I think, instinctively repelled them both. Chaos, even mayhem, yes; but a drab, an austere time, no, even if my mother paid a lot of lip-service to respectability. Love and money only bought me lousy toys in the 1940s and I acceded to my brother's generation, I loved best his plush Micky Mouse and his books, *Alice* and *Pooh*. Times grew less hard; then, at last, I acquired in full measure all the impedimenta of a bourgeois childhood, a dolls' house, toy sewing-machine, red patent-leather shoes with silver buckles, organdie dresses and so on, but these were all a little spooky in a twilight zone and the Cold War was a curious time during which to recreate a snug, privileged, thirties childhood for their daughter. I went to primary school with apprentice used-car dealers and my best friend was a girl whose uncle trained greyhounds, whose mother was an office-cleaner. Not that my parents thought there was anything odd about that. And always, when I came home, the dream-time engulfed me, a perpetual Sunday afternoon in which you could never trust the clocks, until, when I was fifteen, she was ill. And never fully recovered, was never really well again, always an invalid now. And the music of their rowing died to a soft *obligato*.

She once warned me: 'Children wreck marriages.' I had not realised how essentially satisfied they had been with one another until then; not that I think she meant my brother and I had wrecked *her* marriage. If anything, we were too much loved, I don't think she resented us. I do not think she was registering a specific complaint, but making a grand generalisation based on observation, insight yet also, perhaps, she felt a dissatisfaction that was also generalised, had nothing to do with any of us, did not even exist as an 'if only', but as if, perhaps unconsciously, she felt she might have mislaid something important, in the eccentric, noisy trance of that rambling, collapsing house.

But then, I do not think you ever know you are happily married until you have been unhappily married, first.

She once gave me a rose tree.

It was for my tenth or eleventh birthday, I forget precisely which. It was a miniature rose tree, in a pot. I found it on my breakfast table, beside the other presents, of which there were a tremendous many, I was spoiled rotten. It was no more than a foot high and covered with pink blossom. I was a little disappointed with it, at first; I could not eat it, wear it or read it and I was a practical child and could not really see the use of it, though I could see it had been chosen with the greatest loving care.

I misunderstood my mother's subtleties. I did not realise this rose tree was not a present for my tenth birthday, but for my grown self, a present not for now, but to remember. Of all the presents of all the birthdays of a petted childhood, the rose tree is the one I remember best and it is mixed up, now, with my memory of her, that, in spite of our later discords, our acrimonious squabblings, once she gave me a perennial and never-fading rose tree, the outlines of which, crystallized in the transforming well of memory, glitter as if with properties she herself may not have been at all aware of, a present like part of herself she did not know about that she could still give away to me.

The New Review, 1976

As I say, my father returned to his native village shortly after the death of my mother. On the death of his own elder brother and sister, he entered into his inheritance — the family home. Or, rather, the home of his family; my father's house is not my house. It is his house and it was not until I was in my mid-thirties that I was invited to share the patriarchal aspect of the family romance with him.

My Father's House

The dining room, never used except as an ancillary larder, a cool place in which to set jellies and store meat, eggs and fish for the cat, is unchanged in essentials since I first came here in 1945. This room has the air of formal disuse characteristic of the Scots company room of its period. It was assembled long before I was born and is now almost an informal museum of north-east Scots twenties style, heirlooms and memorabilia.

There is a Brussels carpet; a table of brightly varnished, heavily grained yellow pine built by a long-dead local joiner; wallpaper with cowed brown flowers; a mirrored sideboard piled with souvenir china, plastic bowls, flowers made of wood chips bought from whining tinkers, paper bags containing outmoded hats, a number of plastic dolls in blonde wigs and kilts brought back as giftlets for my now deceased aunt by cronies who tripped off to other parts of Scotland for wee holidays.

There is a glass-fronted cabinet where my great-grandmother's tea service is stored, stately shapes of white china teapot and slopbasin – clearly a better class of goods was available in the town in the 1850s than it is today. My father says she was a school-teacher and used to ride to work in Banff, across the Deveron, on a little pony. Banff, a small, granite, seventeenth-century town so obscure that letters directed to it are sometimes sent to Banff, Alberta, in error.

I tentatively identify this great-grandmother as the one whose antique sepia photograph on the wall shows her, good God, in a long cloak, wimple and modified steeple hat – and not as if it were fancy dress, either, but her normal apparel, a little touch of the Aberdeen witches. (In 1636, rope to bind witches at Banff cost eight shillings, a lot of money in those days.) But this lady has the stern face of a kirk-goer. There's the picture of a distant uncle who was killed while working on a railroad in Canada. Other family photographs, no longer identifiable, are curiously poignant. Who the hell were they? Why are they not remembered?

There are several pictures in heavy frames on the walls. Two are reproductions in oils of stags in depopulated Highland glens, school of 'The Stag at Bay'. There are charcoal sketches of similar scenes in all the bedrooms, the house is crammed with stags, there's even a little stag, made of lead, on top of the massive clock in the master bedroom. But there isn't a landscape that could harbour a stag within a hundred miles of this place. It's a purely emblematic Scottishness, this scenery of crags, spruce, glens, tumbling waterfalls, untenanted except for deer, post-clearance landscapes, in which man is most present in his resonating absences.

Clearly this family was once heavily into the mythology of Scotland. I keep trying to interest my father in the history of his people, now he's gone back to them at last. I sent him John Prebble's books about Culloden and the Highland clearances. But he's cast them aside after a preliminary, dutiful browse. He says they're too bloody depressing.

During the whole of his fifty years down South, he never showed any interest at all in his own foreignness. None of your St Andrew's Societies and Burns Nights, those folkmoots of the middle-class Scots expatriate. There's a joke he's still fond of, though. Jock goes down South for an interview and, on his return, is asked: Did you meet any Englishmen, Jock? 'Och, no; I only met heads of departments.' A self-defensive joke. Like the sort of Jewish joke told by Jews. And back he went, eventually. Back home.

It's a long day's drive to a stag-haunted glen from the north-east seaboard – soon, it's rumoured, to be oil-rich. The main evidence of the oil rigs off Peterhead, thirty miles away, is the way property values round here have shot up. Fish and farming remain the basics. The *Banffshire Journal* (sub-headed *and Northern Farmer*) carries stories about the price of fish, the shortage of pigs, the scarcity of fat cattle. Headline: STRAW DESTROYED IN BLAZE. Another: PORTESSIE MAN PRESUMED DROWNED, after he was thrown from the deck of an Aberdeen trawler when an oil rig supply vessel – ah! – ripped an eight-foot gash in her port side. That's the only mention of the oil in this issue.

There is ancient and graceful Banff; and there is the mouth of the beautiful Deveron, 'sweet Deveronside'; and then there is

Macduff, where I come from. Correction. Where my father comes from: I am easily confused by my own roots. Where my father came from and went back to. Two towns separated by a river, and by invisible barriers of class. Brash Macduff was invented virtually as a new town by William Duff of Braco, afterwards first Earl of Fife, during the mid-eighteenth century. They were too busy putting in the harbour to even notice the Jacobite rebellion.

More to the point of this place than the crags and glens on the dining-room wall are the two fine colour prints of clipper ships in frames of birdseye maple. 'Whither, oh, splendid ship, thy white sails crowding, etcetera.' From these tight granite harbours, the clippers set sail for China, the immigrants departed for New Zealand.

I remember, about twenty years ago, a German training ship, some sort of triple-master schooner, put into Macduff harbour. It came floating like a tethered cloud past the little white toy-like lighthouse at the pierhead. It floated, it materialised, out of yet another vulgar, Technicolour, Cinerama sunset. The sun always goes down with amazing splendour over the Moray Firth.

I've never seen the town in such commotion before or since. Ancient fishers, with their flat caps, baggy trousers and characteristic rolling gait, thronged the foreshore, fêting the crew of the ship that shouldered aside the butch little fishing vessels with their touching names – the *Elspeth MacFee*, the *Rose in June*, the *Grace*, the *Fear Not*, the *Intrepid*. The ship came out of the past, carrying an invisible cargo of grandparents' memories. (Later, I think, it went down in the South Pacific.) That was something like an appropriate mythology.

I often wonder where the notion of the bustling industry of the Scots came from. Not from Macduff. They're competent, yes; but it's a sleepy town. Outside the church, there's a cross put up by the second Earl of Fife in 1783, whose pediment is inscribed thus: MAY IT FLOURISH AND LONG INCREASE IN NUMBERS AND OPULENCE WHILE ITS INHABITANTS GAIN THE BLESSINGS OF LIFE BY INDUSTRY, DILIGENCE AND TEMPERANCE. Wishful thinking on the part of the Anglo-Scots aristocracy, I'm inclined to think. 'Everybody takes things easy,' says the man who runs a taxi

22

service, and does a lot of business ferrying drunks home at closing time. Poverty used to make them work hard; they had to. Temperance was always a more notional than an actual virtue round here.

All the same, a godly town. 'If the Lord will, the word of God will be preached on the Lord's Day at 5 pm. All welcome.' So says the sign on the door of the Tabernacle. The North Sea is a killer and those who work upon it pray a great deal, with good reason. 'Lost at sea', 'Lost at sea', 'Lost at sea', reiterate the gravestones in the churchyard, gravestones of Andersons, Pattersons, Shands, names reflecting the Scandinavian influence on this stretch of coast between Aberdeen and Inverness, a region less plastered with phony tartan than a lot of Scotland. I ought to remember that on those occasions when I'm tempted to don the tartan myself.

A couple of generations of my father's family are buried in Doune kirkyard. A theoretical distaste for nationalism, and the knowledge that the Anglo-Scot is the very worst kind, sets up disagreeable tensions within me in the gull-echoing, green place where, with fine self-regard, the dead have their academic qualifications inscribed after their names, BAs and MAs from Aberdeen mostly. Nevertheless, there they are — uncles and grandparents — all degreeless, alas. And another generation back is buried a few miles up the coast, in Portsoy; that's David, who fought at the battle of Waterloo and married a French wife. The stone was erected by his sons in memory of 'the most genial and indulgent of fathers', or so it says; extraordinary epitaph for a Victorian pater-familias in the Calvinist north-east. Either black irony; or else it was true.

He used to live in an earth-floored cottage that now lies in picturesque ruin on the foreshore. We have our little pilgrimages. My father likes to drive out to Davy's grave, Davy's cottage, and we stand and look at the relics, and I try to pretend I don't feel the cold hand of mortality on my heart, of mortality and also of something else. For the circumstances of life in that cottage are unimaginable to me. My family history remains, in some ways, inaccessibly foreign.

It isn't just the great-grandparents who seem impenetrable,

either. My paternal grandmother would not light a fire on the Sabbath and piled all Sunday's washing up in a bucket, to be dealt with on Monday morning, because the Sabbath was a day of rest – a practice that made my paternal grandfather, the village atheist, as mad as fire. Nevertheless, he willed five quid to the minister, just to be on the safe side.

What fictional eccentricities are these? But all true, all perfectly well-documented. Everybody says I look just like my paternal grandmother, furthermore. I can't go out to buy morning rolls, those delicious regional specialities, without somebody who remembers the old lady grappling with me on the pavement and stressing the resemblance.

They're still a bit bewildered by my accent. My Aunt Katie used to explain, almost apologetically: 'Hugh marrit an English girl, ye ken.' And I'd stand there, smiling, feeling terribly, terribly foreign in that clean white town, under that clean, white, un-English light which is nevertheless, in some dislocated way, home – which is where my ain folk are from.

The Japanese have a phrase, 'the landscapes of the heart', to describe the Romantic correlation between inside and outside that converts physical geography into part of the apparatus of the sensibility. Home is where the heart is and hence a movable feast. We used to come here for family holidays when I was a child, but there was bad feeling over my wedding and I hadn't set foot in the place for fifteen years, nor felt the lack of it, until my father decided to go home after an absence of half a century that his ain folk did not even seem to have noticed, so instantly did the town absorb him again. And I felt entirely at home here, the first time I got off the bus beside the harbour again. Nothing, nothing had changed.

Unacknowledged but dreadful pressure of roots? Or the last result of rootlessness and alienation, when you can say – and mean it – 'Anywhere I hang my hat is home'?

'Even the native, who has spent his life among these pleasing amenities, and has every detail imprinted on his mind's eye, is fain, of a Sunday evening, to betake himself to some rising ground, to the Gaveny Brae or the Hill of Doune, and feast his soul for the thousandth time on the well-beloved landscape.' So observed Allan Edward Mahood in his immemorial guide to *Banff and District*, a book my father assures me he kept at his bedside through all his years of London exile. Our rich sentimentality, obverse side to our rigorous cynicism. My ain folk – though they are simple, poor and plain folk. So we proclaim with the characteristic disingenuousness of the colonialised.

Not that there's much nationalism of any kind in my family. When the Scots Nats seemed like so much Ealing comedy, long before they won the local seat, my late Uncle William was leaned on heavily for showing the Union Jack in his shop window at the coronation of Elizabeth the First of Scotland, and took it down for reasons only of pusillanimity. He didn't think his unimpeachable English connections were worth a broken window. England, half-English; Scotland, half-Scottish. Not much of a difference.

It's not even enough difference to make me a mongrel. I never really noticed the difference until I went back there, again, and found how different from home my home was. You don't choose your own landscapes. They choose you.

New Society, 1976

2

ORIENTAL ROMANCES – JAPAN

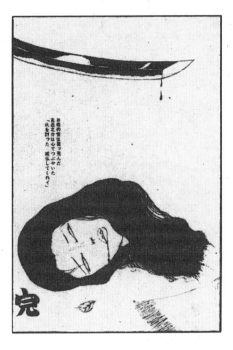

In 1969, I was given some money to run away with, and did so. The money was the Somerset Maugham Travel Award and five hundred pounds went further in those days; it took me as far as Japan — but, all the same, it didn't go much further than that, so there I stuck, for a while, making a living one way and another including working in a bar, and looking at things. Indeed, since I kept on trying to learn Japanese, and kept on failing to do so, I started trying to understand things by simply looking at them very, very carefully, an involuntary apprenticeship in the interpretation of signs.

I wrote the following pieces over the period of two years I lived in Japan, in the early 1970s, when Japan was just starting to boom. I went back for a holiday in 1974, when I went to the fertility festival described here; and will probably never be able to afford to go back again.

Why Japan, though? I wanted to live for a while in a culture that is not now nor has ever been a Judaeo-Christian one, to see what it was like.

In Japan, I learnt what it is to be a woman and became radicalised.

Tokyo Pastoral

This is clearly one of those districts where it always seems to be
Sunday afternoon. Somebody in a house by the corner shop is
effortlessly practising Chopin on the piano. A dusty cat rolls in the
ruts of the unpaved streetlet, yawning in the sunshine.
Somebody's aged granny trots off to the supermarket for a litre or
two of honourable saki. Her iron-grey hair is scraped into so tight
a knot in the nape no single hair could ever stray untidily out, and
her decent, drab kimono is enveloped in the whitest of enormous
aprons, trimmed with a sober frill of cotton lace, the kind of apron
one associates with Victorian nursemaids.

She is bent to a full hoop because of all the babies she has carried
on her back and she bows formally before she shows a socially
acceptable quantity of her gold-rimmed teeth in a dignified smile.
Frail, omnipotent granny who wields a rod of iron behind the
paper walls.

This is a district peculiarly rich in grannies, cats and small
children. We are a 60 yen train ride from the Marunouchi district,
the great business section; and a 60 yen train ride in the other direction from Shinjuku, where there is the world's largest congre-
gation of strip-shows, clip-joints and Turkish baths. We are a
pretty bourgeois enclave of perpetual Sunday wedged between
two mega-highways.

The sounds are: the brisk swish of broom on tatami matting,
the raucous cawing of hooded crows in a nearby willow grove;
clickety-clackety rattle of chattering housewives, a sound like
briskly plied knitting needles, for Japanese is a language full of Ts
and Ks; and, in the mornings, the crowing of a cock. The nights
have a rustic tranquillity. We owe our tranquillity entirely to
faulty town planning; these streets are far too narrow to admit

cars. The smells are: cooking; sewage; fresh washing.

It is difficult to find a boring part of Tokyo but, by God, I have done it. It is a very respectable neighbourhood and has the prim charm and the inescapable accompanying ennui of respectability.

I can touch the walls of the houses on either side by reaching out my arms and the wall of the house at the back by stretching out my hand, but the fragile structures somehow contrive to be detached, even if there is only a clearance of inches between them, as though they were stating emphatically that privacy, even if it does not actually exist, is, at least, a potential. Most homes draw drab, grey skirts of breeze-block walls around themselves with the touch-me-not decorum of old maids, but even the tiniest of gardens boasts an exceedingly green tree or two and the windowsills bristle with potted plants.

Our neighbourhood is too respectable to be picturesque but, nevertheless, has considerable cosy charm, a higgledy-piggledy huddle of brown-grey shingled roofs and shining spring foliage. In the mornings, gaudy quilts, brilliantly patterned mattresses and cages of singing birds are hung out to air on the balconies. If the Japanese aesthetic ideal is a subfusc, harmonious austerity, the cultural norm is a homey, cheerful clutter. One must cultivate cosiness; cosiness makes overcrowding tolerable. Symmetrical lines of very clean washing blow in the wind. You could eat your dinner off the children. It is an area of white-collar workers; it is a good area.

The absolute domestic calm is disturbed by little more than the occasional bicycle or a boy on a motorbike delivering a trayful of lacquer noodle bowls from the café on the corner for somebody's lunch or supper. In the morning, the men go off to work in business uniform (dark suits, white nylon shirts); in the afternoon, schoolchildren loll about eating ice-cream. High school girls wear navy-blue pleated skirts and sailor tops, very Edith Nesbitt, and high school boys wear high-collared black jackets and peaked caps, inexpressibly Maxim Gorki.

At night, a very respectable drunk or two staggers, giggling, down the hill. A pragmatic race, the Japanese appear to have decided long ago that the only reason for drinking alcohol is to become intoxicated and therefore drink only when they wish to be drunk. They all are completely unabashed about it.

Although this is such a quiet district, the streets around the station contain everything a reasonable man might require. There is a blue movie theatre; a cinema that specialises in Italian and Japanese Westerns of hideous violence; a cinema that specialises in domestic consumption Japanese weepies; and yet another one currently showing *My Fair Lady*. There is a tintinnabulation of chinking *pachinko* (pinball) parlours, several bakeries which sell improbably luxurious European pâtisserie, a gymnasium and an aphrodisiac shop or two.

If it lacks the excitement of most of the towns that, added up, amount to a massive and ill-plumbed concept called Greater Tokyo, that is because it is primarily a residential area, although one may easily find the cluster of hotels which offer hospitality by the hour. They are sited sedately up a side street by the station, off a turning by a festering rubbish tip outside a Chinese restaurant, and no neighbourhood, however respectable, is complete without them – for, in Japan, even the brothels are altogether respectable.

They are always scrupulously clean and cosy and the more expensive ones are very beautiful, with their windbells, stone lanterns and little rock gardens with streams, pools and water lilies. So elegantly homelike are they indeed, that the occasional erotic accessory – a red light bulb in the bedside light, a machine that emits five minutes of enthusiastic moans, grunts and pants at the insertion of a 100 yen coin – seems like a bad joke in a foreign language. Repression operates in every sphere but the sexual, even if privacy may only be purchased at extortionate rates.

There are few pleasant walks around here; the tree-shaded avenue beside the river offers delight only to coprophiles. But it is a joy to go out shopping. Since this is Japan, warped tomatoes and knobbly apples cost half the price of perfect fruit. It is the strawberry season; the man in the open fruit shop packs martial rows of berries the size of thumbs, each berry red as a guardsman, into a polythene box and wraps each box before he sells it in paper printed with the legend, 'Strawberry for health and beauty.'

Non-indigenous foods often taste as if they had been assembled from a blueprint by a man who had never seen the real thing. For example, cheese, butter and milk have such a degree of hygienic lack of tang they are wholly alienated from the natural cow. They taste absolutely, though not unpleasantly, synthetic and somehow indefinably obscene. Powdered cream (trade-named 'Creap') is less obtrusive in one's coffee. Most people, in fact, tend to use evaporated milk.

Tokyo ought not be a happy city — no pavements; noise; few public places to sit down; occasional malodorous belches from sewage vents even in the best areas; and yesterday I saw a rat in the supermarket. It dashed out from under the seaweed counter and went to earth in the butchery. 'Asoka,' said the assistant, which means: 'Well, well, I never did,' in so far as the phrase could be said to mean anything. But, final triumph of ingenuity, Megapolis One somehow contrives to be an exceedingly pleasant place in which to live. It is as though Fellini had decided to remake *Alphaville*.

Up the road, there is a poodle-clipping parlour; a Pepsi-Cola bottling plant heavily patrolled by the fuzz; a noodle shop which boasts a colour TV; a mattress shop which also sells wicker neck-pillows of antique design; innumerable bookshops, each with a shelf or two of European books, souvenirs of those who have passed this way before — a tattered paperback of *The Rosy Crucifixion*, a treatise on budgerigar keeping, Marx and Engels on England; a dispenser from which one may purchase condoms attractively packed in purple and gold paper, trademarked 'Young Jelly'; and a swimming pool.

I am the first coloured family in this street. I moved in on the Emperor's birthday, so the children were all home from school. They were playing 'catch' around the back of the house and a little boy came to hide in the embrasure of the window. He glanced round and caught sight of me. He did not register shock but he vanished immediately. Then there was a silence and, shortly afterwards, a soft thunder of tiny footsteps. They groped round the windows, invisible, peering, and a rustle rose up, like the dry murmur of dead leaves in the wind, the rustle of innumerable small voices murmuring the word: '*Gaijin, gaijin, gaijin*' (foreigner), in pure, repressed surprise. We spy strangers. *Asoka*.

New Society, 1970

People as Pictures

Japanese tattooing, *irezumi*, bears the same relation to the floral heart on the forearm of a merchant seaman as does the Sistine Chapel to the graffiti on a lavatory wall. *Irezumi* is tattooing *in toto*. It transforms its victim into a genre masterpiece. He suffers the rigorous and ineradicable cosmetology of the awl and gouge (for the masters of the art do not use the needle) until, unique and glorious in his mutilation, he becomes a work of art as preposterous as it is magnificent.

He is a work of art with an authenticity peculiarly Japanese. He is visually superb; he exudes the weird glamour of masochism; and he carries upon his flesh an immutable indication of caste. Bizarre beauties blossom in the programmed interstices of repression. The puppets of the Bunraku theatre are the most passionate in the world; *ikebana* is the art of torturing flowers. *Irezumi* paints with pain upon a canvas of flesh.

During Japan's first encounter with the West in the 1880s, *irezumi* was banned, but the practice continued to flourish and the laws were later rescinded. Though the art is now in its decline – due, perhaps, to the bourgeoisification of the Japanese working class – the ultimate pictorial man may still be seen in his rococo but incontestable glory on summer beaches around Tokyo; on construction sites; in the public baths of certain quarters; anywhere, in fact, where members of the urban proletariat take off their clothes in public.

Those who traditionally wore tattoos – carpenters, scaffolding workers, labourers, gamblers, gangsters – wear them still, almost as an occupational badge. Among gangsters and the underworld, the practice still has elements of an initiation rite since it is both extraordinarily painful, extremely lengthy and also exceedingly costly. It is often carried out at puberty.

There is an active appreciation of the art, which extends to other styles of tattooing. An Australian prisoner of war among the Japanese happened to have been extensively tattooed in the occidental style. He was often called out from among his comrades to exhibit himself to high-ranking visiting military and received many small gifts of candy, biscuits and cigarettes from his fascinated and admiring guards. This tattoo fancy extends to the collection of skins. In Tokyo there is a private museum, devoted to the display of particularly fine specimens. It is said that, in the heyday of *irezumi*, some enthusiasts would buy the pictures off a man's very back, making an initial down-payment and waiting for the demise of the bearer of the masterpiece to collect it. So, for the poor workmen, tattooing may have been a form of investment or even of life insurance.

The origins of the practice are lost, like the origins of the Japanese themselves, in the mists of antiquity. Tattooing is endemic to Oceania. One recalls Melville's 'living counterpane', Queequeg; and the English word, 'tattoo', is derived from the Tahitian. In the third century AD the custom was ascribed to the Wo, the aboriginal inhabitants of Kyushu, the southernmost of Japan's islands, by the Chinese chronicle, *The Records of Wei*: 'Men, great and small, all tattoo their faces and decorate their bodies with designs . . . They are fond of diving in the water to get fish and shells and originally decorated their bodies in order to keep away large fish and waterfowl. Later, however, these designs became merely ornamental.'

Irezumi has recently been primarily the pursuit of the lower classes but the Edo era (1603-1867) was the classical age. Even the great artist, Utamaro, forsook his woodblock prints in order to design a great number of tattoos. Tattoo contests were held, where firemen, artisans, palanquin-bearers, and dandies of both the merchant and the samurai class, vied in the display of their colours. The geishas of the pleasure quarters were often tattooed with remarkable finesse, especially on the back. In one of his short stories, the modern novelist, Junichiro Tanizaki, with characteristic acumen, ascribes a socially acceptable, but extremely active, sadism to a tattoo artist of the period: 'His pleasure lay in the agony men felt . . . The louder they screamed, the keener was Seikichi's strange delight.'

Today's favourite designs are still based on those popular in the eighteenth and nineteenth centuries. They include the Dragon, giver of strength and sagacity; the Carp (perseverance); folk heroes like the infant prodigy, Kintaro, who stands for success; Chinese sages and Japanese deities. If there are relics of superstitions behind these choices, they are as tenuous as those behind the names of Japanese baseball teams – the Hiroshima Toyo Carp, the Chunichi Dragons, the Osaka Tigers. Many designs have no such significance but are chosen only for their intrinsic beauty. Flowers. The sea. Lightning. Famous lovers. Young ladies astonished by snakes.

Traditionally, the Japanese have always felt a lack of interest, verging on repugnance, at the naked human body. Lady Murasaki, the eleventh-century novelist, wrote with a shudder of distaste: 'Unforgettably horrible is the sight of the naked body. It really does not have the slightest charm.' Even the erotic actors in the pictorial sex-instruction manuals of the Edo era rarely doff their kimono. The genitalia, bared, are rendered explicitly enough, but the remainder of the human form is heavily draped, either because it was considered irrelevant to the picture's purpose or because nobody ever told the Japanese the human form was supposed to be divine.

Modern Japanese men have come to terms with the female nude, to a certain extent, in that there is now an active appreciation of its erotic quality – as though they said, with Donne: 'Oh, my America! My new found land!' But the indifference of 2000 years, whatever created this indifference, lends a peculiarly borrowed quality to the reaction to, for example, a strip-show.

Now, a man who has been comprehensively tattooed – and the *irezumi* artist is nothing if not comprehensive – can hardly be said to be naked, for he may never remove this most intimate and gaily coloured of garments. Stark he may be, but always decent, and therefore never ashamed. He will never look helplessly, defence-lessly, indelicately, nude. This factor may or may not be important in the psychological bases of *irezumi* − which provides the poten-tially perhaps menacing human form with an absolute disguise. In Japan, the essence is often the appearance.

A tattooed Japanese has, in effect, been appliquéd with a garment somewhat resembling a snugly fitting Victorian bathing costume. The finished ensemble covers the back, the buttocks, both arms to the elbow and the upper thigh. The middle of the chest, the stomach and the abdomen are usually left in the natural state. This enhances, rather than detracts from the 'dressed' look, because the bare skin, incorporated into the overall design acquires an appearance of artificiality.

This is the method of *irezumi*. First, the design is selected, possibly from a chapbook of great antiquity. Then the design is drawn on the skin with black Chinese ink, or *sumi*, which gives its name to the technique. *Irezumi* is derived from *sumi* and *ireru*, which means 'put'. The dye is then applied, following these out-lines. A series of triangular-shaped gouges or chisels are used. The full-dye brush is kept steady by the little finger of the left hand, while the gouge is held in the right, rubbed against the brush, then pushed under the skin. This is repeated, until a thick, clear line is achieved. To keep the working surface clean, the master must wipe away blood all the time. Finally, using the full, tradi-tional palette, he works the design into the epidermis.

The traditional palette remains that of the Edo era. The primary tint is, again, *sumi*, which turns an ineffable blue under Japanese skin. Green is also used, together with a light blue and a very subtle red of such extraordinarily excruciating properties that the client can tolerate only a few new square inches of it a week. The brush, and the human form on which it works, together dictate a curvilinear technique. The design flows around the body with the amorous voluptuousness of Art Nouveau. There can be no straight lines in *irezumi*. The effect is that of coarse lace. It is an overall, total and entire transformation.

It is this absolute sense of design that is unique to *irezumi*. Not the eclectic variety of the tattoo produced by the needle − a dragon here, a tombstone marked 'Mother' there, and, on the biceps, the name 'Mavis' surrounded by rosebuds. The master-pieces of the European tattooist are essentially imitative of paint-ing. If they utilise the nature of the body on which they are depicted, it is by way of a happy accident – as when a tattooed hunt follows, in full cry down a man's back, the fox which is about to disappear into his anus. There is nothing whimsical about *irezumi*. No slogans. No skulls or daggers.

It may take as long as a year of weekly visits to a tattooist before the *œuvre* is complete. These visits will last as long as the customer can endure them, perhaps several hours. The process of covering large areas of skin with a single pigment can be extremely painful. Soreness and itching are concomitant with the growth of the garden on one's skin. *Il faut suffrir pour être belle.*

The tattoo-masters themselves tend to inherit the art from their fathers. The apprenticeship is long and arduous, and requires a high degree of artistic skill. They are conscious of the archaic dignity of their profession and may be found in the old-fashioned quarters of Tokyo, where they still cultivate the hobbies of ancient Edo (Tokyo's name before the Meiji restoration), such as keeping crickets in cages and breeding songbirds.

Irezumi is a favourite motif in popular art. Japan produces, for her domestic market, a number of leisurely sagas about the native gangster, the *yakusa*. The word, 'gangster', with its overtones of Capone, does not do full justice to these racketeers, who wear kimonos and often fight with swords. Even today they possess a strange kind of outmoded respectability. The *yakusa* films are usually set in the thirties, though the only indications of period may be the occasional western-style suit, pick-up truck or revolver. The heroes will display handsome, though greasepaint, *irezumi* as a simple indication of *yakusa* status.

The motif of the tattooed bride, the girl from the gangster class or the brothel, who has successfully 'passed' and tearfully reveals the evidence of her past on her wedding night, is not infrequent. Involuntary tattooing, for both men and women, is also a recurring motif. They may be tattooed as punishment for the infringement of group rules, or from revenge. Women are also stripped and lengthily tattooed in certain kinds of blue movie. The tattoo-master, with madly glittering eye, and awl poised above the luscious flesh of his defenceless prey, appears in many stills in the series of publications called *Adult Cinema – Japan*, among pictures of young ladies hanging upside down from ceilings during operations for amputation of the breast.

Masochism and sadism are different sides of the same coin, and perhaps a repressive culture can only be maintained by a strong masochistic element among the repressed. In Japan it is rare to hear a voice raised in anger, and rarer still to see a fight in public. It is considered subtly offensive to show the teeth when smiling, for a public display of teeth may be mistaken for a menacing snarl. If I am angry with my friend, not only do I never tell him so, I probably never speak to him again. More Japanese die of apoplexy than from anything else, as though they have bottled up their passions and bottled them up and bottled them up . . . until one day they just explode.

Perhaps one must cultivate masochism in depth if one is to endure a society based on constant expressions of the appearance of public goodwill, let alone try to maintain it. And, though it is difficult to ascertain the significance of *irezumi*, it is almost certainly one of the most exquisitely refined and skilful forms of sado-masochism the mind of man ever divined. It survives strangely but tenaciously in modern Japan.

New Society, 1970

Once More into the Mangle

They contain practical and explicit advice on sexual problems, and glossy, full-page nudes to cut out and pin up. The nudes are equipped with a variety of phallic props (French loaves or those round-headed Japanese dolls), and they all wear faintly anxious smiles, as if to say: 'Am I being erotic enough?' with that prim lack of inhibition peculiar to the Japanese. Full-page ads feature chubby, immensely trustworthy-looking men holding aloft bottles of magic elixir while demanding: 'Come too quickly? Having trouble with *your* erection?' One can see at a glance these Japanese comics are not for children.

Indeed, from their contents, they would appear to be directed either at the crazed sex maniac or the dedicated surrealist. The picture strips are a *vade mecum* to the latent content of life – pictorial lexicons of the most ferocious imagery of desire, violence and terror, erupting amid gouts of gore, red-hot from the unconscious. However, it is respectably-suited Mr Average who buys them to flick through on his way home to peaceful tea, evening television and continuous, undisrupted, absolute propriety.

The incidence of death, mutilation and sexual intercourse remains roughly constant in Japanese comic books, whatever the narrative. Each book is an anthology of several stories, plus pin-ups, a doctor's column and humorous cartoons. Though there are no specific war comics in Japan, there are often war stories in these comics (and when they deal with the Pacific War, they are often extremely anti-Japanese): no specific horror comics, but the heritage of the *kwaidan* (the ghostly tale and its hideous goblins) cannot be concealed. On the whole, the adult comics deal either with sex and violence against a background of perspectives of skyscrapers, iconographic representations of present-day Tokyo; or they deal with sex and violence among the pine forests, castles and geisha houses of the glorious but imaginary past. They are printed in black and white, with an occasional use of red, on the usual absorbent paper.

The comics of modern life often contain stories based on incidents which actually happened: the exploits of blackmailing bar-hostesses, of bank robbers, of gangsters, of embezzlers and of the abductors of school girls. School girls are a perennial bloom in Japanese erotology, because of their distinctive uniforms, middy blouses, pleated skirts and black stockings, clearly designed by Colette's first husband.

The narratives are stylistically banal and, in the international habit of low art, often take time off to moralise – though the tenor of this moralising can bring the outsider up with a start. Two young girls, in floppy hats, long skirts, high boots, bleached hair and false eyelids, abandon themselves to dissipation. They attend pot parties (where the strip suddenly goes into negative, as in an old-fashioned *avant-garde* movie); fornicate with pop singers; find only ennui; and conclude their careers by jumping, hand in hand, off a bridge. The last picture, where in mid-air, they endearingly clutch their hats, has this caption: 'For life is as fleeting as the dew in the morning and the world is only the dream of a dream.'

The technique of all the comics seems to derive rather from the cinema than from American comic-book art, just as the themes relate more to the B feature film than to the self-conscious whimsy of the super-hero comics. Since the strip, as a form, is essentially a series of stills, unfolding only in the personal time of the reader, the effect is one of continuous static convulsion. This is a condition sufficiently approximating to that of modern Japanese society.

Typically, the strip begins with a pre-credit sequence, sometimes spread over two pages. In the period stories, this may show a detailed, picturesque and action-packed panorama of a battle or an execution. In a modern story, it may show the climax of a horse race or a boxing match, or the hero or heroines, or both, in a striking pose (the heroine lying on her back perhaps, with a racing car roaring out between her legs). This is an overture or appetiser.

The narrative itself is composed in a series of long-shots, close-ups and angle-shots, with an elaborate use of montage. A typical montage sequence in a samurai comic might show: a bird on a bare branch against the moon; the dragon-tailed eaves of a castle roof; an eye; mouth; a hand holding a sword. Some use is also made of techniques equivalent to panning or tracking shots: for example, a series of different sized and shaped shots of a night sky with moon and clouds.

It would be possible to use any of the stories as an unusually detailed shooting script. Latterly, there has been a vogue in Japan for what looks very much like comic-book versions of Italian

Westerns, another form that has a heightened emotional intensity and stylised violence.

Some artists, however, use elements of traditional Japanese graphic art. Until the twentieth century, there was a flourishing trade in pictorial chapbooks, detailing heroic adventure and tales of life in the brothel quarters. The Japanese script itself is more of a visual medium than the Roman one and tends to sharpen the visual sensibility. The comic books, however transmuted, do not in themselves represent a complete break with tradition or reveal the beginnings of a post-literate period. But it is some indication of the mental relaxation they offer that particularly obscure Chinese characters, when they occur in headlines (though not, for some reason, in the text), often have their phonetic transcription in the syllabic *hirogama* printed in little letters beside them.

The period stories especially often borrow their graphic line from the past. This makes them more beautiful than the modern stories. They also sometimes use calligraphic insertions in especially breathtaking scenes, rather than putting the words in balloons coming from the actors' heads.

What is actually going on in the pictures often looks rather odd to me because I cannot read Japanese. When a translation is provided, it usually turns out to be worse than I could have imagined. Why isn't this girl fighting back during a gang rape? Because they forethoughtfully dislocated all her limbs, first. Why is this weeping old lady in bed with this wild-eyed boy? She is his mother; she has given herself to him as rough-and-ready therapy for his persistent voyeurism. Can this really, truly, be a closeup of a female orifice? Yes. It can.

One also finds the marvellous.

The ceiling of a castle hall is pierced with swords, each grasped in a severed hand that drips blood onto the floor below.

A man the size of a flea plants a kiss on the nipple of a giantess as though it were a flag upon a virgin peak. Waking, she cracks him between her fingers.

A feudal lord, afflicted with ulcers, sees the head of the son he has murdered rising up out of each pustule. In a fatal exorcism attempt, he vigorously scoops the damned spots out with his sword until he falls, gashed in his entirety.

The samurai comics offer the most stunning harvest of sadism, masochism, nervous agitation, disquiet and dread, perhaps because the in-built mythic quality of the pseudo-historic time with which they deal excites creative energy. The hieratic imagery occasionally stuns. The virtue of a low-art form is that it can transcend itself. An artist named Hachiro Tanaka stands out from the visual anonymity of his genre by a style of such blatant eroticism and perverse sophistication that, in the West, he would become a cult and illustrate limited editions of *A Hundred and Thirty Days at Sodom*.

Tanaka perpetrates lyrically bizarre holocausts, in décors simplified to the point of abstraction. His emphasis on decorative elements – the pattern on a screen; on a kimono; that of the complication of combs in a girl's hair – and his marked distortion of human form, create an effect something between Gustav Klimt and Walt Disney. His baby-faced heroines typify Woman as a masochistic object, her usual function in the strips.

Formed only to suffer, she is subjected to every indignity. Forced to take part in group sex where it is hard to tell whose breast belongs to whom, her lush body unwillingly hired out to reptilian and obese old men, the eyes of a Tanaka woman leak tears, and her swollen lips perpetually shape a round 'o' of woe, until the inevitable denouement, where she is emphatically stuck through with a sword, or her decapitated but still weeping head occupies one of his favourite freeze-frames. But, whichever way the women go, they all go through the mangle – unless they are very wicked indeed; when they obey the Sadeian law and live happily ever after.

If the ravaged dove is the norm, Woman in the strips is nevertheless a subtly ambiguous figure. One series specialises in erotic futurology. Again, the artwork is at a high level. The latent content presumably reflects the fears that haunt the doctor's columns. ('How can I enlarge my penis?') A race of superwomen has by-passed the male in its search for sexual gratification, and, in designs of a peculiar purity, uses devices, masterpieces of Japanese technology, such as chairs with breast-massaging hands, and electronic lickers. These last are elongated, quivering tongues on legs that produce spasms of extraordinary delight, though (significantly) they often fuse.

In another context, a fat harpy lolls on a cushion of little, crushed men in blue business suits; into her ravenous mouth she crams TV sets, washing-machines and all the other booty of the modern industrialised society. Again, an old woman crouches over a sleeping boy, painting a young face on top of her own withered one with juice extracted from her victim. A culture that prefers to keep its women at home is extremely hard on the men.

But human relations either have the stark anonymity of rape or else are essentially tragic. Even at the level of the lowest art, the Japanese, it would seem, cannot bring themselves to borrow that simplistic, European formula: 'then they lived happily ever after.'

The girl dies from her rape in the arms of the knight who saves her; he walks off alone, Hemingwayesque, into a lonely landscape under a waning moon. The girl and the knight murder the lord who sold her to the brothel; they immolate themselves. The deserted bar-girl consumes sleeping pills. Love is a tragic, fated passion; yet, still, heroically, they love. Japan's is a very romantic culture, even if the Japanese jab enormous daggers in the bellies of the comic-strip girls, and flay them alive, and crucify them, and even jump on them six or seven at a time.

The narratives are interspersed with humorous cartoons. A man raises his bowler hat to reveal a bald head topped with a nipple. A determined lover sharpens his penis with a knife, while a girl watches with justifiable apprehension. An extraordinary cartoon, revealing God knows what stresses in the inflexible family structure, shows a baby at the breast sucking its mother literally dry – until she is nothing but a deflated bag of skin. Unabashed scatological humour proliferates. A man rises above the door of a cubicle propelled by a rising mountain of his own excrement; unperturbed, he continues to read his newspaper. A man strains and strains and eventually excretes his entire bowel. (The indigenous floor-level, seatless lavatory invites a close and painful relationship with one's own shit.)

Essentially, the comic books are plainly devoted to the uncensored, raw subject-matter of dream. They are obtainable at any bookstall for about 10p. They are not meat for intellectuals; when Yukio Mishima disembowelled himself in public, he can hardly have been influenced by the delirious representations of *seppuka* in the comic books. They are read at idle moments by the people whose daily life is one of perfect gentleness, reticence and kindliness, who speak a language without oaths, and where blasphemy is impossible since the Emperor abdicated his godhead. Few societies lay such stress on public decency and private decorum. Few offer such structured escape valves.

In imported editions of *Playboy* and in the home-produced nude and adult cinema magazines, pubic hair, if ever it appears by chance, is scrupulously blacked out with ink; the male genitalia, unless in a comic context (a man bowling a row of penises with a ball shaped like a pair of testicles), might not exist. A knight disgarbs to reveal loins as marmoreal as those in Blake's 'Bright day'. Another paradox.

New Society, 1971

Poor Butterfly

A friend of mine, who is an English teacher of English, asked one of his Japanese students: 'What is the quality that you would require in a wife?' The student, a young lawyer who had graduated from one of Japan's best universities, replied in all seriousness: 'Slavery. I can get everything else I need from bar-hostesses.'

I recently visited a hot springs resort in the mountains near Tokyo; a spot where companies hire hotels to accommodate employees' annual outings. The town was full of souvenir shops, strip-shows and shooting galleries. Most of the latter were deserted, but one was crowded with laughing, shouting men. On examination, the targets at which they aimed their air-guns proved to be small, china statuettes of naked and beautiful women. If you shattered a nude Venus with your pellet, you received, as a prize, a large, cuddly, fluffy toy. This seemed to me a fitting parable of the battle of the sexes in Japan. True femininity is denied an expression and women, in general, have the choice of becoming either slaves or toys. Not long after this epiphanic revelation, I found myself in the front line of the battle.

The *mama-san* explained that, as a special attraction during the festive season, she had originally intended to dress her fifteen resident hostesses in colourful national costumes from all over the world. Owing, however, to a printer's error, the postcards she commissioned to advertise her special attraction read: 'During the days before Xmas, your drinks will be served by charming and attractive hostesses . . . from all over the world.' Therefore she had to go out and search for a clutch of foreigners and she was prepared to pay well over the odds for them, since the notice was so short – 30,000 yen, about £35 sterling, for five nights' work in shifts of two and a half hours.

'This must be the only country in the world where it's cheaper to buy women than to do two bunches of advertising,' said Suzy, a friend who came from Long Island and who once worked as a hostess in a club where an amorous customer, whilst giving her a goodnight kiss, bit her lip so savagely the blood spouted across the room. She also worked, another time, in a club that had a special games room full of pin-ball machines where one directed one's balls towards the pictured orifices of women, and so on.

Our bar was called 'Butterfly', and it was in the most expensive and allegedly exclusive area of Tokyo night life, the Ginza. It was about the size of a largish studio apartment in Hampstead and somewhat tastefully panelled in beige pseudo-wood, with two chandeliers in a tiered, wedding-cake style. A whole lot of tinsel, a white Christmas tree fabricated ingeniously from synthetics, and the presence of Suzy and myself announced that the holiday was at hand. Some of the fifteen hostesses who worked there all the time were indeed decked out in subtly Japanified saris, cheong-sams and other exotic clothing – including one extraordinary costume consisting of a turquoise-satin, crotch-length shift, which had a multiplicity of abdominal slits. 'Harem-style', said the wearer.

However, the hostesses were lumpy girls, on the whole, and, as they say about race-horses, aged. The *mama-san*, a kimono'd pouter pigeon, had the slightly harassed, professional joviality of a woman who has not yet put enough by for her old age − though her place, handsomely subsidised as it was by the Japanese government via the expense account system, was very plainly coining it.

In most bars, the regular visitor purchases his own bottle and drinks from that. But as the drinks are all poured out by a hostess, (there may be as many as five hostesses at a single table at any one time) and also because all the girls quite freely order extras − peanuts, dried fish, chocolate, and so on − the customer has no means of estimating the size of his bill. This will include, of course, a generous charge for the hostesses. In Japan, it is notoriously bad form to question a bill, anyway. Besides, the company usually pays. However, the bill for an evening at 'Butterfly' might cost, perhaps, £30 or £40 − an evening of innocent fun, watered whisky and the company of complaisant young women trained in the art of decorously lewd conversation: the last vestige of the traditional arts of the multi-talented geisha.

Clearly, though, the hostesses do not really need to speak and no doubt soon will cease to do so. They are not selling their charms; they do not usually sell their flesh. If they do, it is strictly a private arrangement; and since, at all costs, the pretence must be maintained that they are not *de facto* prostitutes, they rarely get honest cash paid down for the transaction, but only something useless, like a kimono.

It would be easy to construct a blueprint for an ideal hostess. Indeed, if the Japanese economy ever needs a boost, Sony might contemplate putting them into mass production. The blueprint would provide for: a large pair of breasts, with which to comfort and delight the clients; one dexterous, well-manicured hand for pouring their drinks, lighting their cigarettes and popping forkfuls of food into their mouths; a concealed tape-recording of cheerful laughter, to sustain the illusion that the girls themselves are having a good time; and a single, enormous, very sensitive ear for the clients to talk at.

Japan must surely be the only country in the world where a man will gladly play out large sums of good money to get a woman to listen to him. Possibly slaves do not make good listeners. However, the hostess – the computerised playmate – may conceivably be an illustration of the fact that Japan is just the same as everywhere else, only more so; perhaps she is indeed the universal male notion of the perfect woman.

'Butterfly' is a bar typical of two or three thousand others in the Ginza alone. It is a sufficiently respectable place, patronised by solid businessmen. These include a number of, if not captains of industry, at least first mates and pursers. Of the twenty or thirty men who will visit it during the course of an evening, not one will arrive alone and not one will bring a woman with him. Why, the company man might well ask, bother to bring coals to Newcastle?

Yet a throbbing sensuality is by no means the dominant quality of such places. The atmosphere is curiously similar to that of an English domestic charabanc outing, or even the kind of family New Year's Eve party at which drunken uncles pat the buttocks of their nieces. The plump company men would probably eagerly don paper hats with 'Kiss me Kwik' and 'I am a Virgin (Islander)' on them if some enterprising entrepreneur were to tour the bars selling them. 'I am a naughty boy!' they surreptitiously confide. And 'he is a naughty boy!' they whisper, giggling, about their friends, while, under the table, a continuous groping goes on.

In the warmth and privacy of the bar (as, indeed, of the rush-hour subway), the Japanese abandon their aversion to public heterosexual touching. The hostesses touch and are touched freely, though their status as interchangeable non-persons negates, to a considerable degree, the sensual – or, indeed, purely tactile – connotations of such touching. This depersonalisation process also applies to the customers. Both customers and hostesses are interchangeable commodities. The hostesses move from table to table as fresh customers enter, leaving the drinks, conversations and seduction attempts half-finished. The dirty glasses are instantly removed and the other attentions at once transferred to whichever hostess remains. When a customer leaves, he abruptly terminates interaction as though he suddenly remembers he is paying for it all. Without any warning, he gets to his feet and rarely bothers to bid his hostesses a civil good night, even when the girls move to the door with him in a chattering convoy, carrying him to a waiting taxi if he has become helplessly drunk.

But the price the customer pays, over and above the bill, for such boosts to his male self-esteem is a palpable loss of identity in the warm bath of spurious affection and indulgence supplied by the hostesses. It is hard to say which sex is most exploited by the system; yet both customers and hostesses, as if in diabolical complicity, remain blissfully unaware of the dubious existential status of the interaction. In the course of the evening, the customers, petted, fawned on and indulged, regress to behaviour of a masculine crassness sufficient to make a Germaine Greer out of a Barbara Cartland.

For example, the girls even go so far as to feed their large infants food. 'Open up!' they pipe, and in goes a heaped forkful of raw shellfish or smoked meat. Unaware how grossly he has been babified, the customer masticates with satisfaction. Meanwhile the *mama-san* herself takes ice from the crystal ice-bucket with a pair of silver tongs and pops it into her customers' drinks with gestures of (in the circumstances) ludicrous refinement. And a hostess can hardly call her breasts her own for the duration of the hostilities.

Double entendre, bawdy allusion and a constant reference to sexual performance and phallic dimension stoke the continuous conflagration of mirth, which will occasionally modulate into the authentic, empty hysterical sound of the laughter of the damned.

Such bars will employ Caucasian girls as exotic extras, like a kind of cabaret. A black girl would be far more exotic and could probably command any price she liked for such work. A curious double standard prevails among the clients; a man whose cigarette has just been lit by a Japanese girl will often produce his lighter to light the cigarette of a foreign hostess. Foreign girls also get more pay and exercise far greater job mobility, having different notions of the nature of employment. These things make the Japanese girls overtly hostile to the alien competition, especially when the foreign girls stage strikes for more money, and walk-outs over obscenity. A girl whose livelihood depends on the hostess bars simply cannot afford to have the self-respect to strike.

The Japanese hostess is locked in a remorseless dialectic. Save for the very few who regard hostessing as a profession which – plus, perhaps, a little prostitution on the side – will lead, one fine day, to their very own bars with their very own flock of hostesses, most of these girls are working in bars at night to supplement the monthly income from a daytime job that does not provide them with a living wage. The hostess, poor butterfly, is selling her youth and time and energy at a very cheap rate to people who could not afford to pay for them out of their own salaries. They usually charge her up to a firm which would refuse to give her enough money on which to live if she were officially on its pay sheet. Such are the ambiguities of acute capitalism.

The actual position of a foreign hostess is, however, sufficiently ambiguous as a social phenomenon. We are asked to exercise the customers' English in a kind of dexterous, cross-cultural, tight-rope dance. I transcribe the following conversation verbatim:

Customer: I will provide you with accommodation during your stay in Japan.

Hostess: Will you buy me a house?

Customer: Only if you do it three times a night.

(Roars of delighted applause from the rest of the table, at which are seated three company men and four hostesses.)

Hostess: Will there be room for my children?

(Whoops of appreciation at such wit.)

Customer: I will have my pipes cut (*sic*).

(They all cried the Japanese for: '*Touché!*')

Hostess: I mean, the children I have already.

(Cries of: 'Huzzah! Huzzah! *Bis! Bis!*')

Customer: How many children?

Hostess: Eleven. There will also be my mother; my father; my two sisters; my brother; my aunt; and my husband, a *sumo* wrestler of incredible proportions and invincible strength. . .

At this point, the customer said to his friends: 'Let's move on to the next bar.' They did so, somewhat precipitously. The *mama-san* was a mite peeved and suggested we foreign girls behave in a more lady-like manner, that is – to laugh more and talk back less. She herself laughed almost all the time, even when nothing funny happened.

One customer's English was limited to the single word, 'masturbation', which he pronounced very frequently and with a singular relish. Another raptly muttered the phrase, 'sexual intercourse', over and over again. Suzy claimed to observe a man stifling the signs of an orgasm, while another grasped my thighs quite unexpectedly and then announced: 'I want you tonight.' It is no good turning wrathfully on the poor things and crying: 'What do you think I am? A prostitute?' They *know* you aren't a prostitute. 'No charge, of course,' he added categorically.

After we finished work the first night, Suzy and I walked round to look at the shop on the next block that advertised 'adult toys' and keeps open until all hours. On the way, we passed a mournful transvestite in a kimono, who was warming his hands on a baked sweet potato, hot from the charcoal glowing on a peripatetic vendor's cart. We passed a tea-room that advertised the presence of 'exciting New World bunnies'. It was night-time in the world's most exciting city.

The adult toyshop carried a splendid selection of whips; some tooled-leather chastity belts; all manner of electronically-operated dildos; a variety of books and records, including one entitled *Fornicating Female Freaks*, which offered the authentic sounds of some 'bold butch lesbians having AC/DC sex', imported from America; and many other things. The salesman offered for our inspection a fat fish made of foam-rubber. When he pressed a switch, a red light on top of the fish's head glowed and the whole diabolical contraption started to shudder convulsively. With an enviable, deadpan expression, the salesman explained: 'A masturbatory device for gentlemen.'

Which is, presumably, the same function Suzy and I had performed for the last two and a half hours.

New Society, 1972

A Fertility Festival

Somebody stole the blueprint of hell and, with it, they built Nagoya. The super-express whizzes you to Nagoya from Tokyo in two hours through a landscape of imminent despoliation. Tangerines hang on the trees, tea-bushes cover green slopes, but these pastoral landscape accessories already have a timorous air. Festering industrial blight spreads remorselessly around the artery of the New Tokkaido Line. Soon, one endless city will stretch from Tokyo to Osaka. It won't be a very nice city.

But, thank God, we are only passing through Nagoya, we will not stop there. We are going to attend a fertility festival in the countryside, half an hour or so outside the city. This festival celebrates the marriage of the god called Takeinazumi-nomikoto to the goddess, Arata-hime-no-mikoto. It is a beautiful day in spring, just the season, just the weather, for a fertility festival. Yet all the gods in the Shinto pantheon, working together in one great concerted sacred copulation, could not revivify the concrete desolation of Nagoya.

There is a long queue at the bus station. But they do not look like devotees; most of the potential celebrants carry several cameras and have a prim yet salacious air. They might be about to visit a strip-club. There are more foreigners in the crowd than I expected; we all look a little sheepish. Has anthropological curiosity or mere prurience brought us here? For the focus of this famous fertility festival is a wooden phallus of immense size, borne in triumphant procession through cheering crowds. Surely none of these natty city dwellers has come out of a desire to increase his or her own fertility in this over-populated country that has alienated itself from the sense of the signs that we are about to witness, to the tune of a million abortions a year.

They are running relays of buses to the two temples, one of which enshrines the female principle, the other the male. Since the sexes are polarised in Japan, the two temples are about a quarter of a mile apart. We go to the female shrine first. As soon as I get off the bus, I smell something unfamiliar. Organic pollution.

Horseshit, by God! What a surprise! I've never smelled horseshit in Japan before! Are we about to en:er the unrepressed past?

But a drove of cameramen are here already, bustling about floats set on trucks, about to drive off to the female temple. The floats are decorated with tigers; with Disney deer; a rainbow; the fat-faced, laughing god of joy. And lots and lots of plastic flowers. On each float sits a girl, carrying a plastic rose. I do not know if these girls have any traditional ritual function, or are a modern tribute to the spirit of carnival. They are all dressed in fancy kimonos and their faces made up like geisha, white and impassive as if carved from plaster-of-Paris. They sit quite still.

One float contains an enormous, wood and plaster mushroom, plainly phallic in inspiration. At the end of the float, large, humorous, vulgar, plaster feet stick out on either side. Beneath the phallic mushroom sits – 'Wake me early, mother, for I'm to be Queen of the May' – the plainest of all the chosen girls, wearing a shimmering kimono of gold brocade that must have cost a bomb. She alone has an air of faint embarrassment.

The floats move off slowly down the road towards the female temple. At this shrine is a rock shaped like the female orifice and, in a portable shrine in an auxillary temple a little way away, there is a large clam. Shops along the path are selling live clams, indisputably vulvic in appearance.

The floats reach a junction in the paddies and halt; the rest of the procession approaches to join them. This part of the procession is altogether more hieratic in character. It is lead by a Shinto priest with a bobbing, black, horsehair chignon, in a white robe, mounted on a white horse from whom the horseshit must emanate. The priest is followed by a detachment of middle-aged women in pink and red garments, with red scarves wrapped round their heads and shoulders, carrying staffs decorated with bands of little, jingling bells, trimmed with red ribbons. These women are heavily into the ritual of their roles. All the same, they seem to be daring the spectators to titter. How should a pious lady behave in a situation where piety necessitates obscenity? Aggressively.

Now comes a lorry full of drummers: young men with sweat-bands round their heads, many of them in spectacles, all wearing cotton jackets open to the waist. They beat their drums in archaic rhythms, laugh and shout. And here is a troupe of men carrying bunches of wire sticks stuck with favours of red and purple paper that have white marks at the centre. Possibly stylisations of the female orifice. The crowd, shouting, tussles for these favours the bearers toss to right and left. But it is not a very large crowd, and mostly comprises cameramen.

And now, what we've all been waiting for! The cameras click again and again. Another priest, on horseback – and his retinue bears a waving banner with, painted upon it, a perfectly explicit female orifice which could serve as an illustration in a gynaecological textbook. Hair and clit and everything. Click! Click! Click! And this black and gold portable shrine approaching now must contain the sacred clam. It is being carried along by bare-legged young men, some of them with spectacles, some without.

The shrine bucks back and forth, and it now threatens to topple into the thin crowds standing in the stubbled fields at either side of the path. Good fortune is supposed to spill from the shrine when it does this. Click.

We adjourn to the male temple. Inside the temple itself, men in green, butterfly-sleeved garments flutter about mysteriously behind the paper screens; but outside, in the compound, is all the fun of the fair and lots of people enjoying it in a decorous way. There are stalls selling waffles filled with chopped octopus; goldfish made of barley sugar; hot chestnuts; hoop-la stalls; bowls of real goldfish, that you fish for with a little net and take home in a polythene bag. Toffee-apples. Pop-corn. Hot grilled cuttlefish. Candy floss. Trinkets. Lucky pot cats. Lucky pot badgers. And the round-based, eyeless, gold and red things they buy for luck and paint the eyes in as the luck comes. Or not, as the case may be.

Somebody has asked me to buy them some little clay models, or icons, they thought were sold at this shrine. I've seen samples, bought here years ago. Icons basic as graffiti, two-in-one symbols that combine phallus and vulva in one little pierced knob of white clay. And, really, very beautiful to look at. I look and look for these tokens but they are nowhere to be found. They must have gone out of production. Not kitsch enough for nowadays, perhaps. They illustrate exactly Henry Miller's distinction between obscenity and pornography; it is possible to buy pornography.

One stall sells cocks made of bright pink sugar at 75p a time. In the course of the afternoon, they sell 300 of the things – their entire stock. One other stall, and one other stall only, sells cookies in all manner of phallic and vulvic shapes, as well as lollipops on sticks with a coy little striped candy cock nestling in a bed of pink sugar. But the temple virgins at the amulet booth sell only the tie-pins and charms in brocade bags you can buy at *any* Shinto shrine.

Dozens of kids run about, splashing themselves with water at the holy well as they drink from the bamboo dipper. It is just another fair, to them. A few old men, in cloth caps, with grave faces; they are not here for a cheap thrill. And lots of grannies, pushing empty wicker prams up and down, up and down. Is this not a fertility festival? Their faces are grim, as if to say, Isn't this a serious business? Fierce grannies in drab kimonos, with shocks of grey hair and seamed, wizened faces. The old ladies are out in force, today, attempting to re-establish, by the sheer force of their iron wills, the time – still fresh in their memory – when this festival of the male and female principle indeed revivified the soil, quickened the womb, and so forth.

But who else has come here for a blessing? Some of the family parties, perhaps, who look like gangsters on an outing from Osaka. (Japanese gangsters are repositories of tradition.) But not me, certainly. Nor the parties of holidaying company men, giggling to hide their embarrassment. Nor the cameramen, from the picture magazines. Nor the television crews. There is a gnarled European who says he is from *Paris Match*. My friend Harold hopes to sell his pictures to *Stern*. But all of us, with various emotions, are waiting for the procession that will bring the fabled Mighty Cock back to its home.

Meanwhile, a snake-charmer entertains. A plump, sweating man in shirtsleeves and dark glasses, he talks of the many advantages of owning a snake. How it makes a snug muffler – he wraps it round his neck: you can tie children up with it – eek! the children squeal. And, during the recent toilet paper shortage . . .

at that, he draws the snake back and forth between his legs.

There is a strip-show beside the main temple building. A female barker with a loud-hailer stands outside the entrance; beside her, a window in the tent reveals the head and shoulders, and only the head and shoulders, of the girl inside, who is shortly going to take off her clothes for your pleasure. It is the stately, artificial head of a geisha, matt white, bewigged, hung with shiny ornaments. These sideshows give the scene a medieval quality.

Over the tannoy system, the police, continuously solicitous, urge the crowd not to fall over and injure itself. Not to dart out into the main road in the path of oncoming traffic. Not to trample one another underfoot in their eagerness to witness the procession as it approaches.

Behind the shuttered temple is a shrine containing hundreds and hundreds of phalluses of all sizes. A large crowd is gathered here, taking photographs. In front of this shrine is a large stone phallus, set on a low pediment.

An uneasy, smutty relish pervades the reactions of most of the visitors. They are as much strangers here as we Europeans are; as great a distance separates them from the enthusiasm of the grannies. Perhaps an even greater distance, since they have only just learned the titillation of prudery, while we have struggled all our lives to overcome it.

At last, in the distance, the sound of weird music of bamboo pipes and drums. A breath of strangeness hushes us all. Here it comes – out of the animistic, pagan past, a relic of the days before the Japanese lost their *joie de vivre*. The crowds surge. Click! Click! Click! Someone has climbed into a tree to get a better view. The police order him down. First, a group of Shinto priests, on foot, in white robes and sugarloaf hats of horsehair, bringing a banner which shows a medical illustration of the male organ in a state of advanced tumescence. Then about twenty of those astonishing, prim women who look like members of the local Women's Institute; and each woman cradles in her arms a succinct wooden phallus, about the size of a cricket stump.

Now. Ah! Cheers and lewd cries. The crowd jumps up and down and climbs over itself to fire off its cameras in the direction of the Mighty Cock, as, serene, radiant, triumphant, an explicit glory of varnished wood, golden brown in colour, it sails over their heads. Good heavens, it is eight feet long. Nine feet long. Ten feet long? Immensely long! In a palanquin borne by jovial, obscene ancients, laughing and showing their teeth. The round tip and the immense superstructure of the Mighty Cock emerges from the white curtains of the palanquin. And the ancients shift it this way and that way, so that it seems to move about according to a life of its own.

The photographer from *Paris Match* has broken through the barriers and dances backwards in front of it, clicking away. Harold has joined the procession itself to click at it from close quarters and the ancients are too jovial or too drunk to shoo him away.

The palanquin is attended by acolytes and musicians in white regalia, playing a haunting, archaic melody of drones and beating drums. There are men carrying poles with mops of coloured rags on top of them, all laughing, all singing. And, in spite of the cameras, in spite of our common alienation from the meaning of this ritual, the festival takes hold of us all for a little while – just a few seconds. A magic strangeness, a celebration; the paddies are quickening, it is spring. The god has married the goddess and now returns home. The grannies thrust forward their empty prams and scream shrilly. The old men wave their female favours ecstatically. Here comes a jolly old dancing man bearing yet another phallus in his arms and, after him, a line of dancing men carrying a pole with, hanging from it, a six-foot phallus of unvarnished wood. Phalluses, phalluses everywhere.

All singing, all dancing, they process in authentically orgiastic fashion into the temple. The old folks are having a whale of a time. The priests have an air of suspended disbelief. The children are enjoying themselves, in their pre-pubescent innocence. But the persistent click of the cameras indicates the festival has become one of mechanical reproduction. The day will be fertile only in spool after spool of images of itself processed on film. Perhaps, next year, it will be sponsored by Fujicolor.

It isn't quite over, yet. Amidst screaming and laughter, the priests throw a hail of rice cakes from the balcony of a temple building. The crowd screams and jostles for them; but Harold's girl friend tells him not to go and take pictures of the scene because the rice cakes are hard and might break his lens.

The vendors already begin to pack up their stalls. Dusk draws on. The snake-charmer is gone. The temple virgins have closed the shutters of the talisman booths. Anti-climax. Post-coital depression, perhaps. Over the tannoy, the police now urge the crowd to take care not to get run over in the car park and to drive carefully on the road back to Nagoya. It is getting cold and we must all go back to Nagoya. The restaurant beside the bus stop has upped its prices by 10p per dish in honour of the festival.

New Society, 1974

3

ENGLAND, WHOSE ENGLAND?

When I came back to England, I saw it, refreshed.

At my primary school in Balham, south London, every year in June, they held a celebration known locally as 'Empire Day'. Since this was Clement Attlee's England, the headmistress and stage manager of these proceedings, a woman called Miss Cox who always wore Queen Mary-style dresses in pastel-coloured satins, often with beaded fronts, made a token attempt at retitling the fiesta 'Commonwealth Day', but she had originally dreamed up the whole thing some time in the 1920s and now it was part of neighbourhood folklore, so the old name stuck. (She retired in 1951, year of the Festival of Britain, my eleven-plus year.)

'Empire Day' was a peculiar conflation of themes. One of the top class of eleven year olds, usually the blondest one, was dressed up as Rose Queen in a white shift, and would be pelted with tissue-paper rose petals and crowned with cloth roses. There was country dancing and kids in national dress, i.e. kilt, steeple hat, headscarf, carrying the flags of Scotland, Wales and Ulster. (Oh, that red hand!) We sang songs: 'Rose of England', 'There'll always be an England', and so on, out in the asphalt playground. There was a maypole. Then the tinies, the five and six year olds, would line up, each one carrying a lettercard that combined to spell out the school motto which I believe Miss Cox had invented herself; it was the Kantian imperative; 'Do Right Because It Is Right'.

The strange innocence of these pageants is happily irrecoverable.

The following pieces are explorations of the concept of Englishness, and of certain myths of Englishness as they manifest themselves in various English places.

The reader may note a certain regional bias.

Industry as Artwork

At times, Bradford hardly seems an English city at all, since it is inhabited, in the main, by (to all appearances) extras from the Gorki trilogy, huddled in shapeless coats – the men in caps and mufflers, the women in boots and headscarves. It comes as no surprise to hear so much Polish spoken or to see so much vodka in the windows of the off-licences, next to the British sherry, brown ale and dandelion-and-burdock. Though, again, it might be a city in a time-machine. Those low, steep terraces – where, at nights, gas lamps secrete a mean, lemon-coloured light which seems to intensify rather than diminish the surrounding darkness – and the skyline, intermittently punctuated by mill chimneys, create so consistent an image of a typical Victorian industrial town everything teeters on the brink of self-parody and the public statuary goes right over the edge.

Like monstrous *genii loci*, petrifications of stern industrialists pose in squares and on road islands, clasping technological devices or depicted in the act of raising the weeping orphan. There is something inherently risible in a monumental statue showing a man in full mid-Victorian rig, watch chain and all, shoving one hand in his waistcoat *à la* Napoleon and , with the other, exhorting the masses to, presumably, greater and yet greater productiveness.

The same impulse to ennoble commerce must have dictated the choice of the Gothic-revival architectural style, that of the instant sublime, for which the city is famous. The Wool Exchange pretends to be a far more impressive cathedral than the cathedral itself, and most of the public buildings strive in their appearance to transcend their origins, becoming in the process authentic chapels to Mammon. Mysteriously enough, the city museum is housed in a mansion imitating another kind of grandeur; it and the formal gardens surrounding it are just like the hotel and grounds in *Last Year at Marienbad*, a curiously wistful palace of culture set in a rather romantic public park. The building is guarded by a statue of Diana the Huntress. All this is irrelevantly gracious and unnervingly out of context, reflecting, presumably, the place of the arts in the context of the culture which produced it. The mills, however – reflecting, perhaps, a more honest respect for the muck which signifies brass – are built on heroic proportions.

Their chimneys are monumental in size and design, like giant triumphal columns or pediments for Brobdingnagian equestrian statues. On some days of Nordic winter sunshine, the polluted atmosphere blurs and transfigures the light, so that the hitherto sufficiently dark, satanic mills take on a post-apocalyptic, Blakean dazzle, as if the New Jerusalem had come at last, and the sky above is the colour and texture of ripe apricots. A russet mist shrouds the surrounding moorland, which is visible from almost every street, however mean. On such mornings, it is impossible to deny that the scene is beautiful.

Snow, however, brings out the essential colours of the city. Everything is delicately veiled in soot which fortuitously unifies the eclectic urban scene to such a degree that those public buildings which have been scrubbed back down to their native stone look ill at ease, as though they no longer belonged here, like millhands' sons who have gone to Oxford. But the soot, although it paints in monochrome, does not create a monotonous scene, for here one may appreciate and enjoy an infinitely rich collection of blacks, from the deepest and most opaque to the palest and most exquisitely subtle, through an entire spectrum – brownish-black, greenish-black, yellowish-black and a cosy, warm, reddish-black. The air, which often has the metallic chill of freezing metal, is full of the sweetish smell of coal smoke. Snot is black.

The weather is brutish. The cold has moulded the stoicism of the inhabitants and, perhaps, helped to determine their diet, rich as it is in heat-supplying fats and carbohydrates – so rich in fat, indeed, that persistent local folklore relates how Bradford Royal Infirmary is forced to discard pints of donated blood due to the high fat content it contains.

Fish and chips; pie and a spoonful of reconstituted dried peas the colour of mistletoe, swimming in grey juice; the odorous range of Yorkshire charcuterie, haslet, sausage, tomato sausage, black pudding, roast pork, pigs' trotters, pigs' cheek, jars of pork dripping, every variety of cooked pig the mind could imagine or the heart desire, for the succulent pig appeals to the native thriftiness of its eaters since every part of him may be consumed.

All this powerful cityscape of strangeness and unusual harmonies seduces the eye of the romantic southern visitor so much he finds it easy to forget that, thirty years ago, Lewis Mumford defined such places as Bradford as 'insensate industrial towns'. J. B. Priestley's Bradford was a good place to have come from, bearing in mind one would be able to remember it in tranquillity far, far away; and John Braine's post-war Bradford expressed only an appreciation of those affluent parts of the place that might be anywhere else in Britain. But now it is easy to find it charming here.

It is partly so charming because it is so strange; the presence of so many Pakistanis creates not so much the atmosphere of the melting-pot for, at present, the disparate ethnic elements are held in an uneasy suspension, but an added dimension of the remarkable. Signs everywhere in Urdu; young girls with anoraks over their satin trousers; embroidered waistcoats; unfamiliar cooking utensils in hardware shops; and cinemas with even their names up in Urdu. On Sunday afternoons, the man next door spends perhaps three or four hours practising upon some inexpressibly exotic musical instrument which sounds as though it has only a single string. He chants constantly to his own accompaniment and, to this Asiatic threnody, the wuthering of the Brontë winds from the moors lends a passionate counterpoint.

But thirty years ago would I have found all this charming? Or would I have flinched that human beings should be forced to live and work in these conditions which might well have reminded me of the workers' dwellings in Lang's *Metropolis*; and if, unwillingly, I had found a quaint attraction in the scene, I would probably have identified it as the same attraction/repulsion the late eighteenth-century intellectual experienced at the spectacle of the

Horrid. Just as the uneasy aesthetic of the Horrid modulated into a postive pleasure-reaction to the same spectacle redefined as the Picturesque and thence into that expansion of the sensibility involved in the discovery of the idea of the Sublime, so the Horrid – i.e., the working-class environment, Victorian Gothic architecture, the detritus we now refer to as examples of industrial archaeology – began its modification towards the picturesque twenty years ago, if not before. It is now well on the way to becoming a new type of the Beautiful, although we have not yet found it a fitting name, a type of the beautiful first consciously rendered visually in those British films of the late fifties which featured endless arty shots of gasworks reflected in canals and pit wheels outlined against storm clouds.

A hundred years ago, Daumier found such spectacles perfectly hideous; forty years ago, George Orwell found only a poignant desolation in these industrial cityscapes, marked with the grisly stigmata of poverty. They are probably still seductive principally to the bourgeois romantic intellectual who sees them with the fresh eye of one not born and bred in a back-to-back house or to those afflicted with a sad case of Hoggart nostalgia. (I have a peculiarly rich reaction to Bradford due to a confusion of both kinds of response, plus some piquant memories of an early childhood in a more southerly Yorkshire environment which really looked more like Tolkien's Mordor than anywhere else.) On the other hand, the history of taste may well be that of the obscure and probably warped predilections of the bourgeois romantic intellectual gradually filtering down through the mass media until everybody knows for certain what they ought to like. After all, only a handful of eccentrics enjoyed mountains until a mountain got up and followed Wordsworth across a lake.

I often feel that Manningham Mills are rolling inexorably after me on ponderous wheels down Oak Lane.

Yet Bradford has the virtues of a total environment where work and life goes on side by side, and the hilly streets, following as they do the (indeed) majestic contours of the surrounding hills, retain some kind of organic relation with the countryside in which a chance combination of natural elements, wool and water, produced the city in the first place. It is not a handsome city as Leeds, nearby, is handsome; it does not wear its muck with such conscious, assertive pride. It is more domestic, earthier. The contrast between the splendid front and the squalid asshole are not nearly as great. It is far older than Leeds. At times, it even feels almost medieval, with its windy, winding streets. It is a city with such a markedly individual flavour that even though it will take an aesthetic *volte-face* of seismic proportions before even the most entrenched preservationists hail it as the Florence of the North, that day might some day come; Bradford will indeed be seen by all to be beautiful if it escapes the fate of the rest of Britain, which is plainly that everywhere will be done over to look like a universal, continuous North Cheam. Then we will wake to a shocked consciousness of the visual pleasures we have lost.

New Society, 1970

That was Bradford, Yorks, in 1970, before it changed; this is Doncaster, a few years later. Yes — this is neo-realist England, all right!

The Donnie Ferrets

You get to Doncaster market from the station by going through one of those monumental, multi-tiered shopping precincts with branches of every chain-store you can think of in it, a total merchandising environment with artificially-modulated lighting and controlled temperatures. It must have seemed like a good idea at the time. There are lots of them, as monolithic in design as the buildings of the Thousand Year Reich, constructed in the expectation of universal, everlasting affluence at the end of the sixties.

Now they already have some of the quaint appeal of the ruins of those giant churches built in Paraguay by the Jesuits in the fallacious hope of the conversion of the Amerindians.

This one has a piazza with a concrete pool in it, dry now. The citizens of Doncaster have made an informal agora of this area and sit around it on the seats thoughtfully provided for them, reading the sports pages. When they're finished with their newspapers, they throw them into the dried-up pool. It's busy enough, now, on a Saturday afternoon. But at night, when the shoppers have all gone home, this gleaming temple of Mammon will become the echoing domain of alienation, fit only for vandalisation. It's the spitting image of the shopping precinct in Stephen Poliakoff's *Hitting Town*, where the waitress used to come in the evenings to have herself a good scream.

However, a modest stream of customers now commute between British Home Stores and the branch of Brown, Muff's. Under a black leather poster of Alvin Stardust, menswear in the butchissimo style favoured in south Yorkshire vanishes from the racks with a speed surprising in a recession. The supermarkets are packed, though God knows why. A hundred yards away, belly is king and the stalls are groaning with the sort of food south Yorkshire likes to eat.

Out, then, into the mild drizzle, across the main road; and, like a little touch of Ballets Russes, you see before you the peaked hoods of the market stalls in the distance, beyond O & A's. It's a different world, a different shopping experience, like stepping into a space-time warp. A little town of stalls dominated by the austere classical lines of the Corn Exchange Market and, by the serene and lavishly embroidered towers of Doncaster parish church across the main road.

It's confusing, at first. There's so much of it, and such an extraordinary variety of things for sale, from once-used co-respondent's shoes to plastic tiger lilies. And the market looks like it's been there a long time, which it has. The stallholders are not fly-by-night, here-today-and-gone-tomorrow rip-off artistes, like so many of the stallholders of London's remaining street markets, but solid burghers with a reputation to maintain.

And, furthermore, it's also *meant* to be confusing. These markets are not so much for shopping as for browsing, for a randomly-structured promenade that takes you in a leisurely fashion from stall to stall, comparing prices and qualities, jostled by one's fellow men, exhorted by persuasive barkers, stopping off for peas and chips at Irene's Corner and so forth. A time-and-motion study man would go mad rationalising the movements of a typical weekend shopper in Doncaster market.

Meat, dairy products, bread and cakes are all under cover. The market traders advertise themselves with the up-front self-confidence of the time before advertising became an art-form. 'The egg people,' says one sign; 'pies of perfection', announces another, emphasising the message with a very nice naïve painting of a straight-walled pork pie with a token tomato slice or two at its base. If you look up from the counters long enough, you'll see lots of fine primitives aloft. The stall with the game licence is decorated with medallions of hare, pheasant and guinea fowl. Best beef may be bought under a cameo portrait of a heavy bull with a ring in its nose, all complete, as if to suggest some of the bull's virility will be imparted to those who eat its meat. This is the carnivorous north.

Most of the cheese comes in plasticised cartwheels but some, if you're lucky, may be found in authentic mired bandages and that is often fine. There's a sweetish, musty odour from row upon row of open biscuit tins. I'd forgotten how you used to be able to buy biscuits loose. And lots of cut-price confectionery. 'These are *not* misshapes', says a hand-written sign on a notice on a spilling sack of Mint Imperials. But greedy children who don't pay much heed to symmetry can stock up on warped liquorice allsorts and at very competitive prices.

Cakes. Curd tarts. Slab cakes in various flavours, fruit, seed, coconut, cherry, plain, at 20 pence a small loaf. 'The luxury crumpet.' Balm-cakes. Everything displayed just within reach, as it is on your own tea-table.

There is a lack of reticence about the displays, a lack of guile and artifice in the presentation of the wares, that suggests the food is not designed to appeal to the jaded palate via the eye but directly to the active digestive processes. It grabs you at a visceral level. Meat lies on the slab in moist, bleeding chunks – everything, tongue, liver, kidneys, terribly recognisable as such. They don't hide the eggs away in boxes but heap them up like pebbles on a beach. The baker's stall, called 'The Crusty Cob', tumbles its bread onto the counter prodigally, all dusty with flour and straight from the delivery tray.

There's butter too ('Yorkshire farmhouse butter, 50p a pound') in lavish blocks. These are the very archetypes of basic foodstuffs, not the stereotypes you find jostling promiscuously in the troughs at the supermarket, anonymous sections of meat that might be cunningly synthesised from the look of them, and never even seen a slaughterhouse, and those geometric sections of cheese all sheathed in cellophane so that a hundred hands can shuffle them without the hygiene regulations being broken.

In this market, only the butcher is privileged to handle the meat until you've paid for it. Money is transformed into food before your very eyes, elementary magic of the market-place. The girl at the cheese stall brusquely offers you a sliver of Cheddar on the end of a murderous knife. All is grimly personalised. The rituals of buying and selling involve a direct, face to face confrontation.

This confrontation is especially direct in Doncaster, where they engage in the service industries with a positively Soviet egalitarianism. The cheese lady does not attempt to charm with a smile. She has a black-dyed, piled-up hairdo like a country music star; her eyelids are painted a vivid green. If you don't like her style, so much the worse for you.

The fish and poultry market is even more direct. Under the vaulted architraves, the white marble slabs all aslither with hunks and fillets remind you why they used to call it 'wet fish'. One stall calls itself the 'modern fishmonger' and has a sign showing a very dapper fish in a topper and monocle, smoking a cigarette; modern is a relative term. Eviscerated rabbits lie in mauve mounds, only their kidneys left in the cavities where their bellies were; above them swing racks of rabbits still in their pelts. There are counters where you can buy saucers of whelks and mussels and shrimps and eat them on the spot, from tiny saucers; kids rummage through discarded boxes of whelk shells. It's cold and wet underfoot, here.

It's getting on in the afternoon and they're slapping the fish about something dreadful. The rituals surrounding real food can ravage one's sensibilities, rather.

Fruit and veg outside, mostly; and the occasional flower stall. And clothes; and hats; and used paperbacks; a sheet music stall, a porn stall, a brassware stall – dozens of brassware stalls, some of which have branched out into knick-knacks such as miniature pottery lavatories with money-box slits in them and, written on them, 'Put a penny in the little pot'.

Heavy market-traders in sawn-off Wellington boots against the rising damp, many wearing those characteristic fingerless mittens and the bag of change strapped round their aproned waists, make lavish promises. One offers a ballpoint pen guaranteed to write 40,000 words; but, then, part of the trip is the side-shows, the complete dinner services for a fiver to you, and so on.

And it goes on, stall after stall; and a little roundabout to amuse the kiddies. There's a fire engine on the roundabout, with Doncaster Fire Brigade written on the side. This rambling encampment of goods for sale, where buying is as much of an art as selling and it can all come down to a battle of wits between the stall-holder and you.

Maybe Yorkshire never really left the Third World. These enormous markets of the great northern cities and towns are like the peasant markets of Europe, or even like oriental bazaars, solid, institutionalised – one of the Sheffield markets is housed in multi-storied, concrete erections scarcely distinguishable, from the outside, from any Arndale Centre in the world.

But you can't buy live pigeons in any Arndale Centre that I know of. And there they are, in Donnie, a cage full of beautiful, plump pigeons, their heads sunk into their necks, pigeons all the smoke and slate colours of Doncaster on an autumn morning. A little old man came, and brushed his hand over the outside of the cage, cooing at the pigeons so that they all stirred from their trance and cooed back at him. 'Just you eff off,' said the pigeon vendor, in his flat aggressive cap. 'I've had enough of you.'

But he had more than pigeons to sell. He had canaries, and budgies, and a white dove, and a solid lump of black puppy that separated itself out at random into five puppies, and a tea-chest full of guinea pigs. Also lop-eared rabbits and huge, robust white rabbits with black blotches on them, like Dalmatian dogs, good, I should think, eaters.

And ferrets. I'd never seen a ferret before. Arching its wickedly articulated back, the small, vicious creature, creamy-white, like ermine, snarled delicately at the fascinated children pressed around the cage. Ferrets. Of course they'd sell ferrets. We're in Yorkshire, aren't we? The regional hunting beast, the questing beast; teeth too sharp to make a nice pet, really.

But this little boy wanted a football from the toy stall and even the sight of the ferret wouldn't distract him. He was whinging away about the football until his granny lost patience with him entirely. 'Bugger t' football,' she said, with the air of somebody utterly exhausted by the traditional total south Yorkshire shopping experience, 'Bugger t' football.'

Outside, among the fruit and vegetable stalls, it had started to rain in earnest and the cabbage stalks and shed lettuce leaves were turning to soup in the puddles. It's very tiring, not being alienated from your environment.

New Society, 1976

Between 1973 and 1976, I lived in the city of Bath Spa, one of the most beautiful cities in England, nay, in Europe, a different kettle of fish to Bradford, or Doncaster: or Sheffield, where I spent two years after I moved out of Bath. (Oh, I do like a change . . .) I always find beautiful places obscurely troubling, especially beautiful English places, and I wrote the following piece, a formal reverie about the City of Bath, on purpose in a style that matched it, Fine Writing, the evocative voice, the dying fall. Bath was a lovely place in which to live. Yet it is England at its most foreign to me; as self-conscious a performance as Miss Cox's 'Empire Day'.

Bath, Heritage City

Getting a buzz off the stones of Bath, occupying a conspicuous site not fifty yards from the mysterious, chthonic aperture from which the hot springs bubble out of the inner earth, there is usually a local alcoholic or two on the wooden benches outside the Abbey. On warm summer afternoons they come out in great numbers, as if to inform the tourists this city is a trove of other national treasures besides architectural ones. Some of them are quite young, one or two very young, maybe not booze but acid burned their brain cells away, you can't tell the difference, now. Jock will dance while his mate attempts to play the concertina. I remember a demented youth banging a cider bottle against the bench and singing a tuneless song with the refrain, 'I am an angel', which clean French and Scandinavians − we only get upper market tourism − ignored.

I once saw a man puking exhaustively inside the Abbey, surrounded by memorial plaques of soldiers and sailors who seem to have come to die here in large numbers. Bath is dotted with blue plaques, Wordsworth was here, Southey was here, Jane Austen was here, almost everybody came for a weekend but Malthus was actually buried here. My favourite plaque is in Brock Street. 'Here dwelt John Christopher Smith (1712-1745), Handel's friend and secretary.' Such English self-effacing modesty! Why not come out with it; 'I was a sycophantic arsehole-licker.'

On the Abbey façade, angels climb up the ladder towards God, sort of nutty Disney. The Palladians who turned Bath into what it is today pulled down almost everything else, they must have left the Abbey façade standing because it was so charming. Charm, the English disease; charm, mask of dementia? The fine-boned, blue-eyed, characteristically English madness; foreigners, who see both charm and madness at the same time, tend to diagnose the combination as hypocrisy. I had a Japanese friend who said: 'When I see a pair of blue eyes, I think of the Opium War.'

There's a lot of fine-boned, blue-eyed English madness in Bath, part of its charm, a population with rather more than a fair share of occultists, neo-Platonists, yogis, theosophists, little old ladies who have spirit conversations with Red Indian squaws, religious maniacs, senile dements, natural lifers, macrobiotics, people who make perfumed candles, kite-flyers, do you believe in fairies?

Down the Lansdowne Road stride a blue-eyed, Aryan, straightly tall couple garbed in colourful rags and chinking with crucifixes; the young man carries an open Bible, from which he declaims in a stentorian voice the more lugubrious assertions of Ecclesiastes. Past Hedgemead Park, favoured venue of the local flashers, bearing the word of the Lord. Past Steve the Tattoo Artist's shop. Steve can inscribe a nice Pietà on your back if you want, and he's got a pamphlet stuck in his window called, 'The Fall of Babylon', Radical Traditionalist Pamphlet No. 2, 'A message of comfort to the latter-day citizens of that great city'. The peripatetic evangiles skirt the West Indian grocer as he loads yams into his mobile shop, he's a member of the New Testament Church of God, himself; crying, 'Hallelujah!' they disappear into the heart of heritage Bath. Nobody turns to look. Too much fine-boned, blue-eyed English dementia around here already to raise an eyebrow.

Constructed in a navel-like depression of hills, Bath's ompholoid location induces introspection, meditation, inwardness, massive sloth. Some of us disappear right down our own navels and never come up again, in fact; famous madmen lived here – William Beckford; the irrascible Captain Thickness, enshrined in that monument to the English disease, Edith Sitwell's *English Eccentrics*. But the Anglo-Saxons wouldn't live here, they thought it was haunted. Too cack-handed and primitive themselves to build in stone, they thought that only giants or devils could have done so and left the Roman ruins well alone. There is an Old English poem describing their superstitious dread of the place.

Some of the anti-conservationists, even some of the City Fathers, seem to feel the same terror, as though this masterpiece of planning had been built with the aid of unholy powers and so presents a dreadful menace to we punier beings. Best let the old place quietly fall down. Such things are not for us. Of course Bath is a masterpiece of town planning. As the alternatives murmur to one another over their halves of cider, anywhere you live, you're only ten minutes walk from the Social Security; apart from the sheer convenience of everything, the Georgian city has the theatrical splendour, the ethereal two-dimensionality of a town of dream.

It has crazy skies, like those beneath which the blue-eyed dements of the novels of John Cowper Powys, also occultists and neo-Platonists, disport themselves. And certain luminous skies of early evening irradiate with gold the haze through which the church towers in the valley are always peeking, so that, then, the terraces thrown with such artful assymetry across the hillsides have a deserted look. The beautiful trees in this city are so huge they look as if they had been here before the houses and will outlast them. Marvellous, hallucinatory Bath has almost the quality of concretised memory; its beauty has a curiously second-order quality, most beautiful when remembered, the wistfulness of all professional beauties, such as that of the unfortunate Marilyn Monroe whom nobody wanted for herself but eveybody wanted to have slept with.

In front of Lansdown Crescent, that stunning bone-white terrace which contrives the perfect solution to the middle-class English desire to live in a town house in the heart of the country, a horse grazes on the downward dipping hillside. It is so peaceful you can hear him crunch. All those magisterial chestnuts in the hollows! From this elevation, the entire city is laid out before us, like a splendid toy for the very rich who still live here in large numbers, people of rank and fashion, taste and means. Bath is enjoying a revival. Such a civilised place to live. In a green dishevellment of waste-land and disused allotments a little way along, sprightly young foxes tumble and cuff one another. Soft, mauve shadows cast by the golden light.

That golden light, the light of pure nostalgia, gives the young boys in their bright jerseys playing football after tea in front of Royal Crescent the look of Rousseau's football players, caught in the amber of the perpetual Sunday afternoon of the painter. The sound of the voices of the children contains its own silencing already within it: 'Remembered for years, remembered with tears.' Nostalgia is part of the aesthetic, time's sweet and inevitable revenge.

The haunting silences of Bath are those with which the Engish compose intimacies.

The uselessness of the city contributes both to its charm and to its poignancy, which is part of its charm. It was not built to assert the pre-eminence of a particular family or the power of a certain region. It had no major industry in the eighteenth century, except tourism. The gentleman whose tastes this city was built (speculatively) to satisfy had no interest in labour as such, only in his profits from a labour he hoped would take place as far away from his pleasures as possible; Bath was built to be happy in, which accounts for its innocence and its ineradicable melancholy.

The younger and elder Woods did not even build the Circus and Royal Crescent, those monumental pieces of domestic design, the Olympian apotheosis of the terraced housed, to glorify themselves, as a Renaissance architect might have done. They, and Baldwin, and Palmer, and Finch, and Eveleigh, and Goodrich, and so on designed to demonstrate and also help to create the taste of a certain class, a taste the dominance of that class would help to institutionalise as 'good taste'. The demonstration and embodiment of that taste was also the demonstration of greatly enlarged economic power of a greatly enlarged upper-middle class, but, in one sense, this was incidental to the main plot. Only rich madmen like Beckford went in for conspicuous consumption and vulgar display.

Order, space, harmony, what Mumford calls the Olympian qualities. A residential town for a gentleman, which could also house the service industries that catered to his elegant and civilised pleasures. His main indulgences were not the gross pleasures of boozing and fornication, but the subtler debaucheries of dandyism, that is, systematised narcissism and gambling, an activity that performs at least one radical function, that of robbing money of its exchange value and making it, at least temporarily, a plaything. He liked to dance primly under the stern eye of Beau Nash, surely one of the most boring men who ever lived, boring and totalitarian, a veritable Stalin of good taste.

The narrow, cluttered alleys of the medieval city did not suit such a gentleman's needs, although he liked to keep one or two of them around because they were so charmingly picturesque. No. Best of all, he liked to bowl along in a curricle or a gig, in control of his own direction, high above the mob that plodded through the mud his wheels had agitated, so he enjoyed wide boulevards. Poultney Street, the perfect neo-Classical street. On foot, the walk to the two-dimensional focal point of what is now the Holbourne and Menstrie Museum, an amazing bit of architectural *trompe l' oeil*, soon palls. The wide road, flat as a pancake, the front doors passing by with the grim regularity of telegraph poles. You are not meant to linger here. On the other hand, a car goes much too fast. You whizz past the splendid façades in a moment; they hardly impinge upon the eye at all. But, in a horse-drawn carriage, the twin terraces flow past on either side like exquisite back projections, to be viewed as part of a city of views, to be decorously enjoyed at a distance and to be soon – but not *too* soon –. over.

The lucid and serene architecture of this city confronts me with an Englishness I attempt to deny by claiming Scottish extraction. I always give Jock a shilling when he pan-handles me.

Bath, in its romantic, dishevelled loveliness, is no longer the city the Woods built; two hundred years of the history of taste have modified the crisp outlines of its rational harmony, and this has changed its appearance far more than time itself has done. Our perceptions of the city are modified by those of everybody else who has ever been here and thought that it was beautiful. It is more than the sum of its parts.

The softly crumbling stone; those tumultuous skies across which, now and then, the wild swans fly; that light, with the elegiac quality that brings a lump in the throat; that sense of pervasive pastoral, the feeling for the countryside typified in wild gardens, it isn't really anything to do with the countryside at all but a liking for parks, for landscaped meadows, for contained nature, for garden cities . . . the water-colour aesthetic as of English art, whose favourite seasons are the moist ones, early spring, early autumn, and all of whose landscapes are gently haunted. Bath, a city so English that it feels like being abroad, has been so distorted by what Pevsner called the Englishness of English art that the city itself has become almost an icon of sensibility. This particular Englishness, this particular sensibility, had a last major high art revival in the late forties, in the pictures of John Piper and Michael Ayrton and the Nashes. Mervyn Peake showed its demonic aspect. In fiction, the novels and anthologies of Walter de la Mare; in music, Britten's setting of 'The splendour falls on castle walls'.

It devolves on an aesthetic of mood and feeling, not of form or idea; the sensibility is common to all the examples above, regardless of the medium in which they were executed. It is an art that does not bear the marks of having been jostled in the market-place, and such a jostling would have brushed away a good deal of its melancholy bloom. It is not so much bourgeois art — that would be vulgar — as a truly middle-class art, and, since the English middle class is unique, then perhaps this class origin is what gives the sensibility itself its characteristically English charm. It is reflective, the production of reverie and introspection. It is typical of Bath's quality as a product of the English artistic sensibility that one of its ghosts should be a lyrical creature who manifests its presence by an odour of jasmine.

On the hill beyond the river, they illuminate at night, a folly called 'Sham Castle'.

New Society, 1975

These landscapes insist on being peopled, some more insistently than others. You cannot, for example, keep Wordsworth out of the Lake District.

Poets in a Landscape

Ghosts of dead poets don't walk the Lake District, no – they hike. Fell-walking ghosts as mad as hatters, high as kites . . . you feel you might surprise them at the rim of Rydal Water, or spot their phantom reflections in the magic mirrors, Grasmere, Windermere – I bet the glassy tarns looked terrific on opium! Although the story goes the Wordsworth sibs, ace pedestrians and compulsive water-viewers, only took laudanum for medicinal purposes, your honour. In Lakeland, among daffodils shuddering in April snow, how easy to imagine the Wordsworths, freaked out as all hell, trudge, trudge, trudging the miles from Dove Cottage to Windermere to check if their connection (probably Humphrey Davy) had delivered.

For surely they *must* have been smashed out of their skulls all the time, Wordsworth and his sportive sister with her crazy eyes ('wild and startling eyes', opined de Quincey, noting, no doubt, and who more knowledgeably, her expanded pupils). Why else should they have gone striding off in all weathers, whirling blizzard, serrating frost, braving the peculiarly wet Cumbrian rain, to take in yet another peak or mere in a different light? How else could they have stood it, had they not been smashed? They took bits of cold pork or mutton in their pockets, to snack on. Wordsworth, absent-minded as only a genius or an incompetent, kept forgetting his gloves or his cardigan and having to go back for them.

Behind every great man is a silly woman who thinks the sun shines out of her darling's arse-hole and believes his over-sensitive fingers will rot off if he does the washing-up. Conversely, behind every great woman is some irascible fellow who says, for example: 'Of course you can't tie a clove hitch, don't be silly; give me the rope.' And she gives it to him, all right, The Reverend Patrick Brontë is a perfect example of this latter type; his daughters were bound to be geniuses, in order to spite him. But, alas, poor Dorothy Wordsworth, how could she protest her own genius in the face of a man who freely acknowledged it, yet couldn't have tied a clove hitch to save his life? There is no role so thankless as that of the muse of a person who needs looking after.

All the same, the addiction to hiking. Of course, the Wordsworths were fleeing a stress situation at home. In the confined space of Dove Cottage, they must have been bumping into one another all the time and then jumping apart as if they'd both simultaneously touched a live wire, mumbling 'Sorry' and looking out the window to see if it had stopped raining. What a finely-wrought atmosphere of sexual tension! Where else to go – even if it hadn't *quite* stopped raining, yet – but out into God's good fresh air, among the insolent grandeur of the snow-clad mountains, let the boisterous winds blow it out of their systems. Look, William; daffodils.

And we know that William looked.

Sometimes, on their walks, Dorothy was so overcome with *everything* that she had to stick her head into a babbling mountain stream to cool off. Then, when they'd got home, she'd take to bed.

There is no denying that the home life of William Wordsworth at this time was rather odd. The Dove Cottage years; William and Dorothy, he just a year older, turning thirty, at his creative peak. *Lyrical Ballads* in the bag, *The Prelude* on the boil. She, his amanuensis, his willing victim, his sycophant, glorying in it. They were acquainted with plenty of solid members of the Lakeland bourgeoisie and even one or two peasants but it is their junky friends, Coleridge (a frequent visitor) and de Quincey (although he arrives a little later) who finally complete the group.

English artists are supposed never to congregate together and form groups in the way that French artists do. Indeed, it is the proud boast of modern masters like Kingsley Amis and Margaret Drabble that the whole point of the thing is the bourgeois individualism with which it is done. Nevertheless, form groups they always have, in fact, ever since Shakespeare and Jonson at the Mermaid Tavern: the Pre-Raphaelite Brotherhood, the Camden Town Group, the Bloomsbury Group. The Lake Poets are not unique in their peer bonding.

These congregations operate with that hypocrisy of which

foreigners so often accuse us, for not only do they exist when they should not, and while their very existence is denied, but they also embrace deviant behaviour with considerable enthusiasm, the while overlaying it with such a thick coat of plain living and high thoughts that the man in the street thinks all artists are great bores until the biographies appear after they are dead and the laws of libel no longer apply.

Sexual aberration and dope (in which I include ethyl alcohol) are the prime specialities of these groups, sometimes simultaneously, occasionally favouring one rather than the other. Offhand, I cannot recall any Bloomsbury junkies but their deviance rating was high enough to recall the zero-population growth slogan coined years ago by Anthony Burgess: 'It's sapiens to be homo.' The Lake Poets, on the other hand, tended to concentrate on laudanum and whatever it was Humphrey Davy concocted in his test tubes.

Wordsworth and his sister were, however, very close. All agree on this. Impossible not to start to see such entries in Dorothy's journal of the first two years in Grasmere, when they lived in picturesque isolation together: 'I petted him on the carpet.' But Wordsworth wasn't Byron, of course. He was quite clear on that point. They must have lived together as in a perpetual latency period where puberty was postponed; and these rare nursery caresses were permitted only on those rare, sweet evenings beside the parlour fire, when William had not taken himself to bed early with a bad head. Since all art springs from repression, it is no wonder that parlour nourished great poetry. Since Dorothy had less access to sublimation, one may assume most of the tension came from her. But what did *she* get out of it? Reflected glory?

We all know what William got out of it. Oh, that delicacy of observation of hers! Ah, the exquisite language of her journals, the filigree precision with which she logs the lovely scenes around her! And was she not his unique reference book where flowers and trees and the quality of weather were concerned? Which was just as well since, as Robert Graves crustily observed; 'Wordsworth had a very cursory knowledge of wild life; he did not get up early enough in the morning.' Certainly the journals never note a breakfast earlier than nine o'clock, which was past lunchtime by the standards of the peasant farmers around them. Sometimes they have breakfast about the time I have my tea.

They were playing at the simple life, of course. William would stake out a row of peas in the vegetable garden and then retire, clapped out with manual toil, to his bed – he spent a lot of time in bed – leaving the rest of the plot to Dorothy. She did the washing; cooking; endless baking – bread, bread, bread, and giblet pies, which seems to have been her speciality. (Nowadays, this type of person is into health foods.) She coped with the servants for, although the Wordsworths were not rich, they were quite far from poor. She dealt with the beggars, the two or three a day who asked for a crust and ha'pence, she interviewed those one-legged soldiers, idiot boys, orphaned children, itinerant leech-gatherers, gypsy ladies, whose dossiers her brother later versified so diligently. She copied out the interminable results of his labours, she edited, she criticised, she polished, not ever the muse herself, but the hand-maiden of the supplicant to the muse. Funny role. Rum.

Now and then, William's one wild oat would raise its ugly head, Annette Vallon, seduced and abandoned in France years before. 'Letter from Annette', Dorothy notes impassively from time to time. These entries are usually followed by the announcement of a headache, for Dorothy, too, was prone to headaches. They are both of them always reeling under terrible headaches. Toothache; colic; piles; insomnia. 'I lay down unwell.' 'William still poorly.' Gastric troubles. Colds – a five-mile tramp soaked to the skin always leads to a week in bed, but any fool, I should have thought, could have foretold that!

So that sometimes it looks almost as though they went in for all that healthy outdoor activity simply in order to procure the temporary refuge of sickness. But both of them were sick as dogs half the time yet rarely with anything catching; I submit that the evidence in Dorothy's journals of the chronic, low-level, ill-health in the household and the exultant submission to sickness when it came is proof-positive of acute, long-term nervous strain.

Yet not, I think, the strain of repressed sexuality so much as the strain induced upon them both by Dorothy's importunate, obsessive, self-abnegating devotion to the brother who is her more-than-self. 'The fire flutters and the watch ticks. I hear nothing else save the Breathing of my Beloved and he now and then pushes his book forward and turns over a leaf.'

This is not the language of love; love is more abrasive. It is the language of the fourth form. She must have had a crush on him. Poor Dorothy; poor William, trying to read his book uneasily conscious of her crazy eyes. Eyes mad not with passion but her own ambition for, if he is *not* a genius, then she might as well be dead.

Later on, when he was married and famous and she was paralysed and demented, she could still recite her brother's poetry perfectly. Perhaps by then, resurrecting her stillborn self-esteem in the privileged licence of madness, she thought she had written it all herself.

New Society, 1978

4

LOOKING

The piece called 'Notes for a Theory of Sixties Style' was one of the first of my pieces published by the magazine, New Society. That was in 1967, when things were peaking. It makes me feel very odd, and rather old, to read 'Notes for a Theory of Sixties Style', now. I note that it is over-written and over-literary, but a person can only walk the one way and that is the way I still walk ... but, oh! the nostalgia that floods me! When I was Writer-In-Residence at the University of Sheffield, in the mid-seventies, kids would come up and ask me, in hushed voices: 'What were the sixties really like?' (This doesn't happen so much, now; the sixties must no longer seem like that Golden Age that people who were twenty in 1976 missed by a whisker, but either pure myth, or pure camp, or pure ennui, the period in which one's parents lived, as the thirties was for me.)

Anyway, they'd say: 'What were the sixties really like?' Impossible to answer except, well, it wasn't like they say in the movies. It was the best of times, it was the worst of times, etc. etc. etc. The pleasure principle met the reality principle like an irresistible force encountering an immovable object, and the reverberations of that collision are still echoing about us.

I learned how to look at things in the sixties, and I have carried on looking.

Notes for a Theory of Sixties Style

Velvet is back, skin anti-skin, mimic nakedness. Like leather and suede, only more subtly, velvet simulates the flesh it conceals, a profoundly tactile fabric. Last winter's satin invited the stroke, a slithering touch, this winter's velvet invites a more sinuous caress. But the women who buy little brown velvet dresses will probably do so in a state of unknowing, unaware they're dressing up for parts in our daily theatre of fact; unaware, too, how mysterious that theatre is.

For the nature of apparel is very complex. Clothes are so many things at once. Our social shells; the system of signals with which we broadcast our intentions; often the projections of our fantasy selves (a fat old woman in a bikini); the formal uniform of our life roles (the businessman's suit, the teacher's tweed jacket with leather patches and ritual accessory of pipe in breast pocket); sometimes simple economic announcements of income or wealth (real jewellery – especially inherited real jewellery, which throws in a bonus of class as well – or mink). Clothes are our weapons, our challenges, our visible insults.

And more. For we think our dress expresses ourselves but in fact it expresses our environment and, like advertising, pop music, pulp fiction and second-feature films, it does so almost at a subliminal, emotionally charged, instinctual, non-intellectual level. The businessmen, the fashion writers, the designers and models, the shopkeepers, the buyers, the window dressers live in the same cloud of unknowing as us all; they think they mould the public taste but really they're blind puppets of a capricious goddess, goddess of mirrors, weather-cocks and barometers, whom the Elizabethans called Mutability. She is inscrutable but logical.

The inscrutable but imperative logic of change has forced fashion in the sixties through the barriers of space and time. Clothes today sometimes seem arbitrary and bizarre; nevertheless, the startling dandyism of the newly emancipated young reveals a kind of logic of whizzing entropy. Mutability is having a field day.

Let us take the following example. A young girl, invited to a party, left to herself (nc mother to guide her), might well select the following ensemble: a Mexican cotton wedding dress (though she's not a bride, probably no virgin, either – thus at one swoop turning a garment which in its original environment is an infinitely potent symbol into a piece of decoration); her grandmother's button boots (once designed to show off the small feet and moneyed leisure of an Edwardian middle class who didn't need to work and rarely had to walk); her mother's fox fur (bought to demonstrate her father's status); and her old school beret dug out of the loft because she saw Faye Dunaway in *Bonnie and Clyde* (and a typical role-definition garment changes gear).

All these eclectic fragments, robbed of their symbolic content, fall together to form a new whole, a dramatisation of the individual, a personal style. And fashion today (real fashion, what real people wear) is a question of style, no longer a question of items in harmony. 'What to wear with what' is no longer a burning question; in the 1960s, everything is worn all at once.

Style means the presentation of the self as a three-dimensional art object, to be wondered at and handled. And this involves a new attitude to the self which is thus adorned. The gaudy rags of the flower children, the element of fancy dress even in 'serious' clothes (the military look, the thirties revival), extravagant and stylised face-painting, wigs, hairpieces, amongst men the extraordinary recrudescence of the decorative moustache (and, indeed, the concept of the decorative man), fake tattooing – all these are in the nature of disguises.

Disguise entails duplicity. One passes oneself off as another, who may or may not exist – as Jean Harlow or Lucy in the Sky with Diamonds or Al Capone or Sergeant Pepper. Though the dis-

guise is worn as play and not intended to deceive, it does nevertheless give a relaxation from one's own personality and the
discovery of maybe unsuspected new selves. One feels free to
behave more freely. This holiday from the persistent self is the
perpetual lure of fancy dress. Rosalind in disguise in the Forest of
Arden could pretend to be a boy pretending to be a seductress,
satisfying innumerable atavistic desires in the audience of the play.
And we are beginning to realise once again what everybody always
used to know, that all human contact is profoundly ambiguous.
And the style of the sixties expresses this knowledge.

The *Bonnie and Clyde* clothes and the guru robes certainly don't
indicate a cult of violence or a massive swing to transcendental
meditation (although *Rave* magazine did feature a 'Raver's
Guide' to the latter subject in the November issue); rather, this
rainbow proliferation of all kinds of fancy dress shows a new
freedom many people fear, especially those with something to lose
when the frozen, repressive, role-playing world properly starts
to melt.

Consider a typical hippy, consider a typical Chinese Red Guard.
One is a beautiful explosion of sexually ambiguous silks and beads,
the other a sternly-garbed piece of masculine aggression, proclaim-
ing by his clothes the gift of his individual self to the puritan ethic
of his group. The first sports the crazy patchwork uniform of a
society where social and sexual groupings are willy-nilly disintegrating, the second is part of a dynamically happening society
where all the individuals are clenched together like a fist. One is a
fragment of a kaleidoscope, the other a body blow. One is opening
out like a rose, the other forging straight ahead.

Of course, one does not have to go so far afield as China to see
this dichotomy of aim. If you put the boy in the djellibah next to a
middle-aged police constable, each will think of the other: 'The
enemies are amongst us.' For the boy in the djellibah will be a very
young boy, and the class battle in Britain (once sartorially symbolised by Keir Hardie's cloth cap) is redefining itself as the battle of
the generations.

The Rolling Stones' drugs case was an elegant confrontation of
sartorial symbolism in generation warfare: the judge, in ritually

potent robes and wig, invoking the doom of his age and class upon the beautiful children in frills and sunset colours, who dared to question the infallibility he represents as icon of the law and father figure.

The Rolling Stones' audience appeal has always been anti-parent, anti-authority, and they have always used sartorial weapons – from relatively staid beginnings (long hair and grime) to the famous *Daily Mirror* centre spread in superdrag. They are masters of the style of calculated affront. And it never fails to work. The clothing of pure affront, sported to bug the squares (as the Hell's Angels say), will always succeed in bugging the squares no matter how often they are warned, 'He only does it to annoy.'

The Hell's Angels and the other Californian motor-cycle gangs deck themselves with iron crosses, Nazi helmets, necklets and earrings, they grow their hair to their shoulders and dye their beards green, red and purple, they cultivate halitosis and body odour. Perfect dandies of beastliness, they incarnate the American nightmare. Better your sister marry a Negro than have the Oakland chapter of Hell's Angels drop in on her for coffee.

But this outlaw dress represents a real dissociation from society. It is a very serious joke and, in their Neanderthal way, the Hell's Angels are obeying Camus' law – that the dandy is always a rebel, that he challenges society because he challenges mortality. The motor-cycle gangs challenge mortality face to face, doing 100 mph on a California freeway in Levis and swastikas, no crash helmet but a wideawake hat, only a veneer of denim between the man and his death. 'The human being who is condemned to die is, at least, magnificent before he disappears and his magnificence is his justification.'

In the decade of Vietnam, in the century of Hiroshima and Buchenwald, we are as perpetually aware of mortality as any generation ever was. It is small wonder that so many people are taking the dandy's way of asking unanswerable questions. The pursuit of magnificence starts as play and ends as nihilism or metaphysics or a new examination of the nature of goals.

In the pursuit of magnificence, nothing is sacred. Hitherto sacrosanct imagery is desecrated. When Pete Townshend of The

Who first put on his jacket carved out of the Union Jack, he turned our national symbol into an abstraction far more effectively than did Jasper Johns when he copied the Old Glory out in paint and hung it on his wall. Whether or not Pete Townshend fully realised the nature of his abstraction is not the question; he was impelled to it by the pressures of the times.

Similarly, fabrics and objects hitherto possessing strong malignant fetishistic qualities have either been cleansed of their deviational overtones and used for their intrinsic textural charm, or else worn in the camp style with a humorous acknowledgement of those overtones. Rubber, leather, fur, objects such as fish-net stockings and tall boots are fetishes which the purity of style has rendered innocent, as sex becomes more relaxed and the norm more subtle.

Iconic clothing has been secularised, too. Witness the cult of the military uniform. A guardsman in a dress uniform is ostensibly an icon of aggression; his coat is red as the blood he hopes to shed. Seen on a coat-hanger, with no man inside it, the uniform loses all its blustering significance and, to the innocent eye seduced by decorative colour and tactile braid, it is as abstract in symbolic information as a parasol to an Eskimo. It becomes simply magnificent. However, once on the back of the innocent, it reverts to an aggressive role: to old soldiers (that is, most men in this country over forty) the secularised military uniform gives far too much information, all of it painful. He sees a rape of his ideals, is threatened by a terrible weapon of affront.

A good deal of iconic clothing has become secularised simply through disuse. It no longer has any symbolic content for the stylists and is not decorative enough to be used in play. Mutability has rendered it obsolescent. The cabaret singer in her sequin sheath which shrieks 'Look at me but don't touch me, I'm armour-plated' survives as an image of passive female sexuality, the *princesse lointaine* (or, rather, the *putain lointaine*) only in the womblike unreality of the nightclub or on the fantasy projection of the television screen. The tulle and taffeta bride in her crackling virginal carapace, clasping numinous lilies, the supreme icon of woman as a sexual thing and nothing else whatever, survives as part of the potlatch culture at either end of the social scale – where the pressures to make weddings of their daughters displays of conspicuous consumption are fiercest.

On the whole, though, girls have been emancipated from the stiff forms of iconic sexuality. Thanks to social change, to contraception, to equal pay for equal work, there is no need for this iconography any more; both men and women's clothes today say, 'Look at me and touch me if I want you.' Velvet is back, skin anti-skin, mimic nakedness.

New Society, 1967

The Recession Style

A poster advertising a certain women's magazine has been decorating the London underground for some time. It shows a girl wearing an assemblage of what are evidently supposed to be very high-style garments, so high-style as to represent an extreme of dandyism. The slogan rams this point home: 'Most girls wouldn't wear it.' This is the famous 'dare to wear' challenge – dare you blind 'em with your style, or are you (it is implied) content to remain a fuddy-duddy stick-in-the-mud.

But if you didn't know she was a fashion model, the girl in the poster would, in fact, look like nothing so much as a bag lady (or rather, person), in her asexually shapeless jacket, loose trousers and sagging socks, with a scarf of a dubiously soiled colour wrapped round her head, like a bandage beneath a hat jammed firmly down. Indeed, you can sometimes see, slumped on benches beneath this very poster, people in much the same get-up, utterly unconscious of their daring, or their involuntary dandyism, or anything at all.

In Green Park station, this poster has acquired the graffiti: 'Most girls couldn't afford it.' But to look like this need not necessarily cost much. You could put the look together for pennies. It has some of the qualities of late sixties thrift-shop chic, and many women of my generation have been going around looking like that for years, and looking like hell, in fact. Only the model's exquisitely painted face indicates that *her* get-up is intentional, and not some haphazard makeshift arrangement; that she has been paid to dress up like this, and hasn't been snapped at random at the Greenham Common peace camp. (As if to emphasise this resemblance, the poster has elsewhere been inscribed: 'Embrace the Base.')

She seems to be carrying a gasmask for a handbag, and is walking across a version of J. G. Ballard's 'terminal beach', – an arid stretch of pebbles devoid of the evidence of life beneath a sunless sky.

It is a very striking image, a gift for the spraycan commentators, and it captures the mood of the times almost to the point of parody, as if to say: we are all paper-bag persons, now, refugees in an empty world where, as well as all the other problems, you can no longer depend even on rouge to tell you what is male and what is female. Now that boys paint their faces, too, we only know she *is* a girl because the slogan tells us so.

The poster represents a public breakthrough for the aesthetic of poverty that has been operating strongly at street level since the punk styles of the mid-seventies, and may well prove (and is it any wonder?) to be the dominant mood of the eighties. It is a way of dressing that makes you look like the victim of a catastrophe.

Obviously, an aesthetic of poverty is quite different from looking poor because you *are* poor. The sisters with the spraycan interpreted the spirit of the poster correctly. The cash nexus enters into the whole thing as soon as you pay two hundred quid for your disintegrating leather flying-jacket, instead of digging it out of a garbage can.

Paying through the nose to look poor may well be a self-protective measure among those in work whilst the unemployment figures stack up. But it is ironic that rich girls (such as students) swan about in rancid long-johns with ribbons in their hair, when the greatest influence on working–class girls who *are* holding down jobs at ludicrously low wages, would appear to be

Princess Di, herself always impeccably turned out and never short of a bob.

Princess Di look-a-likes work at the check-outs of every super-market, often looking much prettier than her pictures, but, to quote *Honey* magazine: 'The way for clothes to look now is battered and crumpled, as though they've stood the test of time.' This is in itself an elitist concept, because only high-class, expensive fabrics *do* stand the test of time and, like the rich, look better as they get older.

Few can afford *real* old clothes of that kind. But cheap fabrics can simulate age if purposely crumpled, faded, torn and stained. (Leather, both real and artificial, is synthetically aged – the process known wittily as 'distressing'.) A poor fit is essential because garments must look twice-used, as if rescued from some nameless disaster. In its own unique way, the rag trade has acknowledged the recession.

According to the coverage, lavish as inscrutably ever, of last autumn's Paris fashion shows, the Japanese designers now in vogue seem to have been waiting in the wings until the time was ripe to off-load onto the backs of prosperous Occidentals a whole cornucopia of shapeless, arbitrary Zen styles, executed in impeccably Zen shades of earth, granite, foam and dung, and in fabrics which would appear to have been stored in cesspits since early Edo period. Now, clearly, they judge the time has come.

To force the filthy rich, in the name of high fashion, to dress up in garments derived from the Buddhist equivalent of Franciscan habits, the garb of conspicuous and unworldly poverty, may well seem richly humorous to the perpetrators of the jape and, perhaps, some small revenge for World War II, or the entire history of European imperialism, depending on the personal bias of these designers. I suspect, too, a degree of class vengeance in some of the British designers (like Vivienne Westwood), who have arrived in international couture via anarcho-Dada.

All the same, imitation cast-offs, shrouds and coveralls are the coming thing. Up-market couture coincides with the sort of real cast-offs those people who are so down-market they scarcely figure fiscally within it have been making the best of since the economy first began to show stress.

This, as ever, leaves the middle class out in the cold, where they stay snug in their Marks and Spencer sweaters and Laura Ashley frocks. They usually remain in work, and are therefore at liberty to indulge in wishful thinking about eternal values and 100% pure natural fibres.

These days, the thing that really determines whether you look 'nice' (ie, clean, neat and unprovocative) or 'nasty,' (ie, messy, spiky, ominously black clad, riotously painted or tattooed) depends very much on whether you are in work or not. It behoves most of those in steady employment, especially white-collar work, to keep that white-collar scrubbed and trim because there are lots of people after it. Perhaps *that's* why most girls won't dare to wear the bag lady look until circumstances force them to it – though they might wrap a few token rags around their ankles.

Only top executives 'dare to wear' jeans to the office any more, or, indeed, jeans anywhere. Jeans have lost their outlaw chic since the class of '68 took them into the senior common room by a natural progression. They are now, more or less, a sign of grumpy middle age.

But, if you are *not* in work, you can wear what you bloody like. And they do. This emphasises more and more the basic distinction between those participating in the economic process and those exiled from it, a distinction which becomes daily more and more marked. The rich – which, nowadays, means almost everyone who has a steady job (except for those notable exceptions in the NHS and elsewhere) – may adopt the aesthetic of poverty for fun. Those who have no other option adopt it with ferocity and aggression. Once they know what they're doing, that is.

And often they do. Semiotic theory has clearly permeated the whole business. (I blame the art schools, especially their general studies departments; and the theory and practice of performance art has something to do with it.) Not only has the idea of the 'language of fashion' become a boring shibboleth, but much of the apparel you see about is clearly intended to be 'read', in no uncertain terms, as complex statements of affection and disaffection.

Literally, read. To hang around sheathed in leather covered

with unimpeachable slogans like 'PEACE', 'BAN GOVERNMENT' and 'UTOPIA NOW', whilst writing 'CHAOS' on walls, gobbing a lot and lobbing crushed beer cans at passing cats, is to engage in a complicated piece of street theatre, which an illiterate person could be forgiven for getting entirely wrong.

The idea of appearance-as-visual-confrontation resurfaced with the punks in '76 after its first Situationalist outing in the heady days of '68. Its roots go right back to Zurich '17, and Petersburg just before the deluge. It is now common property, and it is used consciously by people who sometimes do not appear to be fully in control of what, precisely, they are expressing.

Pariah chic is more serious than outlaw chic. It produces ambiguities of which a girl with an anarcho-feminist lapel badge and a ring through her nose – the kind of ring with which animals are traditionally led to slaughter – is but the innocent victim.

Turning yourself into a slogan is, in the first place, a confrontational thing to do. Then comes the problem of the nature of the slogan, and who reads it.

The most extreme, and permanent way of turning yourself into a slogan is to tattoo that slogan on your skin, as if to say: My attitudes won't come off in the wash. But since tattooing is a form of self-mutilation, like pierced ears and noses, there is already an ambivalence about the tattooed provocateur. You must suffer in order to be provocative in this manner. And this kind of provocation can seem intended to prove suffering.

There was this skinhead, on the bus. He was adorned with two tattoos, both obviously self-inflicted. One went round his neck. It was a serrated line plus the instruction: SLIT HERE. The other, on his forehead was a swastika. He was twitching a lot, probably junked up to the eyeballs to give himself courage for the project he had evidently decided to embark on. He got off the bus at Vauxhall, and strode off in the direction of Brixton.

But to walk through Brixton with a swastika on the forehead, and an exhortation to slit the throat under one ear, is not so much provocative as suicidal – even if, along Electric Avenue, his appearance was certainly read as an advertisement of his own psychosis rather than a political statement. This kid had turned

himself into a walking piece of racist graffiti. He filled me with
rage, pity and terror.

The Dadaists used pity, rage and terror as the tools of the art
that was supposed to end art, just as the first world war put an end
(or so they thought) to civilisation. They sang, danced and
screamed the scenarios of the end of the world in Zurich, among
the cuckoo clocks. They caused a lot of fuss.

Something like fifty years ago, Yeats opined that things were
falling apart, and many believed him and were distressed. Now
the rough beast may well be amongst us, having chiselled the
mark on his own forehead, and nobody makes much fuss.
So accustomed have we become to the violent and desperate
extravagance of the visual language which has accompanied
economic catastrophe.

We must brace ourselves and wait while the Chinese curse
works itself out: 'May you live in exciting times.'

New Society, 1980

The Wound in the Face

I spent a hallucinatory weekend, staring at faces I'd cut out of
women's magazines, either from the beauty page or from the ads
– all this season's faces. I stuck twenty or thirty faces on the wall
and tried to work out from the evidence before me (a) what
women's faces are supposed to be looking like, now; and (b) why.
It was something of an exercise in pure form, because the magazine models' faces aren't exactly the face in the street – not low-
style, do-it-yourself assemblages, but more a platonic, ideal face.
Further, they reflect, as well as the mood of the moment, what the
manufacturers are trying to push this year. Nevertheless, the
zeitgeist works through the manufacturers, too. They do not
understand their own imagery, any more than the consumer who
demonstrates it does. I am still working on the nature of the

imagery of cosmetics. I think it scares me.

Construing the imagery was an unnerving experience because all the models appeared to be staring straight at me with such a heavy, static quality of *being there* that it was difficult to escape the feeling they were accusing me of something. (How rarely women look one another in the eye.) Only two of the faces wear anything like smiles, and only one is showing a hint of her teeth. This season's is not an extravert face. Because there is not much to smile about this season? Surely. It is a bland, hard, bright face; it is also curiously familiar, though I have never seen it before.

The face of the seventies matches the fashions in clothes that have dictated some of its features, and is directly related to the social environment which produces it. Like fashions in clothes, fashions in faces have been stuck in pastiche for the past four or five years. This bankruptcy is disguised by ever more ingenious pastiche – of the thirties, the forties, the fifties, the Middle East, Xanadu, Wessex (those smocks). Compared with the short skirts and flat shoes of ten years ago, style in women's clothes has regressed. Designers are trying to make us cripple our feet again with high-heeled shoes and make us trail long skirts in dogshit. The re-introduction of rouge is part of this regression; rouge, coyly re-introduced under the nineteenth-century euphemism of 'blusher'.

The rather older face – the *Vogue* face, as opposed to the *Honey* face – is strongly under the 1930s influence, the iconographic, androgynous face of Dietrich and Garbo, with heavily emphasised bone structures, hollow cheeks and hooded eyelids. Warhol's transvestite superstars, too, and his magazine, *Interview* – with its passion for the tacky, the kitschy, for fake glamour, for rhinestones, sequins, Joan Crawford, Ann-Margaret – have exercised a profound influence. As a result, fashionable women now tend to look like women imitating men imitating women, an interesting reversal. The face currently perpetuated by the glossies aspires to the condition of that of Warhol's Candy Darling.

The main message is that the hard, bland face with which women brazened their way through the tough 1930s, the tough 1940s and the decreasingly tough 1950s (at the end of the 1950s, when things got less tough, they abandoned it), is back to sustain us through the tough 1970s. It recapitulates the glazed, self-contained look typical of times of austerity.

But what is one to make of the transvestite influence? Is it that the physical image of women took such a battering in the sixties that when femininity did, for want of anything better, return, the only people we could go to to find out what it had looked like were the dedicated male impersonators who had kept the concept alive in the sequined gowns, their spike-heeled shoes and their peony lipsticks? Probably. 'The feminine character, and the idea of femininity on which it is modelled, are products of masculine society,' says Theodore Adorno. Clearly a female impersonator knows more about his idea of the character he is mimicking than I do, because it is his very own invention, and has nothing to do with me.

Yet what about the Rousseauesque naturalism of the dominant image of women in the mid-1960s? Adorno can account for that, sociologically, too. 'The image of undistorted nature arises only in distortion, as its opposite.' The sixties face was described early in the decade by *Queen* (as it was then) as a 'look of luminous vacancy'.

The sixties face had a bee-stung underlip, enormous eyes and a lot of disordered hair. It saw itself as a wild, sweet, gipsyish, vulnerable face. Its very lack of artifice suggested sexual licence in a period that had learned to equate cosmetics, not with profligacy as in the nineteenth century, but with conformity to the standard social and sexual female norm. Nice girls wore lipstick, in the fifties.

When the sixties face used cosmetics at all, it explored imports such as kohl and henna from Indian shops. These had the twin advantages of being extremely exotic and very, very cheap. For purposes of pure decoration, for fun, it sometimes stuck sequins to itself, or those little gold and silver 'good conduct' stars. It bought sticks of stage make-up, and did extraordinary things around its eyes with them, at about the time of Flower Power. It was, basically, a low-style or do-it-yourself face. Ever in search of the new, the magazines eventually caught up with it, and high-style faces caught on to flowered cheeks and stars on the eyelids at about the time the manufacturers did. So women had to pay considerably more for their pleasures.

The sixties look gloried in its open pores and, if your eye wasn't into the particular look, you probably thought it didn't wash itself much. But it was just that, after all those years of pancake make-up, people had forgotten what the real colour of female skin was. This face cost very little in upkeep. Indeed, it was basically a most economical and serviceable model and it was quite a shock to realise, as the years passed, that all the beauty experts were wrong and, unless exposed to the most violent weather, it did not erode if it was left ungreased. A face is not a bicycle. Nevertheless, since this face had adopted naturalism as an ingenious form of artifice, it *was* a mask, like the grease masks of cosmetics, though frequently refreshingly eccentric.

At the end of that decade, in a brief period of delirium, there was a startling vogue of black lipstick and red eyeshadow. For a little while we were painting ourselves up just as arbitrarily as Larionov did before the Revolution. Dada in the boudoir! What a witty parody of the whole theory of cosmetics!

The basic theory of cosmetics is that they make a woman beautiful. Or, as the advertisers say, more beautiful. You blot out your noxious wens and warts and blemishes, shade your nose to make it bigger or smaller, draw attention to your good features by bright colours, and distract it from your bad features by more reticent tones. But those manic and desperate styles – leapt on and exploited instantly by desperate manufacturers – seemed to be about to break the ground for a whole new aesthetic of appearance, which would have nothing to do with the conformist ideology of 'beauty' at all. Might – ah, might – it be possible to use cosmetics to free women from the burden of having to look beautiful altogether?

Because black lipstick and red eyeshadow never 'beautified' anybody. They were the cosmetic equivalent of Duchamp's moustache on the Mona Lisa. They were cosmetics used as satire on cosmetics, on the arbitrary convention that puts blue on eyelids and pink on lips. Why not the other way round? The best part of the joke was that the look itself was utterly monstrous. It instantly converted the most beautiful women into outrageous grotesques; every face a work of anti-art. I enjoyed it very, very much.

However, it takes a helluva lot of guts to maintain oneself in a perpetual state of visual offensiveness. Most women could not resist keeping open a treacherous little corner on sex appeal. Besides, the joke went a little too near the bone. To do up your eyes so that they look like self-inflicted wounds is to wear on your face the evidence of the violence your environment inflicts on you.

Black paint around the eyes is such a familiar convention it seems natural; so does red paint on the mouth. We are so used to the bright red mouth we no longer see it as the wound it mimics, except in the treacherous lucidity of paranoia. But the shock of the red-painted eye recalls, directly, the blinding of Gloucester in *Lear*; or, worse and more aptly, the symbolic blinding of Oedipus. Women are allowed − indeed, encouraged − to exhibit the sign of their symbolic castration, but only in the socially sanctioned place. To transpose it upwards is to allow its significance to become apparent. We went too far, that time. Scrub it all off and start again.

And once we started again, red lipstick came back. Elizabeth I seems to have got a fine, bright carmine with which to touch up her far from generous lips. The Victorian beauty's 'rosebud mouth' − the mouth so tiny it was a wonder how it managed to contain her teeth − was a restrained pink. Flappers' lips spread out and went red again, and the 'generous mouth' became one of the great glamour conventions of the entire twentieth century and has remained so, even if its colour is modified.

White-based lipsticks, colourless glosses, or no lipstick at all, were used in the 1960s. Now the mouth is back as a bloody gash, a visible wound. This mouth bleeds over everything, cups, ice-cream, table napkins, towels. Mary Quant has a shade called (of course) 'Bloody Mary', to ram the point home. We will leave our bloody spoor behind us, to show we have been there.

In the thirties, that spoor was the trademark of the sophisticate, the type of Baudelairean female dandy Dietrich impersonated so well. Dietrich always transcended self-pity and self-destruction, wore the wound like a badge of triumph, and came out on top. But Iris Storm in Michael Arlen's *The Green Hat*, the heroines of Maurice Dekobra, the wicked film star in Chandler's *The Little Sister* who always dressed in black to offset her fire-engine of a mouth — they all dripped blood over everything as they stalked sophisticatedly to their dooms. In their wake, lipstick traces on a cigarette stub; the perfect imprint, like half a heart, of a scarlet lower lip on a drained Martini glass; the tell-tale scarlet letter, A for adultery, on a shirt collar . . . the kitsch poetry of it all!

Elizabeth Taylor scrawls 'Not for sale' on her bedroom mirror in her red, red lipstick in *Butterfield 8*. The generosity the mouth has given so freely, will be spurned with brutal ingratitude. The open wound will never heal. Perhaps, sometimes, she will lament the loss of the tight rosebud; but it has gone forever.

The revival of red lipstick indicates, above all, I suppose, that women's sense of security was transient.

New Society, 1975

Frida Kahlo

Frida Kahlo loved to paint her face. She painted it constantly, from the first moment she began seriously to paint when she was sixteen up till the time of her death some thirty years later. Again and again, her face, with the beautiful bones, the hairy upper lip, and batwing eyebrows that meet in the middle. She liked to be photographed, too, but she could not do that for herself so other people did it for her, although portrait photographs of Frida Kahlo resemble the face in her own pictures so closely that her eyes seem to have had the power to subvert the camera, making it see her as she saw herself, as she makes us see what she sees when she paints.

Women painters are sometimes forced to specialise in self-portraiture because they can't afford models. Gwen John, for example. That wasn't the case with Frida Kahlo. I think it was the process of looking at herself that engaged her. Because the face in the self-portraits is not that of a woman looking at the person looking at the picture; she is not addressing *us*. It is the face of a woman looking at *herself*, subjecting herself to the most intense scrutiny, almost to an interrogation.

But we will never know what this urgent self-interrogation concerns. Frida Kahlo uses narcissism, exhibitionism, as a form of disguise.

This is the face of a woman looking into a mirror. We cannot see the mirror but we must always remember that it was there. These paintings are a form of self-monitoring. She watches herself watching herself. When she does that, she is at work.

The painted face is that of a woman working at transforming her whole experience in the world into a series of marvellously explicit images. She is in the process of remaking herself in another medium than life and is becoming resplendent. The flesh made sign.

The wounded flesh.

Her raw material was herself, just as the raw material of the New York performance artist, Cindy Sherman, who also specialises in self-portraiture, is herself. (In many ways, Frida Kahlo was ahead of her time; hers is a remarkably total kind of artistic vision, including such things as shoes and bed-linen.)

But, with Frida Kahlo, the raw material remained – raw. The wounds never healed over.

Her husband, Diego Rivera, said: 'Frida is the only example in the history of art of an artist who tore open her chest and heart to reveal the biological truth of her feelings.' How painful he makes it sound. It *was* painful. The expression on that painted face, unchanging over the years, is one of enigmatic stoicism and she displays her wounds like a martyr. The woman who would dig an ornamental comb through her hair deep into her scalp with what a friend called 'coquettish masochism' was a connoisseur of physical suffering.

Speaking of hair, what she does with it in the pictures is extra-ordinary. If wild, flowing hair is associated with sensuality and abandon, then note how the hair of Frida Kahlo, the most sensual of painters, hangs in disorder down her back only when she depicts herself in great pain, or as a child.

Sometimes her hair is scraped back so tight the sight of it hurts; or it is unnaturally twisted into knots; plaited with flowers and ribbons and topknots and feathers in any one of 50 different ways; arranged in fetishistic, architectural compositions of braids. She puts her poor hair through such torture it is a relief, in the picture of 1940, after her divorce from Rivera, to see it all cut off at last and lying on the ground, as if she'd finally got rid of an unpleasant, demanding pet.

But there is a phrase from one of the popular songs she liked to sing at the top of the picture:

look,
if I loved you, it was for your hair
now you are hairless
I love you no more.

And she wears, not the folkloric Mexican finery with which we associate her but a man's suit. When she was a girl, before her accident, before she married Rivera, she used to pose for photographs *en travestie*. Even for family photographs. Quite the little dandy. But in *this* picture, the jacket and trousers are much too big, billowing, voluminous. Has she put on her enormous ex-husband's clothes, in order to comfort herself? Or do men's clothes no longer fit her, as they once did? One thing is plain: whoever no longer loves her like this, she certainly does not love herself. They were remarried later that year. She grew her hair and braided it again.

Although Frida Kahlo, born in 1907, liked to give 1910, the year of the Mexican revolution, as the date of her birth, you could say she was not really born until the disastrous accident that broke her. Her work as a painter came out of that accident; she painted in order to pass the time during the lengthy period of recovery nobody had really expected. (Before the accident, interestingly, the woman who was to become the lifelong patient of doctors had intended to study medicine and become a doctor herself.)

The accident and its physical consequences not only made her start to paint; they gave her something to paint about. Her pain. In fact, the accident itself, horribly, turned her into a bloody and involuntary art object. After a streetcar ploughed into the bus on which Frida Kahlo was travelling through Mexico City, a metal bar pierced her back; somehow all her clothes came off in the crash and the bag of gold powder carried by a fellow passenger spilled over her. It is an image from a nightmare, more horribly glamorous than any she imagined, or recreated.

There's a deer with Frida Kahlo's face, its habitual changeless intensity of gaze; the deer's side is pierced with arrows. She is not often so subtle. She depicts her body enclosed in one of the plaster-of-Paris corsets prescribed for her crumbling spine, her torso stuck with tacks; she paints the fresh incision of the surgeon's knife; her own blood, and other people's, too; her miscarriage; her restless dual nature, part European, part Mexican; her broken heart.

She made of her broken, humiliated, warring self a series of masterpieces of mutilation and she did so in real life, too, submitting herself to more than thirty surgical operations between 1925 and 1954, culminating in the amputation of a foot.

And that loss seems to be what killed her. What made her not want to live any more, finally. As if they could cut her, carve her, burrow away within as much as they pleased, just so long as they did not take anything away.

Most of her operations did not alleviate the many and various conditions that ailed her; possibly some of them, at least, were needless, even harmful. If she was an invalid all her life, she did not act like an invalid unless forcibly bedridden; had she treated her physical fragility with more respect and less awe, she might have lived longer, and painted more still lives of fruit and flowers, more portraits of monkeys and children. More cruel truths. As it was, she became addicted to pain-killers and to alcohol. In addition, she may have suffered from syphilis. In the circumstances, her narcissism becomes triumphant, a carnival. (Never forget the black humour in her paintings.)

Married to Rivera almost all her adult life with only the brief respite of a year's divorce, she was tormented by jealousy and paid back his infidelities in kind although her husband's own jealousy prevented her from the pleasure of regaling her conquests to him, as he did to her.

Monstrously ambiguous couple – Frida with her moustache, Diego with his fat man's breasts. The sexiest couple in Mexico, who did not fuck. (According to Rivera, one of the conditions Frida made for their remarriage was, no more sex.) Mr and Mrs Jack Spratt, he so fat, she so skinny. Their division of labour was absolute: he did the large scale public works, the great political murals. She did the colour postcards of heightened states of mind, the politics of the heart.

Rivera, I suppose, was her muse. At least two self-portraits, one of 1943, one of 1949, show he of the bullfrog features ensconced upon her forehead, in the place where I imagine that Cain was marked. Obsession. Devotion. Inspiration. Muses aren't supposed to make you happy, after all. Then, again, men are warned against marrying their muses. Women sometimes have no option.

She became a great painter because of, not in spite of, all this.

Women painters are often forced to make exhibitions of themselves in order to mount exhibitions. Fame, notoriety, scandal, eccentric dress and behaviour – Rosa Bonheur, Meret Oppenheim, Leonor Fini, Georgia O'Keeffe. Frida Kahlo. Fame is not an end in itself but a strategy. Being famous means she can stake out her own territory, can even determine, wholly or in part, the way her paintings will be looked at. Frida Kahlo's transition from the status of maker of tiny, charming paintings on tin in the naïve style to publicly acknowledged major artist was assisted, not hindered, by her growing fame as the beautiful wife of the Mexican muralist. Indeed, she became famous as a symbol of *Mexicanness*.

After her marriage, after she gave up trousers, she always wore the most elaborate Mexican traditional dress and quantities of jewellery, pre-Columbian antiques, beads bought from the market, anything, everything. She spent hours arranging herself for the day. She turned herself into a folkloric artefact at a time when the Mexican bourgeoisie, from which she came, did not indulge in fancy dress and even high Bohemia, to which she now belonged, only kept it for parties.

If she started to wear her long petticoats to hide her crippled leg, then the enchantment of disguise, of the perpetual festival of fancy dress, soon overcame her. In New York, children followed her in the street: 'Where's the circus?' When she dressed up for some big event, she took the plain gold caps off her incisors and replaced them with caps set with rose diamonds. Even the dazzle of her smile was artificial, and her living exposition of the vitality of the peasant culture of Mexico which turned her appearance into a piece of political theatre could easily find itself trapped in the world of commodity high fashion. In Paris in 1939, Schiaparelli liked her dress so much that she designed a *robe Madame Rivera* and Frida Kahlo's hand, with its crust of market stall rings, graced the cover of *Vogue*.

Like Walt Whitman, if she contradicted herself, it was because she contained multitudes.

After her death in 1954, Diego Rivera turned the blue painted house in Coyoacan, a suburb of Mexico City, where she had been born, where they lived, into the Museo Frida Kahlo. He didn't have to change a thing; she had already made of their home a shrine dedicated to their entwined, if complicated, lives. Herself a work of art, she produced art works inside another one. Rivera left the unfinished portrait of Stalin on the easel in her studio, with her wheelchair next to it. The little earthenware mugs spelling out DIEGO Y FRIDA on pegs in the kitchen. Her most precious fetishes in her bedroom, for this thwarted mother kept a pickled foetus in a jar by her bed, surrounded herself with dolls.

In the magic and artful universe of this house, a beautiful and wholly invented life of flowers, fruit, parrots, monkeys and other people's children went on while Rivera paused from mural painting to conduct visiting Hollywood film stars on guided tours of the work of the Revolution in Mexico. (Both husband and wife were more than the sum of their contradictions.) She, sometimes in her orthopaedic corset, sometimes in her wheelchair, sometimes in bed and painting with the aid of a mirror, sometimes miraculously whole, plaited and unplaited her hair; sang rude songs and violent ballads; laughed and was enchanting. Yes. I believe that. I believe that she was enchanting.

When she was well enough, she painted the strangeness of the world made visible. Her face. Her friends. A bowl of fruit. Flowers. The victim of a *crime passionel*. The sun. A dead child. The curse of love, the disasters to which the female body is heir. 'VIVA LA VIDA', she scrawled on her last painting, when she was about to die.

Images of Frida Kahlo, Redstone Press, 1989

The Bridled Sweeties

Underwear exemplifies the existence – indeed, the chronic persistence – of the cultural taboo against nakedness that seems universal to all people at all times. In symbolic terms, a penis sheath or an ochre body rub is as good as a white tie and tails. We may see as stark naked many a man who perceives himself adequately, even impeccably, dressed. In the same way, a woman covered from neck to ankle in a woollen dressing-gown wouldn't dream of going down to the shops for a quarter of tea because she perceives herself as provocatively undressed.

Robert Graves prissily distinguishes between two kinds of unclothing. The naked (he poetically opines, I leadenly paraphrase) is sacred but the nude, rude. In other words, the pagan spectacle of the ritually and consciously unclad is the human in a glorious state of holy nature, which is why it is taboo. The nude, dressed up to the eyeballs in a lengthy art tradition, is clad in an invisible garment composed of generations of eyes.

Elsewhere – in *The White Goddess* – Graves describes how a numinous young Celtic person solved an enigmatic request to appear before her lover neither clothed nor unclothed by wrapping herself up in a fishing net. This non-garment performs none of the essential functions of clothing, neither protection from the elements, nor chaste concealment of the parts, nor sign of status. Yet it fulfilled, while it subverted, the conditions of the taboo against absolute nakedness. Similarly, Baudelaire made his girl-friend take off all her garments but for her necklace. This made her look more naked by contrast, while offering a talismanic protection against what Graves might call the unleashed power of the goddess (though in that case she was a black one). From here, it is but one short step to the magical *deshabillée* of the Janet Reger catalogue.

Women's sexy underwear is a minor but significant growth industry of late twentieth-century Britain in the twilight of capitalism. In this peculiar climate, the luxury trades prosper. Perhaps a relationship with post-imperialism may be postulated; some folks call it 'decadence'. 'This collection has received enthusiastic acclaim wherever an appreciation for excellence as part of life's enrichment is sought,' declares the brief preface to Miss Reger's picture book of her wares. The cover depicts a handsome pair of legs in gold kid mules, caressed in an auto-erotic fashion by a hand whose red fingernails are of a length that prohibits the performance of useful labour. The whole is sheathed in the unfolding drapes of a peach-coloured, lace-trimmed, full-length negligée; the eye automatically follows the line of the leg upwards, to a tasselled garter: the Rowena G. Garter. One size only. Colours: snow, champagne, palest green, soft apricot, ebony. The garter – than which there could not be a finer example of the luxury non-garment. The price list at the back of the mail-order catalogue offers it at £10.

Most of the colours of these fetishistic adornments are those of the archetypal luxury non-food, ice cream – with the inevitable addition of black which, for some reason, remains synonymous with naughty underwear. The Reger catalogue hints subtly at the naughtiness: the girl posing legs akimbo in Corinna C. Negligée Ebony has scarcely perceptible bags under her eyes, and two black-clad models are pictured reclining on fur throws, perhaps to make some point about sophisticated carnality.

This luscious and expensive (£2) catalogue acts as a *vade mecum* via the post to the enrichment of your life through the non-garment. In itself, too, it is an *objet de luxe*, an invitation to voluptuous or narcissistic fantasy, depending on the sexual orientation of the browser. It also has enough of the air of the come-on brochure for an up-market knocking shop to risk causing creative confusion in those countries where brides as well as negligées are obtained through the post. This is part of the 'fantasy courtesan' syndrome of the sexy exec, a syndrome reflected admirably in the pages of *Cosmopolitan* magazine. Working women regain the femininity they have lost behind the office desk by parading about like a *grande horizontale* from early Colette in the privacy of their flats, even if there is nobody there to see.

The erotic point is inescapable. The models are dressed up in undress, in a kind of clothing that is more naked than nudity. Their flesh is partly concealed by exiguous garments in fabrics that mimic the texture of flesh itself – silk, satin-finish man-made fibres, fine lawn – plus a sublimated hint of the texture, though (heaven forbid!) never the actuality, of pubic hair.

The models are very heavily and ostentatiously made up, as if to demonstrate this civilised voluntary exile from the natural. They, too, are *objets de luxe*, as expensive to manufacture as the fragile ambiguities which adorn them. (The Leilah N. Nightdress, colours: rose, beige, black, in French lace, is really nothing more than a very sophisticated version of the Celtic young person's fishing net.) They are also elaborately coiffed, though occasionally in a style of reticent dishevellment, often with flowers in the hair, as if for some kind of bedroom *fête champêtre*. However informal, these garments are obviously public dress.

I remember reading somewhere how, in the fifties, model girls were often reluctant to do lingerie jobs. Swimwear was fine; but respectable girls drew the line at modelling knickers, on the grounds that they should only be photographed in clothes in which they might be seen in public in normal circumstances. This quaint scruple seems to have vanished. The ostentatious glamour of the new lingerie (of which Janet Reger is only the most widely-publicised purveyor), and certain changes in social relations, have created a climate in which this kind of non-garment is socially acceptable. It is breathtakingly expensive, and high cost is, in itself, a great moral antiseptic. The rich are different from us. The single-minded pursuit of excellence neutralises all kinds of waywardness.

Lingerie has become simply another kind of the non-garments characteristic of what you might call 'hyper-culture'. Others are some furs, evening dresses and ball gowns, real jewellery. All are, first and foremost, items of pure conspicuous consumption. Yet they also fulfil elaborate ritual functions. They are the garb for the Good Life in an opposite sense to that of the TV eco-serial – the pursuit of anti-nature. This includes the opera, eating in restaurants, parties, and, increasingly, sexual relations in which the gibbering old id, the Beast in Man, the manifestation of nature at its most intransigent, is scrupulously exiled. In hyper-culture, human relations are an art form.

The precious, costly fripperies on Harrods' underwear counter must do a roaring business among transvestites, whom I trust wear it in good health. For transvestites, the appearance of femininity is its essence. As I grow older, I do begin to believe this might be so. I'm just waiting, now, to aspire to the sexless grandeur of the ancients in Shaw's *Back to Methusalah*.

Of course, the whole notion of the 'natural' is an invention of culture, anyway. It tends to recur as an undertow in hyper-culture times as some sort of corrective to the excesses of those who see life as an art form without knowing what an art form is. But to say that nature as an idea is an invention does not explain the idea away. Clothing as anti-nature – as the distinction between beings under social restraint and beings that are not – can be seen in action in any circus. It is amazing what a number of non-garments – bridles, plumes, tassels – even the liberty horses wear, to show to what degree they have suppressed their natural desire to run away. Relations between the non-garments of circus horses and those of professional strippers is obvious: they are seldom wholly naked, either.

Even the hippies were reluctant to strip off completely in their pursuit of the demystification of the human body. They could never resist the temptation to add a string of beads or two, or daub themselves here and there with greasepaint. Perhaps the promotion of the non-garment as decent wear shows a streak of culture within hyper-culture itself. This would come as no surprise to students of the whole messy business.

However, the real complexity of the taboo against nakedness may be seen most clearly in the catalogue of a firm like Frederick's of Hollywood – who, interestingly enough, use line-drawings rather than photographs. This is probably for reasons of cost, but it enables, all the same, a far greater degree of physical distortion. Mr Frederick is the man who offered you panti-girdles with padded or 'uplift' buttocks, and padded brassieres that elevated the nipples while leaving them bare. Downmarket sexy underwear has a long, murky history.

In the early sixties, even before permissiveness hit the West Coast, Mr Frederick – a world away from Serena French Knicker and Hattie Brief – was advertising the Pouf (sic) Panty, which had a puff of maribou at the front like a bunny girl's tail put on the wrong way round. His scanty bikini briefs were 'embroidered with lips at the nicest spot'. He urged his mail order clients how it pays to advertise: 'Wear our ''Try it! You'll like it!'' panty! Chances are . . . he will!' The acetate (no natural fibres here) non-garment bore this slogan stitched athwart the pelvic area. A vogue for sloganising knickers (and, indeed, underpants) has been a consistent feature of the downmarket, 'raunchy' lingerie market for years. Just, the slogans get ruder as time goes by.

Of all Mr Frederick's offerings the most striking is the 'all-nylon sheer lace brief pantie' that has 'daring *derrière* cutout edged in lace'. He calls this steatopygous gesture 'Back to Nature'. You couldn't put the whole ambiguous message of women's sexy underwear – upmarket, downmarket or in my lady's chamber – any fairer than that.

New Society, 1977

All prices quoted are from the 1977 Janet Reger Catalogue.

A Well-Hung Hang-Up

Cock modestly detumescent, Andrew Cooper III, *Playgirl's* Man for June, leans against the bonnet of an extremely powerful car, both car and boy studies of potency *in potentia*. The winged symbol on the radiator suggests the erection the young man decently fore-bears to unfurl but it's plain to see he's superbly hung. The centre-fold show him fresh from a sunset sea, white towelling robe falling away from his emblematic virility. He also displays himself for women's pleasure in tennis kit; in blue-jeans and Tee-shirt; and in a sort of Chinese shroud.

Playgirl, the magazine for women, gives us Andrew Cooper III unclothed, as if his flesh were his function, like that of a beautiful woman, but his biography equates male sexuality with money and power in the traditional manner; 'he raked in his first million by the time he was twenty-one.' The biographical notes authenticate him; he has a history as well as a torso. We read of his endearing habits, he likes to climb mountains in the nude. Freedom, he says, is everything to him. He water-skis like a champ, plays tennis like a demon, handles a camera like a pro. Therefore, he exists. He has a soulful look, reminding us that his iconic derivation may be as much from the pin-ups of the rock stars in fan-mags of the sixties as it is from his lascivious sisters in the tit mags who part their legs and leer with far greater a culturally-sanctioned abandon. He looks too butch to be true. He is hairy as an ape.

The pin-ups of male nudes in *Playgirl* and *Viva* serve at least one socially useful function; they gratify early adolescent curiosity as to the actual appearance of the male sex-organ, which exercises pre-pubescent girls a good deal until they are traumatised by their first flasher. But the magazines do not appear to aim at the pre-bra set, the tone of the contents is resolutely sophisticated, so their purpose cannot be simply educational.

Playgirl, like *Playboy*, of which it is not the stable-mate, has a philosophy, which is one of responsible sexual freedom. The editor declares: 'I do not trumpet behind the banners of women's liberation, yet I am not so foolish as to deny that the success of individual liberation is the quintessence of our survival. I believe vehemently in femininity and will do everything in my power to promote it.'

The nature of this femininity is demonstrated by ads for vaginal deodorants, vibrators, slenderising devices, bust developing creams, and exotic underwear. The exotic underwear ad offers something called 'Bosom Buddies', which seem to be artificial nipples, good heavens, out of style since the *Directoire*. 'Soft rubber nipple pads help nature along. Natural look and feel even under see-through tops.' There is certain egalitarianism in that men are not spared these excesses, either; the *Playgirl* shopping guide suggests, 'Give your man "Hot Pants" for Father's Day. Either "Super Cock" or "Home of the Whopper" styles. 100% cotton stretch waist band. Specify style and size (small, medium, large).' 'Small' and 'medium' is poignant. One letter on the doctor's page asks: 'Can they really double penis size?'

Viva, stablemate of *Penthouse* and *Forum* so truly in the vanguard of the sexual revolution, is less up-front, rather less brash than *Playgirl* with, perhaps, some pretensions to feminism as well as to femininity; nevertheless, the *raison d'être* of both publications is the full frontal, male nude pin-up, and, from the context, one can assume the purpose of these pin-ups is, like all pin-ups, purely titillatory. And I assume, from the context, that the person they want to titillate is a maturish professional woman not unlike, perhaps, me.

Fat chance, I tell you, fat chance.

The poverty-stricken aesthetic behind these nudes cancels out all the erotic promise of the flesh itself and all flesh, even that of Andrew Cooper III, is potentially erotic. For one thing, in the ideology behind the aesthetic lurks the notion that, as a general rule, women are looking for love and therefore the flesh, to please a woman, may not be presented specifically as flesh-in-itself. It is well known that women are not aroused by hardcore porn so the titillation has a top-dressing of sentiment. A picture-story in *Viva* actually depicts, in saccharine soft focus, a wedding night. The sensitive, open-pored face of Jerry, *Viva*'s 'sexy yachtsman', spreads across an entire page and he talks about love: 'First, of course, I'm attracted to the body, but then the mind becomes important. The relationship is really in the mind.' Ross, Case, Shep, Greg – such butch, emphatic, deliciously brutal mono-syllables! – make themselves and their limp pricks available for romantic fantasies rather than erotic ones.

The pseudo-biographies of the models in the tit-mags have, in contrast, a sprightly fakery; Marisa, Portland, Tracy know that nobody would recognise them with their clothes on, anyway, that they exist exclusively as ingenious articulated toys in a porno-Disneyland, and do not need to pretend to have hearts.

The aesthetic of the prick-and-bum mags is, butch is beautiful. Jerry, 'young, light-hearted master of the waves', thrusts master-fully through the ocean, proudly naked steers his yacht. A pair of nude skiers have been snapped in mid-flight; naked sky-divers, even . . . the necessity to portray the male nude in action, demon-strating Hemingwayesque conspicuous virility, drops them straight into the absurd. It's not even kitsch, it's ridiculous. (*Playgirl* has a circulation of a million and a half, *Viva* something less.) Jaques Perrault runs eight miles a day to keep himself in trim, it says. Almost all the young men exhibit pale bikini marks on their deeply tanned, terribly hairy frames. They are joy through strength. The beaux of Muscle Beach engaged in as narcissic a cult of the body as Hitler Youth.

Yet this must be an atavistic memory, in however vague and distorted a form, of the nude, discus-throwing youths, the Beau-tiful Athletes, the figures on vases, the pin-ups of the locker-rooms of Athens and Sparta so dear to the classical tradition, the principal models of the male body as an image of beauty and delight in our culture, hallowed by the public school tradition and the notion of a healthy mind in a healthy body.

And so, as images of delighted male sexuality, *Playgirl* and *Viva* toss we maturish professional women a few muscle-bound hustlers left over by a couple of millenia from the Symposium because the models we do have for lovely boys are too few to create a tradition and, perhaps, express far too explicitly the notion of the male body as an object of desire, as an instrument of pleasure – but not of woman's pleasure. Donatello's delicious David is, according to the colour supplements, a 'masterpiece of homosexual art'; hands off, girls! Similarly with Michaelangelo's celebrations of vulnerable, narrow-chested striplings and Caravaggio's fat, sinister Bacchus with his fruit-hat à la Carmen Miranda; not a trace of such imagery as this to be found in *these* glossy pages. No room for complex sensuality, only for simple virility.

The picture of a naked man belongs to a different aesthetic convention than that of a naked woman. The female nude's nakedness is in itself a form of dress, since the lengthy tradition of European art clothes even the vulgarest pin-up with a heavy if invisible cloak of associations. She knows how to wear nothing; further, she is perfectly secure in that, so garbed, she can always expect approval. But what is sauce for the goose is not necessarily sauce for the gander.

The articles which will accessorise the nakedness of the pin-up, her erotic apparatus of beads, feathers, white stockings, black stockings, corsets, scarves, bodices, frilly knickers, hats, are sanctioned by a tradition that extends back as far as Cranach and beyond. Andrew Cooper III's towelling robe has no such cultural resonance; his blue-jeans belong only to the modern tradition of porno-kitsch in which he himself is so firmly ensconced.

The dreamy narcissism of Dolores or Marsha, one hand straying towards her crotch, refers directly back to the slumbrous Venuses of the Renaissance; Hélène, Natasha, Jane are continually peeking into little hand-mirrors with the intense self-satisfaction of a Titian goddess. Boucher's Mademoiselle O'Murphy is a Penthouse Pet already. It is a central contradiction in European art that its celebration of the human form should involve subsuming the particularities of its subjects in the depersonalising idea of the nude, rendering her – in the name of humanism – an object.

But women have the advantage of their disadvantages. Our relation to our own bodies is both more intimate and more abstract than that of most men to theirs. Naked, a woman can never be less than herself for her value in the world resides more in her skin than in her clothes. Though, naked, she loses her name and becomes a 'blue nude', 'the bather', 'woman dressing', 'Suzie', 'Gina', 'Europa', 'Eve', 'Venus', this personal anonymity is the price of a degree of mystification of her naked body that means she can accede to a symbolic power as soon as her clothes are off, whereas a man's symbolic power resides in his clothes, indicators of his status. The story of the Emperor's new clothes would have a different meaning were the hero an Empress; the spectators would have thought she had done it on purpose, that now she was displaying her real, female authority.

The tranquil and unconcerned pride with which nude women since the Renaissance display their usually generous breasts which are the rendezvous (remember) of love and hunger, means that, if not in the world, then, at least as art, the women have been certain of creating a positive response when they pretend to be a triumphant icon of nourishment and sexuality, of love, in fact. Mademoiselle O'Murphy and her look-alike, Marilyn Monroe might have been very confused about everything else but at least knew exactly who they were when they took their clothes off; their skin itself was the sign of their status, their nakedness their sole but irrefutable claim to existential veracity. The male models of *Playgirl* and *Viva* do not exhibit such self-confidence; and no wonder. There is a specific vocabulary of gestures and attitudes of sexual expression available for women in relation to men that does not exist for men in relation to women and so, erotically speaking, Andrew Cooper III and Gerry and Woody and all the chaps are posing in a void.

Further, they are playing deeply against the cultural grain. For there *is* a tradition of the male nude in European art and one so deeply part of our culture we don't even think of it as a male nude, which is what it is, though the genitals are not displayed. (They're not in any female nudes outside graffiti, either.) The icon of the naked woman as the source of nourishment and sexuality is balanced by the icon of the naked man in physical torment. 'It is no accident,' says Kenneth Clark in *The Nude*, 'that the formalised body of the ''perfect man'' became the supreme symbol of European belief.' However, the formalised body of the 'perfect man' had to become a supreme icon of sado-masochism before that happened and the only heir to that tradition in our merciful age of unbelief is Francis Bacon. And it isn't simply two thousand years of crucifixions and pietàs working against the male body as an image of joy; it is two millenia of St Sebastian transfixed by arrows, St Lawrence with his gridiron, St Bartholomew being flayed, decapitated Holofernes, Prometheus with the birds gnawing his liver, martyrdoms, executions, dissections. Marat stabbed in his bath. Against this rage can beauty hold a plea? Not, certainly, in the timorous hands of the male pin-ups.

New Society, 1975

At the Zoo

Last week, summer holidays, ice-cream weather, the apes at the zoo were drawing the usual huge crowds with their comic antics and their wistful air of being almost human. Part of the fascination of the monkey-house is the arbitrariness of it. The primates are behind bars and we, apparently quite fortuitously, have escaped this fate; visiting a mad-house in the eighteenth century must have been rather like this. There is pleasure in the relief with which we leave the monkey-house – 'There but for the grace of God'.

At London Zoo, of course, there are only invisible bars in the monkey-house; the apes live in a nice, low-rise, brick-built complex and their apartments have huge picture windows in which visitors can see their own reflections almost as if moving about inside the apes' lovely homes, with their Design Centre exercise bars, their Habitat stylishness.

Only a whimsical quirk of evolution has separated Guy the gorilla, in his massive, obsidian repose, from an executive desk in an international corporation. As it is, he is trapped behind his glass panel as if on a TV screen, the daily functions of his life performed before an impersonally curious audience, the helpless star of a long-running soap opera of ape life – you could call it, 'My Brother's Keeper'. The most intimate details of his domestic life are on display; when Lomie, Guy's mate, struck a blow for the

Women's Movement by showing herself a careless and unnatural mother, it caused as much stir as the death of Grace Archer years ago. Since Lomie had been forcibly impregnated by another ape, the whole episode smacked more of Peyton Place than the Archers, but we were spared the dreadful scenes that must have taken place in the relative privacy of their sleeping quarters as her time drew near.

After the birth there followed a most touching spectacle, that of the infant gorilla, repellently named 'Salome' (why?), cradled in her green-uniformed keeper's arms as he sat in her enclosure, the cynosure of all eyes. The gorilla couple achieved a certain revenge on their script-writers; they managed to get one of them written into the serial.

The terminology of the animals' attendants brings home the analogy with the mad-house. They are 'keepers', as in an old-fashioned lunatic asylum, not 'guardians', as in a poor-house, even if the apes do not engage in productive labour. Yet the keepers, although men, perform functions that are not altogether human, such as teaching baby giraffes how to walk and suckling orphaned baboons from bottles. They are ambiguous link-men between the world of men and the world of beasts and the animals may well regard the keepers as entirely in complicity with them, though their discreet presence ensures we never forget the fact that a zoo is a world of beasts, for beasts, built entirely by men for their own purposes.

The Zoo's Royal Charter of 1829 gives the objects and aims of the Zoological Society of London, which owns both London and Whipsnade Zoos, as: 'The advancement of zoology and animal physiology, and the introduction of new and curious subjects of the animal kingdom.' In the zoological gardens, the beasts are themselves like sentient plants, laid out as in flower-beds, objects of study, contemplation, surmise and fantasy. Like lilies of the field, they are not bred for food or service. They have another function, they are there just to *be*, in the best conceived of all possible paternalist utopias.

The mandrills at London Zoo have a spacious garden to play in, with climbable rocks and exercise bars; a hedge of roses divides it from the visitors, such a hedge that, if untended, would grow into as huge and thorny a barrier as protected the lapse of consciousness of the Sleeping Beauty. In their lives as mobile vegetation themselves, in their great wastes of perpetual leisure, what can the apes be thinking of?

The patriarch of the mandrill family (*Mandrillus Sphinx*, West Africa) has a face indeed like a tropic flower. A luscious snout of the tenderest red; white, bulbous, blue-veined cheeks like the calyx of a pitcher plant; and delicate, pointed, leprechaun ears almost hidden in a foliage of speckled fur. He is the most magnificent, the least human-looking, therefore superbly dignified. Like all the enclosed patriarchs, he ceaselessly patrols the perimeter of his enclosure. He has a sunset-coloured rump.

Last week, however, most of the rumps of most of the primates appeared to be in full-bloom; must be the season. The sexual organs of the Sooty Mangaby (*Cercocebus atys*, West Africa) are undeniable as mouths, like the transposed orifice in Magritte's 'The Rape', sore, enflamed, a visible reminder of the persistent irritation of the flesh. Carnal. A wound. It is almost as if they were doing it on purpose.

The chimp patriarch patrols the chimpanzee enclosure, round and round and round, on all fours, his flaming rump jutting well out and his tongue, also, stuck out at full length; on his tongue, he balances a great lump of the bright yellow shit produced by a fructarian diet. 'What's he doing that for, mummy?' Possibly a too scrutable sign. What *can* they be thinking of, in their chronic unemployment, their ideal housing, their life as objects of instruction and amusement.

There are nice monkey-houses and nasty monkey-houses. The nastier the monkey-house, the more exemplary the quality of ape life, the more they seem to be staging some sort of primates agitprop.

The baboon enclosure in Turin Zoo is like a penal colony. Twenty or thirty of the animals are housed in a perfectly round, shadeless, concrete arena with some branches of a dead tree in the middle in which one or two immobile baboons usually perch. These yellow baboons have curious, leonine muzzles with virtually concave noses, enraged eyes and well-barbered, bristling manes. Like crew cuts. Like convict cuts.

It was midday and very hot. In spite of, or because of, the heat, the baboons were engaged in almost ceaseless activity, some copulating, some masturbating, others stalking about the concrete floors. Many were engaged, with some tenderness, in delousing others and gobbled up the lice as they picked them off the pelts with mechanical relish. Often, the louse-pickers would form a busy chain of three or four baboons. Directly below us, for a terrace offers a god's eye view of this microcosm, we would see how white their flesh was as one baboon parted another's scanty fur, and how pitted with the bites of insects.

Their buttocks were so extravagantly in bloom they seemed to experience some difficulty in walking. The thin skin over the purple cushions of flesh was stretched so tight it shone like cheap satin and looked as if it would spout pus if it were lanced. This grotesque appendage appeared to cause some difficulties with hygiene, one way and another, there was a lot of shit around the baboon pit. All the despair emanating from this pit had a specifically anal quality. Genet.

Too much like Genet. Konrad Gesner observed baboons in the sixteenth century and noted: 'When he is signed to, he presents his arse.' A sexual offer, but also a general token of humility. Male baboons of low rank display female mating behaviour towards those of high rank. 'The smaller and younger male can obtain a good many advantages by submitting to a more powerful male. The superior male will protect his favourite against the attacks of other apes. When the stronger partner is about to take food away from the weaker, the young male will frequently offer himself sexually and in return will be allowed to keep the food.' (*Sex Life of the Animals*: Herbert Wendt).

Suddenly one baboon stopped delousing another and raised his head, as if all at once on the alert. Then he barked sharply. One after another, they all started it, after that – each stopped whatever he was doing and began to bark until every baboon in the pit was barking in unison in the still heat of lunch-time, when the other animals in the zoo were fast asleep.

They went on barking for a long time, almost a minute. Then stopped. Three of them began to drearily work the treadmill for a while; the delousing parties began again; and one or two of them started to pick over the piles of straw-coloured shit on the floor of the arena, extract from it undigested husks, and eat them.

They order their monkey-houses more existentially than we do in Turin; grief, despair, degradation, defiance, hopelessness. A pecking order. A lice-picking order. Easy to see what *these* chaps are thinking of – such a pitch of rage they'd never be fobbed off with a Habitat lounge-suite; I had thought that one baboon was buggering another but, when I looked more closely, I saw the one had climbed upon the other's back only in order to reach, to claw as high as he could up the perpendicular surface of the perfectly smooth concrete wall that surrounded them.

There was a lovely zoo in Verona, though, that seemed to have been designed by people who saw the beasts' side of things almost completely. At the entrance was a notice: 'Attention – this is the only chance most animals have to observe the behaviour of human beings. Make sure they receive a good impression.' The yaks had a hillside to run in, the vultures obscured themselves in the branches of real trees. Next to a somnolent tiger, another notice announced didactically: 'When a man kills a tiger, we call it sport; when a tiger kills a man, we call it ferocity.'

A small colony of monkeys inhabited a roomy cage full of greenery; all was not oppressively chic, but green and decent. As in a very good sanatorium, all was order and decency. A pair of baboons sat together on a bough like Darby and Joan. In an adjoining cage, a very nice black gibbon with a white beard did a few press-ups.

He swung to the front of his cage when he saw us and thrust both his long arms through the bars, opening and closing his black, wrinkled, distressingly humanoid hands but not quite as if he were begging for food, more as if beseeching us for something. And he must have known we would not give him food for there were notices everywhere: 'It is vehemently forbidden to feed the animals.' (When I was working at the zoo in Bristol, once, I saw a man feed a little rhesus monkey with a ball-point pen.) No. It seemed as if he wanted to hold hands.

When nothing was forthcoming from us, no reciprocal gesture, he reached right out to the grass that grew outside his cage, pulled up a few stalks, all that he could reach, and munched them. So it *was* goodies he was after! But his bowl was full of lots of delicious looking fruit; did the grass outside his cage have a different flavour? Or perhaps, since we had not responded to him, he was saving face, was now showing us that of course he had not been reaching out to us at all, at all.

But, as we turned away from the cage, he thrust his hands out towards us again; and followed us, padding after us as far as his commodious cage would let him, and then he pursued us further and further with his dreadful speaking eyes as we went off.

The nicer the zoo, the more terrible.

When darkness falls and the crowds are gone and the beasts inherit Regents Park, I should think the mandrills sometimes say to one another: 'Well, taking all things into consideration, how much better off we are here than in the wild! Nice food, regular meals, no predators, no snakes, free medical care, roofs over our heads . . . and, after all this time, we couldn't really cope with the wild, again, could we?'

So they console themselves, perhaps. And, perhaps, weep.

New Society, 1976

Fun Fairs

The idea of 'fun' is an odd one. Fun is quite different from pleasure, which has obscure overtones of the erotic. Barbarella's machine killed you with too much pleasure; a machine that killed you with too much fun suggests a far less swooning death. Death by tickling, perhaps. (*The World's Fair* advertises tickling sticks, 'ideal for Glasgow Fair'.) Fun is also quite different from delight, which is a more cerebral and elevated concept. You might get

121

pleasure, or delight, from a good performance of *The Marriage of Figaro*; if you found it fun, or worse, 'great fun', it would only go to show what a camp little number you were.

According to the OED, 'fun' originally meant a cheat, a hoax, a practical joke; widened to involve ridicule ('to poke fun') and, heartlessness, always an aspect of the comic, only finally settled to a significance of guiltless enjoyment at around the turn of this century. Perhaps some folk memory of its earlier meaning is what lends a certain ambivalence to fun fairs. (Which are not the same as fairs.)

Since fun is pleasure without guilt, as in the euphemistic 'fun-loving', we are bound to feel it must be inherently trivial; in a Judaeo-Christian culture, half the fun of the thing is the guilt, any-way. Adultery is never fun; look at Anna Karenina. Swapping *is* fun, or so the writers to *Forum* claim. Promiscuity isn't fun and will land you in approved school but 'having a bit of fun' with a consenting adult suggests that nobody minds a slice off a cut loaf. Fun is pleasure that does not involve the conscience or, further-more, the intellect. (Hegel is never fun.) Fun, in fact, might be the pleasure of the working class, as defined from outside that class.

Nevertheless, it's a shibboleth that socialism can never be fun; it won't be much *fun* after the Revolution, people say. (Yes; but it's not all that much fun, now.) But perhaps this means that a degree of alienation is necessary before the full 'fun' effect takes place; unalienated fun might be something unimaginably else.

You cannot be overwhelmed by fun, as you can be by pleasure. This kind of estranged fun is in the nature of a holiday; doing something 'for fun' is to act gratuitously. Yet fun is *per se* harm-less; it is often good and clean, while pleasure can be unnatural. Even de Sade couldn't think up unnatural *fun*. Fun costs some-thing – what doesn't? – but, like thrills, may often be obtained remarkably cheaply.

Fred Loades' vast model fairground, working models exactly to scale of roundabouts, coconut shies, big wheels, swingboats, rock stalls, all the fun of the fair, constructed between 1929-77, a life-work, features midget pantechnicons bearing such legends as: 'Loades of Fun, Fun On Tour', etc. You press the time-switch;

the lights go on; everything clicks into motion. Then stops. Until you press the switch again. Discontinuous as the peripatetic fair itself.

There was a man in Hammersmith market, he sold shirts, he used to shout: 'We're not here today and gone tomorrow, we're here today and gone today!' Fun is peripheral to one; here today and gone today, unless you have it in your heart. To the provider of fun, of course, it is so much hard work, dismantling the ride at two in the morning, driving a hundred miles, getting your ride built up again when you get there and so on. The technology of fun is a hard task-master; its reward is a consciousness you do no harm to anyone. And an unusually cohesive life-style. The In Memoriam columns of *The World's Fair* are even more affecting than those of the *Morning Star*; the wedding announcements suggest grand alliances between friendly clans, reports of parties staggering folkmoots.

In 1934, Mitcham fair covered seventeen acres. There were 35 riding devices, 168 hooplas or similar, ten circuses, 50 darts stalls, 14 coconut shies, 59 refreshment stalls, palmists, ices, the fattest lady, the biggest rat, boxing booths, performing fleas and Wild West shows. Those were still heroic days. By the time I started going to the fairs on the South London commons, it was post-war, lean times, menace of Teds and flick-knives, no more fat ladies or sharp-shooters to gawp at. Candy floss had come in – women with turquoise eyelids and stacked hair twisting the bouffant pink stuff on to sticks out of the whirling drum; and lots of peppermint-rock and toffee-apples, because none of these things were covered by sweet coupons, were, in fact, 'off ration', somehow legally illicit, oddly similar to the fair itself. But, no hot dogs; absent, that pervasive aroma of dehydrated onion simmering in a vat of hot water that hits you between the eyes at fair-grounds nowadays.

Yet there are still gallopers on the road, gallopers staked through the back with the barley-sugar stick supports to which you clung, gallopers with scarlet nostrils and gilded manes, after which real horses seem such a bitter disappointment. In my child-hood, only the very youngest children rode them, everybody else preferred the dive-bombers, caterpillars, dodgems, speedy, flashy things that whirled you round and sometimes turned you upside down. Yet round and round the gilded horses still went, to the music of an organ that emitted a bronchitic wheeze of pure nostalgia, and so they do still, those marvellous horses whose feet never touch the ground, although, one by one, Victorian round-abouts retire to the museums. Just as fun art, with the passing of time, turns into fine art, so the frivolous technology of the round-about turns into industrial archaeology.

The fun of the fair, like the magic of music-hall, has a capacity for procuring instant nostalgia in the hearts of people whose parents probably never let them go to fairs at all in case they picked up germs, and who can't even remember music-halls. The bour-geoisie always prefer to experience popular art at second-hand, in museums, art galleries and the pages of coffee-table books; that way, you run no risk of actually having any fun, or being forced to submit to the indignity of the Demon Whirl or the Lightning Jets. Since the fun of the fair is entirely sensational – that is, a direct, visceral assault on the senses – and may be experienced cheaply and without guilt; it has connotations, not of the erotic, which is all in the mind, but of the straightforwardly sexual, which is all in the flesh and blood. Best to keep it in the quarantine of other people's experience, then. At the fair, you play games with vertigo, the quaking attraction of gravity that makes us want to plunge when we see an abyss – falling, spinning, the system-atic derangement of all the senses and no harm done. All in fun. Oh, the titillation of the infernal apparatuses for whirling, bouncing, whizzing, swooping down! People scream when the dive-bombers swing out on their chains; all the fun of the centri-fuge. Pleasures of incipient nausea; of feeling danger when one is absolutely safe. Of concealment and revelation; do you remember the Caterpillar, that sped round its circumscribed track under a retractable awning of green canvas? Young couples loved it, the awning creaks up, creaks down at mechanical random.

Exhilaration of speed; and of not being in control, somebody else is in control, the gnarled, muscular showman for whom all this secular magic is only so much real life. 'It's thrilling.' 'It's terrifying.' 'It's exciting.' 'It's fun for all,' opine the signs in their ineffable agitated lettering. All around, the shrieks and crazed hysterical laughter of those in the grip of orgiastic physical excitation. And the inescapable music, remorseless as the juke-boxes of hell.

In the exhibition of fairground art at the Whitechapel Gallery in 1977, there was an electric-shock machine, built around 1900, the first ever to utilise electricity for amusement. This comes as no surprise. All the fun of electro-convulsion. No doubt the ancient Chinese, had they got around to inventing electricity, would have thought it best to keep it exclusively for fairground sideshows, just as they couldn't think of any other use for gunpowder but fireworks.

A fairground is a fun cathedral for the poor. It is visually a hard-edged world, in which most of the decorative detail is two-dimensional, executed in that kind of *trompe-l'oeil* which deceives nobody and is intended to deceive nobody, not so much rococo as almost a conscious parody of rococo. Compare the work of the fairground artist, Fred Fowle – or you could even buy the set of Twist Cars decorated by him advertised in the fairground and circus trade paper, *The World's Fair*, if you had the nerve – anyway, compare a scenic panel by Fred Fowle with the effects inside a thirties super-cinema, the Tooting Bec Granada, say. Fowle's work is up-front, straightforward, it hits you in the eye; it was he who introduced primary colours into the fairground, in the thirties. It is decoration which is part of machines whose function is not to procure dreams but to excite the senses. Not the delineation of an invented reality but an exaggeration of concrete images to do with real sensation. On the other hand, Tooting Bec Granada, with its cyclorama of moving cloud and gallery of mirrors, is an interior constructed wholly of fantasy, of illusion. That is why the marble there is real.

Fred Fowle uses marbling techniques, but knows that it must not even *look* real, for his purposes. 'The thing about marble is that you exaggerate it more than it is. If you go in the Natural History museum you see marble there, but if you were to copy them . . . it wouldn't have the same effect, of course' (interviewed by Ian Starsmore in *The Fairground*).

Super-cinema architecture, with its red velvet drapes, crystal chandeliers, marble interiors, post-Symbolist murals and ritualistic screenings of movies showing, in the main, very rich people behaving extremely oddly, was designed for consolation during the Depression; you paid your money and you entered a better world. Fairground design was dedicated to the proposition that even if you didn't have a penny to bless yourself with, you could still have a bit of fun. Admission to the site was free; you could just walk around, look at the bright lights, enjoy the paintings, listen to the music and the ululations of those actually undergoing the ordeals by speed and mild terror. Fun, in fact, not unlike that which the Catholic church offers in its rococo pleasure domes in Southern Mediterranean countries.

Certain crafts turn into art when people stop doing them, so you see that the craftsman was an artist all the time because the things they made stay beautiful after they have ceased to be functional. The beautiful beasts from old fairgrounds that Lady Bangor has collected together will probably convince the Chinese archaeologists that a particularly jolly kind of totemism flourished in Europe in the nineteenth century; the preternaturally alert gallopers, a furred, saddled seal, a cow with a golden horn, a fluorescent ostrich, a cat with a fish in its mouth, a llama, a cockerel. To ride round and round on one of them a hundred years ago must have made you feel you were the Lord of motion; it is around these items from the archetypal fairground of the pseudo-memory of nostalgia that the lustre of an actual art-object begins to gather. They are ceasing to be fun; now, on their stands, where you can walk all round them and see how perfect the finish is, they give quite a pure kind of delight. The fairground, of course, with its project of sensual immediacy, has rendered them obsolete; even the kiddies' rides in open-air markets have more fire-engines and motorbikes aboard than gilded goats, nowadays.

I once read an interview with Fred Fowle in the *Evening Standard*. He said: 'Balham was a Disneyland to me when I was a kid and every place outside was as foreign as the moon . . . I used to ride on the swings at old Bedford Hill Fair and wonder if there really was anything outside of south London.'

I suppose there isn't, really, if you have an eye like that. On his own terms, he is a great social-realist painter. The fairs he works for are themselves stylisations of, exaggerations, heightenings of real life, as, ideally, holidays should be – not time off or out, but time, as it is, enhanced. The time of your life.

New Society, 1977

5

SCREEN AND DREAM

These are pieces about the movies or television, mostly the movies, these ones mostly
about women in the movies, done from an
angle of committed feminism. (For, should I
ever have a daughter, I would call her, not
Simone, nor even Rosa, but Lulu — and
Jane, for her grandmother.)

Femmes Fatales

Prince Escerny: Can you imagine a greater happiness for a woman than to have a man wholly in her power?
Lulu (jingling her spurs): Oh, yes!

This illuminating exchange comes from Frank Wedekind's *Earth Spirit*, the first of the two 'Lulu' plays that Wedekind thought were about abnormal psychology but turned out to be really about everyday life, as these things so often do. What is interesting about this repartee in the dancer Lulu's dressing-room (hence the spurs – part of her costume), is that Escerny does not pay the slightest attention to her reply.

With a little probing at this point, Lulu might have been willing to give him the answer to that version of the riddle of the sphinx – 'What do women want?' – that was exercising the mind of a certain Viennese *savant* at this very time. But Escerny is not concerned with that. In a roundabout way, he is telling Lulu what *he* wants, which is for her to destroy him. Since she is a good-natured girl, she would probably be prepared to gratify this desire were it not for the exigencies of the plot, that must now whirl her away to lesbianism, murder, incest and a final epiphanic *crise* at the hands of Jack the Ripper. Which is what, presumably, Wedekind thought an attractive girl like Lulu would actually prefer to having a nice time.

But Wedekind himself could not consult Lulu as to the nature of her own real wishes since she does not exist except as the furious shadow of his imaginings. But at least he gives her credit for some kind of life beyond his imaginative grasp; it was left to one exceptional actress and one exceptional film-maker to flesh out that life and show that it is in absolute contradiction to the text.

Pabst's screen version of the Lulu plays, *Pandora's Box*, remains one of the great expositions of the cultural myth of the *femme fatale*. It is a peculiarly pernicious, if flattering, myth which Pabst and his star, Louise Brooks, conspired to both demonstrate irresistibly in action while, at the same time, offering evidence of its manifest absurdity.

They've just shown this particular piece of emotional dialectic at the National Film Theatre as part of the Surrealist season. Brooks is the greatest of all the Surrealist love-goddesses, pitched higher in the pantheon, even, than Dietrich and Barbara Steele because she typifies the subversive violence inherent in beauty and a light heart. She is the not at all obscure but positively radiant and explicit object of desire – living proof, preserved in the fragile eternity of the film stock, that the most mysterious of all is, as Octavio Paz said, the absolutely transparent. And, indeed, Lulu is transparent as sunshine; which is why her presence shows up all the spiritual muck in the corners. So she gets blamed for the muck, poor girl.

Time and permissiveness has dimmed neither the medium nor the message one whit. Brooks' face and presence remain unique; God knows, one would think she was quite enough woman as she is, but nobody, of course, can leave her alone for one moment. Desire does not so much transcend its object as ignore it completely in favour of a fantastic recreation of it. Which is the process by which the *femme* gets credited with fatality. Because she is perceived not as herself but as the projection of those libidinous cravings which, since they are forbidden, must always prove fatal. So Lulu gets off with the countess and obligingly sets up an Oedipal situation for her stepson when she shoots his father.

The conviction that women ought to live for love remains implicit in the idea of the *femme fatale*, despite the continual evidence of the behaviour of the *femme fatale* herself that this is not so. But the main contradiction inherent in the *femme fatale* is that, though she seems to live for love and often lives by it, she is, in fact, quite incapable of it. Or, so they say.

Lulu keeps repeating cheerfully that she has never been in love. This is the main thing that is wrong with her, according to Wedekind. No heart, see. A lovely flower that, alas, lacks perfume. Her loyalty to her old friends; her fidelity to her first seducer, the repulsive Schön; her willingness to support her adoptive father and effete stepson by the prostitution she loaths – Wedekind records all this but cannot see it as any evidence of human feeling at all. She is the passive instrument of vice, he says. That's all.

Pabst concentrated on the physical integrity of his leading lady and so the plot turns into something else. Lulu's negative virtue, her lack of hypocrisy, illuminates the spiritual degradation of every single other character in the movie, with the possible exception of the honest Egyptian brothel keeper. This slight imbalance is created, in part, because Pabst had to tone down the part of the lesbian countess who exploits Lulu less viciously than anybody else does. The hypocrisy of censorship has, therefore, only served to strengthen the point that the movie is actually making about hypocrisy.

There are, of course, not one but two classic German expressionist cinematic *femmes fatales* and if Louise Brooks is the more magical, then Marlene Dietrich is the most succinct. At every point, these two women present mirror images of one another, just as their names – Lulu, Lola-Lola – teasingly echo one another. Dietrich was Pabst's second choice for Lulu if Paramount had not released Louise Brooks. *Pandora's Box* is a silent film; Brooks speaks with her body. The image of Dietrich in *The Blue Angel* is inseparable from her plangent, sardonic voice.

The Blue Angel, made by Joseph von Sternburg, né Joe Sternburg of Brooklyn, made of Dietrich not a cult legend but a major icon of the cultural imagination of the twentieth century, serene, heartless, androgynous, a lovely cobra poised to strike, and so on. This is a curious transformation wrought on the actual character in the movie by, again, those strange projections of desire that have turned Lola-Lola into a drag-queen.

At the core of the didactic Pabst's abstract melodrama of bourgeois hypocrisy is the American Brooks' exhibition of lyrical naturalism. That is part of the artistic tension of the movie. The central jewel in the formal rococo of von Sternburg's parody of provincial life is, in fact, a virtuoso piece of harsh realism –

Dietrich's attractive, unimaginative cabaret singer, who marries a boring old fart in a fit of weakness, lives to regret it but is too soft-hearted to actually throw him out until his sulks, tantrums and idleness become intolerable. If that is the story of a *femme fatale*, then some of my best friends are *femmes fatales* and anybody who feels ill-used by them has only himself to blame.

Lola-Lola can't love, either. She's much too sensible. She sings 'Falling in love again' with the ironic self-indulgence of one about to embark on a sentimental interlude that might give her a little fun but not much lasting profit. She has the look of somebody planning a brief holiday. So much the worse for the unfortunate professor, who is vain enough to think she is offering him her all. But as for him, is he so capable of human feeling himself?

He doesn't actually propose to Lola-Lola ('Men don't marry women like that,' as Schön, her seducer, says of Lulu) until he gets the sack for making a fool of himself over her. Maybe he thinks she owes him that much. Why? His marriage to Lola-Lola looks less like the surrender to a fatal passion than a grab at the chance of a lifelong meal ticket. How anybody has ever been able to see this film as the tragedy of an upright citizen of Toytown ruined by the baleful influences of a floozy is quite beyond me. The professor is a monster at the beginning and a monster at the end; he has toughened Lola-Lola up a bit and, perhaps, that is *her* tragedy, but clearly she will not brood. Neither will the toughening process kill her, as it does Lulu.

Dietrich's Lola-Lola is, of course, another wonder of the cinema and quite sufficient, in its sheer self-confidence, to serve as the projection of a fatal woman. And she is far more of an affront to male self-esteem than Lulu could ever be, because Lulu, being a child of nature and not a professional woman, has very little self-esteem herself. So *Pandora's Box* is never as criminally misread as *The Blue Angel* is. I have only ever seen one interpretation of *The Blue Angel* that seemed to tally with the movie I've seen and that is by the Surrealist, Ado Kyrou.

Kyrou, however, is so *bouleversé* by Lola-Lola that he goes right over the top. He simply can't believe Emil Jannings' luck. The famous scene, often regarded as the apogee of the ex-professor turned clown's humiliation, where he helps Marlene Dietrich on with her stockings: Kryou shakes and stammers at the very thought. Is there a man living, who would not regard a lifetime spent helping Marlene Dietrich on with her *stockings* as the very highest fate to which he might aspire? Kyrou can hardly bear it; he wants to jump right into the screen, knock Jannings out of the frame and takes his place tenderly at her feet. The professor's real tragedy, opines Kyrou, is that he is offered, if not love then a reasonable simulacrum of it, by a woman who is patently well worth a bit of hard work, and he is too great an idiot to see it.

'A woman blossoms for us precisely at the right moment to plunge a man into everlasting ruin; such is her natural destiny,' states the spineless sponger, Alwa Schön, in Wedekind's play. The horrid professor might have said the same. But what about her own life, if she can retain it, after the ruin has been accomplished? That is a gap in the scenario which, if she manages to get out of the mess, she must fill in herself. The pragmatic Dietrich packs her bags and exits with a sympathetic vaudeville performer, who will not ask of her more than she is willing to give. The more metaphysical Lulu can only hope, now, to accede to death as if it were some kind of grace.

So Lulu, the reluctant prostitute who never wished to sell the body she regarded as an inalienable possession, will be murdered by a sexual maniac, a man whom repression has turned into a monstrous scourge of whores, and on Christmas Eve, too, poor girl. She pays the price of expressing an unrepressed sexuality in a society which distorts sexuality. This is the true source of the fatality of the *femme fatale*; that she lives her life in such a way her freedom reveals to others their lack of liberty. So her sexuality is indeed destructive, not in itself but in its effects.

Repressive desublimation – i.e. permissiveness – is giving the whole idea of the *femme fatale* a rather period air. But this is only because the expression of autonomous female sexuality is no longer taboo. To clarify the point, a remake of *Pandora's Box*, or even *The Blue Angel*, ought, perhaps, to star a beautiful boy in the *femme fatale* role. Fassbinder could direct it. The significance of the *femme fatale* lies not in her gender but in her freedom.

New Society, 1978

Louise Brooks

by Barry Paris, Hamish Hamilton

I once showed G. W. Pabst's 1929 film version of Wedekind's *Lulu* plays, Louise Brooks' starring vehicle, *Pandora's Box*, to a graduate class at the University of Iowa. I was apprehensive. These were children of the television age, unfamiliar with the codes of silent movies, especially of German silents – the exaggerated gesture, the mask-like make-up, the distorted shadows – but I badly wanted to show them this great film about the unholy alliance between desire and money as part of a course about twentieth-century narrative I'd titled, quoting from Thomas Wolfe, 'Life is strange and the world is bad'. Nothing else but *Pandora's Box* would do.

Happily, they did not fidget or shuffle but sat like mice. Finally Jack the Ripper stabbed Lulu just as, or just because, she turns towards him the full force of her radiant sexuality; like the sun, he cannot bear to look at her for long. The film was over. There was a silence. Then a young man said: 'That was the most beautiful woman I've ever seen in the movies.'

And they all said, yes. The most beautiful. The best performance. Who is she? What else did she do? This biography provides a comprehensive answer to that question. Note how no attempt has been made to gussy up the title; Louise Brooks is a name that carries with it all the resonance of a quotation. The name that instantly evokes her personal logo, that haircut, those eyebrows. There are sumptuous photographs on front and back flaps – oh! the patented Brooks version of the Giaconda smile, the one that, as Barry Paris says, isn't so much a 'come hither' look as a look that says, to each and every gender, 'I'll come to you.' (If, that is she likes the look of you, a big if, in fact.)

That straightforward look of hers is what makes these sixty-year-old photographs of Louise Brooks so provocative, so disturbing, so unchanged by time. Like Manet's Olympia, she is directly challenging the person who is looking at her; she is piercing right through the camera with her questing gaze to give your look back, with interest. 'This provocative eyeful,' as *Picturegoer* magazine called her in the brief springtime of her youthful fame, is not presenting herself as an object of contemplation so much as throwing down a gauntlet. She is 'the girl in the black helmet', she'd have you know. She is the one they call 'the exotic black orchid'. She has a Cartier watch and a copy of *A La Recherche du Temps Perdu* tucked into her purse. Essentially, her attitude is one of: 'Now show me what *you* can do.'

It is still an unusual attitude for a woman to adopt. Many men, even if aroused by it, would think it was a bad attitude; so would those women who were neither aroused, nor felt complicitous with her.

'Women of exceptional beauty are doomed to unhappiness,' says Theodor Adorno. Beautiful is as beautiful does; Brooks' features in repose can look doll-like, chocolate boxy. The spirit that animated them was the exceptional thing. Roddy McDowell, who knew her in old age, said, 'when she was young she must have been like a whirling dervish. She must have been like a shot of oxygen right into the brain.'

And, on the evidence of this book and of her own book of essays, *Lulu in Hollywood*, I don't think she was unhappy, exactly. She was certainly, as she says, 'inept' at marriage, trying it briefly twice; it never took. She quarrelled with her best-loved brother shortly before he died, as if to insure herself against grieving for him. She was a vain, imperious bitch with a tongue like a knife, yet she was loved far more than she deserved, or acknowledged, and, even during her bleakest periods of despair, she always seems to have been buoyed up by a mysterious, self-sustaining glee. Drunk or sober (more often the former than the latter), flush or destitute, star, salesgirl, call-girl, or, final incarnation, *grande dame* and *monstre sacrée*, she never lost a talent for living memorably. Born a self-dramatiser, she always enjoyed the spectacle of herself.

It was an unusually picaresque life, for a woman, one of varied sexual encounters, booze, violent reversals of fortune, a good deal of laughter, and fairly continuous intellectual activity – Lotte Eisner, the critic, first spotted Brooks on the set of *Pandora's Box*, immersed in a volume of Schopenhauer's *Essays and Aphorisms*. She thought it was a publicity stunt, but changed her mind after they became friends.

Neither guilt nor remorse were items in Brooks' repertoire. It was a life like a man's, complicated by her beauty, and by the unimpeachable fact she was *not* a man. Far from it.

It was a life centred around, given meaning by, an extra-ordinary accident – that this young American adventuress and budding glamour star, on the advice of her handsome but sinister millionaire lover, accepted, without reading the script beforehand, the role of the Life Force incarnate, Wedekind's earth spirit, the Dionysiacally unrepressed Lulu, who must die because she is free. She went off to Berlin to shoot the film because she and her lover felt like an ocean cruise.

The role of Lulu itself is one of the key representations of female sexuality in twentieth-century literature. Brooks, under Pabst's direction in the movie, perhaps did nothing more than what came naturally. As Dorothy Mackail, a colleague from early Hollywood days, remarked: 'All they had to do with Brooksie was turn the camera on.' Mackail did not realise that therein lay the essence of a great screen performer. Pabst did.

But Brooks' chaotic life had an enormous artistic logic to it, as if Mr Pabst himself defined its parameters that day in Berlin, when Brooks was twenty-two, hungover from partying till all hours with rich American friends; finally Pabst, exasperated, said to her: 'Your life is exactly like Lulu's and you will end the same way.'

Another Pabst movie, *Diary of a Lost Girl*, also 1929, shows that *Pandora's Box* isn't a fluke, that Brooks could do it twice. It isn't as good a film as *Pandora's Box* but Brooks is, if anything, even more luminous, more like a transparency through which joy and pain, pleasure and heartbreak are transmitted directly to the audience. The 'lost girl,' seduced and abandoned, finds herself in a brothel.

At one point, Brooks is raffled off as a prize. Brooks, laughing, preening her extraordinary neck like a swan, looks as if it is the most exciting adventure in the world, that random chance will bring her partner for that night. Her particular quality is, she makes being polymorphously perverse look like the only way to be.

In her thirties, after she hit the skids, was doing a bit of this, a bit of that in New York, she and her great friend Tallulah Bankhead used to go out on the town together, bar-hopping, up to God knows what. Behaviour of Henry Miller buddies. But, however scabrous the circumstances, Brooks never lost a thoroughly un-Millerian elegance and self-irony and when she finally took up her pen and wrote, in her sixties and seventies, she wrote, not about life in the lower depths, but about her work in the movies, and if she wrote very little, she wrote very well, with an acute critical intelligence, and much showing off. (She was a culture vulture, an intellectual snob, an autodidact – good for her!)

Although her life spiralled downwards, like Lulu's, no victim, she. She died, unregenerate, in her own bed, at the ripe age of seventy-eight. But she was also the lost girl; in 1976, she wrote to an admirer, 'Remember when the prodigal son returned the father said, 'He was lost and is found.' It was the father who *found* the lost son. Somehow I have missed being found.' But this kind of existential rhetoric may only be the gin talking. Barry Paris makes it plain that somebody, somewhere, always did arrive in the nick of time to bail Brooks out. Always magnificently ungrateful, she would then scornfully retreat to the tried and tested company of 'my beloved Proust', her Ortega y Gasset, her Goethe.

We are dealing with a complex phenomenon, here.

She was born deep in the American grain, in Kansas, in 1906, of pioneer stock – her father, aged three, had been brought out West in a covered waggon. Her first dancing teacher had a name straight out of Mark Twain, Mrs Argue Buckspitt. In *Lulu in Hollywood*, she describes an unconventionally idyllic childhood, full of books, music and freedom. It sounds too good to be true; yet proves to be true in every detail, even to the music her beautiful, unhappy mother played all day on the piano. Bach, Debussy, Ravel . . .

All true. Except that Brooks edited it. Her parents preferred the company of books and music to that of their children, whose freedom was the product of indifference. Louise, the elder daughter, the image of her beautiful mother, was 'more or less a professional dancer by the age of ten,' performing at fairs, junkets, jamborees all over South-Eastern Kansas, whether to fulfil her mother's thwarted ambitions or, more simply, to coax from her, however fleetingly, attention and praise is now beyond surmise. Probably a bit of both.

At fifteen Brooks left home, an act most bourgeois parents would consider premature even in these permissive times; Brooks père was a highly respected lawyer. Nevertheless, with parental blessing, off she went to join a modern dance troupe, the Denishawn company. Barry Paris is succinct about Denishawn: 'In effect, Denishawn founded American modern dance.' It was also as chaste an establishment as a convent.

One of Denishawn's then stars was Martha Graham. Later, Brooks would say she learnt to act by watching Martha Graham dance, and to dance by watching Charlie Chaplin act. This explains her technique.

Brooks wrote in her journal, reminding herself how hard she must work 'as I someday intend to rise high in the ranks'. There is something very touching, something uncharacteristically earnest, about that phrase. She worked extremely hard, but it did her no good. Yet dance was Brooks' first and probably abiding love; at seventy, hair scraped austerely back from her vividly mobile face, the lovely old bones sticking out everywhere, she looks not in the least like an antique movie star but exactly like a retired dancer, as if, as a final indulgence to herself, she has decided to allow herself to look like the thing she'd wished she'd always been.

She never became a match for Martha Graham because she was thrown out of Denishawn after two years, not for dancing badly but for hell-raising. Sex, mostly. The sexual double standard was to haunt her for the rest of her life. No young man would have been censured in this way for sexual experimentation. At the same age, the impenetrably respectable Kafka regularly spent one evening a week at a brothel and was not dismissed from his insurance company. Nor turned out of home.

Her revenge on Denishawn and all it stood for in the way of

High Art and Plain Living was swift and spectacular; soon, in beads and feathers, she starred in Zeigfield's *Follies*, and engaged in a brief but highly visible affair with Chaplin, then at the dizzy height of his fame. *The Gold Rush* was freshly out. Crowds followed them in the streets of New York.

The dedicated dancer, moved by some 'inner vision' that Martha Graham, for one, saw in her, was now well on the way to becoming a *grande horizontale*. Men bought her furs. She let them take her out to tea. The management accused her of 'using the theatre simply as a showcase – a place to publish her wares'. She was capricious, promiscuous, petulant; she could have said, in the words of another great 1920s beauty, Lee Miller, the muse of the surrealists, 'I was terribly, terribly pretty. I looked like an angel but I was a fiend inside.'

Almost absent-mindedly, because it was the thing for showgirls to do, she started to make movies. Then came Hollywood.

I'd always assumed her Hollywood movies were negligible, her career there a non-starter, but Barry Paris makes out a convincing case, based on the amount of fan mail she received, the sheer *attention* she got, her rise from supporting player to fledgling star, that she was set fair to be one of the major stars of the 1930s. Sound would have posed no problem; she went to make a very successful stab at radio, dramas and soaps, in New York in the 1940s, before she trashed *that* career, in a fit of pique.

But that terrible accident intervened. She fell in love, broke up her new marriage, broke up her contract, went off to Berlin and made a huge flop of a movie. Because, in its time, *Pandora's Box* proved dead on arrival at the box office in both Germany and the USA. The last great silent, it was rendered obsolete before the première by the arrival of sound. She stayed on in Europe to make a couple more movies that scarcely saw the light of day and when she finally got back to California, she found her own career was floating belly up, expired in her absence, beyond recall.

Perhaps it had to do with her capricious libido; although accustomed to follow the promptings of her own desires wherever they might lead, they tended to stop dead at the casting couch. For a year or two, she coasted, doing bit parts in lousy films, until at last she was offered a chance at rehabilitation – the lead in *Public Enemy*, opposite James Cagney. When in doubt, Miss Brooks always burned her boats. She turned it down. It went to Jean Harlow.

And that, barring a few minor roles in 'B' features, was that. Eventually she went home to Wichita; home is where you go when nobody else will have you. But they wouldn't have her there, either. Her blue period began.

Until, like a miracle, *Pandora's Box* emerged in the 1950s after years of neglect as one of the greatest of all silent movies, and the young woman who always believed she could not act, and was not beautiful, either was too 'black and furry', who approached the movies as though it were modern dance, became, retrospectively, a great star, and one of the iconographic faces of the cinema, because of a role she had forgotten, in a film she had never seen all the way through.

She could have got the Myrna Loy role in *The Thin Man* series, opines Barry Paris. And, God . . . think of missing out on *Public Enemy*! What a great star Hollywood lost!

So what. Think of this as a possible analogy. After *Niagara*, Marilyn Monroe got a phone call. Let us bend time a little, and say it was from Tarkovsky, who had read in a smuggled copy of *Photoplay* how she'd always wanted to play Grushenka in *The Brothers Karamazov*. It just so happens, if she can get a release, that Mosfilm are preparing a production he has scripted. Puzzled, flattered, Monroe accepts. No problem about her English. She'll be dubbed.

After six months in Moscow, with no Russian, she's no longer sure if she's shooting *The Brothers Karamazov* or *Carry On, Comrade*. Tarkovsky pours mud over her and barks at her to keep her clothes on every time she tries to take something off. However late she is on the set, she is always the first one there. She lets her hair grow out. And *being* Grushenka all that time breaks something inside her. She stops shaving her armpits. She stops worrying about her weight. She returns home to find she has gone out of fashion overnight; no place in Hollywood for overweight brunettes with too much body hair. Because I am fond of Marilyn

Monroe, I will find her congenial work – in a children's home, perhaps. How the children love her! Count your blessings, Marilyn; you missed out on Arthur Miller.

Meanwhile, back in the USSR, the Tarkovsky movie is shelved for painting a negative picture of life in the Urals. The years pass. Glasnost. Tarkovsky's *The Karamazov Brothers* opens at the Venice Festival. His greatest picture. Who is the stunning girl with the blonde halo? Can it be possible she is still alive? So the lovely, fat old lady, resurrected, becomes a staple of film festivals. She is in a position of absolute security. Fame has come too late to bewilder or corrupt; it can only console. She is something better than a star; she is an eternal flame in the holy church of cinema.

I'm sure that Louise Brooks could have been, had she wished, had she even so much as lifted her little finger, as big and as durable a star as her contemporary, Joan Crawford. But she was presented, without either her knowledge or consent, a choice between Art and Fame, as straightforwardly as it might have been offered in a Renaissance allegory, and, without even being aware of it, she plumped, as it were, for the eternity promised by the poet. I do believe that, in her heart, she knew just what it was she wanted. She wanted 'to rise high in the ranks'. It was the reverse of a Faustian bargain. She bartered her future in exchange for her soul.

London Review of Books, 1990

Acting it up on the Small Screen

The main difficulty about television drama is that it has to compete with old movies. When I watch British television drama, especially the sort of prestige production for which they use well-known 'classic' actors, that is, actors trained for the theatre, I remember why I stopped going to the theatre (it was some time in the late fifties) and started going to the movies, instead.

'Live' theatre – though it might be better to call it 'undead' theatre – used to embarrass me so much I could hardly bear it, that dreadful spectacle of painted loons in the middle distance making fools of themselves. But these loons have truly come into their own, now. They have inherited the small screen and are inescapable, they spread themselves across all three channels mopping and mowing and rolling their eyes and scattering cut-glass vowels everywhere.

Television has extraordinary limitations as a medium for the presentation of imaginative drama of any kind. It has an inbuilt ability to cut people down to size, to reduce them to gesticulating heads or, in long shot, to friezes of capering dwarfs. The *Rock Follies* series and Dennis Potter's *Pennies from Heaven* utilised this diminished reality effect in various sprightly ways and British actors, given good scripts, can do quite nicely under these conditions. Two-dimensional characters present them with no problems, unless the script is by Noël Coward. (Oh, that dreadful *Design for Living*.)

This is because most of them can't stylise for toffee. Two dimensions, yes; four dimensions, no. They think stylisation means over-acting. But the problem remains; the image on the television screen is very small. Television drama is more like the movies than it is like the theatre, obviously, but it is like the movies through the wrong end of a telescope. Watching *real* movies on television is very much an all-round reduced experience, though the opportunity to catch up on something like the current Douglas Sirk season is the main reason for owning a set.

In the cinema, we accept the convention that the images on the screen are much larger than life without even thinking about it. This means that we accept, also without thinking about it, a far higher degree of expressionism than television could ever tolerate on its own terms.

Double Indemnity turned up – what a treat – as the midnight movie a few weeks ago. Take the famous close-up of Barbara Stanwyck's high heels, with the teasing anklet, as she walks down the staircase in order to lure Fred MacMurray to his doom. What this shot means, of course, is that MacMurray's whole attention is focused, not on the woman but on the erotic potential he, she and we know she is exploiting. On television, this whole point is lost. The image of Stanwyck's lower limbs is simply no longer large enough to sustain a metaphor. In television drama itself, there is not sufficient artistic space to contain this kind of device, and when directors try to perpetrate it it looks phony and contrived.

A close-up on television is about the size of one's own face in a mirror. Two is a crowd; scenes involving three or more people involve abrupt changes of the focus of attention. In three-quarter shot, the actors are already receding rapidly backwards, turning into wee folk before your very eyes. This question of scale, that only faces are life-size and everything else is far smaller, means that television narrative is somehow always composed at a distance, in the third person.

Movies aren't. There is always someone to identify with, even if its only the director. And scheduling that cruelly juxtaposes vintage Hollywood classics, great movies, quaint movies, boring movies, freaky movies against inept American telefilms and worthy but dull British high-class custom-made drama suggests only that television drama has not yet found its Lilliputian D.W. Griffiths.

Nevertheless, one test of the viability of television drama *as* television is whether or not it would look better on a big screen. If it would, then it's lousy television. I would have thought this stood to reason, due to the limitations of the form creating the aesthetic of the form. But sometimes one suspects television drama is made for preview theatres rather than transmission. It is interesting to see television falling into some of the old Hollywood traps, though.

For example, it is a well-known fact that good novels make bad movies. Obviously, what makes a novel good are just those qualities that make it difficult to translate it out of fiction into anything else. (Conversely, who'd want to read the book of the film of *Citizen Kane*?) Why, then, should it be accepted as a self-evident fact that great novels make great television? God knows. But the BBC keeps on churning out its 'classics' series, working remorselessly through Tolstoy, Hardy, Robert Graves (*Robert*

Graves?) amid a chorus of sycophantic yawns.

These series certainly give the painted loons a chance to show their paces. British actors adore period costume and facial hair; that's what they went to RADA for. The just-ended *Crime and Punishment* on BBC 2 really brings out the worst in them, even more than Chekhov does. They love to get their tongues round those lilting patronymics, they seem grotesquely liberated by personating groovy Slavs, it's an excuse to act your head off. Everybody knows how histrionic Russians are. Yet what looks, if not good, then at least lifelike in a parodic kind of way on a stage, looks like the theatrical equivalent of S. J. Perelman's pastiches of Dostoievsky when it is virtually delivered into your lap, which is what television does.

At the end of *Queen Christina*, Garbo was presented with the problem of a lengthy close-up as she sailed away from Sweden, having given up her throne to run off with a gentleman who had unfortunately just been eviscerated. Should she look glum? brave? Reuben Mamoulian told her to keep her face a perfect blank, so that the audience could read into her features whatever they felt should be the appropriate response. It works, too. Triumph of reticence; her face has the weary immobility of the obsessed. In this benighted *Crime and Punishment*, John Hurt feels it necessary to contort every single facial muscle, until the very hairs within his nostrils seem to rhumba, in a baulked effort to convey spiritual turmoil. This is no way to sift out the human truth from a script based on a writer whose strong suit was just that very thing. Mind you, I don't want to put John Hurt down. He is a highly competent character actor in the classic British theatrical style; but that style, as Norman Mailer suggested in another context, is designed to evade truth and celebrate simulation.

In an interview (in the *Radio Times*) Hurt is quoted as saying: 'If an actor can make you listen and watch and believe him, he's achieving quite something.' This fetchingly modest statement contains within it the very definition of that sort of 'naturalistic' acting that drove me out of the theatre, blushing for them, all those years ago.

He's talking about the fictive reality of naturalism, which

necessitates the creation of an illusion as an end in itself. (No wonder British actors make such a pig's breakfast out of Brecht.) But 'naturalism' as a mode which deals with the recreation of reality as a credible illusion is quite a different thing from the mode of realism itself, which is a representation of what things actually *are* like and must, therefore, bear an intimate relation to truth or else, well, it isn't any good. (And, of course, it doesn't have to *look* real.)

Hurt's remark reminds me of something gnomically ambiguous that Erving Goffman says about the fictive reality of commercial photography: 'It is through such practices that those who make a living reproducing appearances of life can continue further to stamp the real things out.'

Television, as a medium for drama, is, as I said, more like the movies than it is like the theatre. In fact, it is more like the movies than the movies are themselves, since so much of it is done in close-up. Most British actors are trained to project emotion rather than embody it. Nobody needs to project in close-up, unless he or she is selling something. British actors are very good at television commercials.

In fact, by far the most *realistic* acting in *Crime and Punishment* was Frank Middlemass as Marmeladov, but Marmeladov is a piece of cake for any British actor because Marmeladov is a posturing fake. The peculiarly external quality of the British school of acting, as if it were done in the third person, suits the personation of posturing fakes very well. It also suits the personation of other actors and of people who live with a high degree of self-consciousness; the upcoming *Brideshead Revisited* serial ought to turn out rather nauseatingly well because of this. It was also probably, in another way, why ITV's gangster series, *Out* worked.

John Hurt was terrific, truly, as Quentin Crisp, though *Crime and Punishment* hit the high peak of embarrassment, for me, when he threw himself at Sonya's feet with such an abrupt lurch that one half-expected the poor girl to snap: 'What you obviously have in mind will be five roubles extra.' But it certainly wasn't John Hurt's fault he couldn't bring off Raskolnikov's spontaneous act of homage from the murderer to the pious harlot. Probably only somebody as vulgarly Dostoievskian as Douglas Sirk would have known how to orchestrate Hurt's theatricality with the demented theatricality of the image.

I doubt if it would occur to a BBC2 classic serial television director to watch Sirk to pick up tips, though I hope I'm wrong. But the only thing at all like this exchange between Raskolnikov and Sonya that I've seen on television recently was when Susan Kohner threw herself on her mother's coffin in Sirk's *Imitation of Life*. Funnily enough, in the terms of British classic theatre, Susan Kohner probably can't act at all.

The BBC 'classic' serials are really no more than upmarket versions of the Classic Comics on which I was raised and which did indeed lead me in time to a curiosity about great literature that I eventually satisfied. It is probably unfair to discuss them as if they were drama, really. After all, as somebody pompously opined about *Crime and Punishment*, if it makes one person who had never heard of Dostoievsky pick up the book and start to read, it will have served its purpose . . . and also have the rather self-defeating result of, presumably, making him switch the telly off.

But if the BBC really does feel a compulsion to tackle projects like *Crime and Punishment*, it seems shabbily unimaginative of them not to treat the insane melodrama about guilt and redemption, which is, after all, Goffman's 'real thing', as richly unnatural as life, in the mode of realism. Maybe they could have thrown it open to the school of television social realism – Garnett-Loach-Allen *et al.*, let the cast make up their lines as they went along, shot it in Bradford which really does look like a Russian city, instead of what a Russian city is supposed to look like. Television pseudo-documentary social realism, after all this time, remains the only genre of television drama in this country that has the marks of a coherent style in which form and content fuse so that the actors appear to believe in what they are doing rather than trying to put one over on you.

New Society, 1979

Japanese Erotica

The blowfish (*fugu*) is the Japanese culinary speciality *par excellence*, the greatest treat of all, but one to be approached with caution. It is exceptionally delicious, it is a delight to the eye, it is inordinately expensive and, if you aren't careful, it will – the final thrill – kill you! Certain of its internal organs are fatally toxic. The Japanese feel about blowfish like they feel about the love of women.

Maybe *The Blowfish Feast* might have been a better title for Nagisa Oshima's sumptuous period piece – you can't call it a costume drama, because the principal actors usually appear unclad, (contrary to the lengthy tradition of Japanese eroticism). *The Bullring of Love* is a rough translation of *Ai No Corrida* though the image of the bullring does express the erotic antagonism between men and women that the film so amply illustrates: sex as an exhibition of athletic skill and physical stamina, in which the man is the blundering, witless, phallic bull, the instrument of female pleasure, the passive, adoring victim, perpetually desired, easily exhausted. And the woman, the toreador, derives her ultimate orgasm from the *coup de grâce* with which she then dispatches him.

But it is not as simple as that.

Kichi knew what was coming to him, all right, just as somebody who wilfully consumes the blowfish out of season knows he stands a running chance of taking his after-dinner nap in the morgue. And, in Japan, nowhere but the morgue is the right, true end of passion. Innkeepers near famous waterfalls, precipices, volcanoes (love suicides like beauty spots), cautiously refuse to let rooms to young couples who arrive late, indecorously hand-in-hand, suspiciously without baggage.

In a country happily free from the notion of original sin, ethics is part of the process of socialisation. A society in which, traditionally, the common goal is the good of all and marriage a liaison of reason, it is erotic passion that turns the communard into the bourgeois individualist. It turns Oshima's Kichi from complacent stud to clapped-out murderee, Sada from submissive maid-servant to demented castratrix.

Libidinal gratification may be pursued with wholehearted enthusiasm and nobody pay it any attention. It is the unique assertion of the self in erotic passion that is the secular sin which necessitates a self-inflicted punishment. At some point in all this, just to fall in love becomes an act of rebellion against society, as the Surrealists always said it was. But the lovers of *Ai No Corrida* have no consciousness of the nature of the society from which they retreat into emotional seclusion. You could call them rebels without a cause.

Yet the events *Ai No Corrida* describes took place in 1936, when Japan, in the thick of imperialist expansion, was purging the left wing through a series of assassinations and preparing for war. A time of rage, despair, violence, hysteria and frustration. Juxtaposed against this is the story of Sada.

The story of Sada, as all those who read the film reviews will know, is: maidservant runs off with employer's husband and eventually strangles him in the course of a sexual game. (Accidents will happen.) What happened then seems to me to belong solely to the realm of psychopathology; she sheared off his penis, wrote SADA AND KICHI-SAN FOREVER in blood on his hapless trunk, wrapped his penis up in a handkerchief and was found, a few days later, wandering the streets of Tokyo with the bloody relic in her bosom. She told the police she cut it off because she didn't want him to sleep with another woman. She received a very light prison sentence because, I was told, most people thought she was nuts – a reasonable hypothesis Oshima does not explore. She ended her days, I believe, again as a maid in an inn. People would come for miles to have her pour saké for them.

It is a singularly bizarre variant on the classic theme of the love suicide; and the lightness of her sentence and the levity, albeit terrified levity, with which her crime is discussed, suggests the lack of seriousness with which women are treated in that country. Oshima certainly does not treat her with levity. He treats her with such lugubrious solemnity that the movie made me wish that men would just leave off making films about female sexuality until they stop feeling threatened by it, for good intentions can lead them into old traps.

Coming out of the Gate Cinema after Sada had finally strangled and castrated the poor hulk, after an infinitely prolonged session of foreplay, I overheard some idiot braying: '*That* was a liberated lady for you!' As if erotic anti-feminism wasn't one of the great staples of all romantic art and we hadn't just seen a particularly glittering celebration of it. For all I know, Oshima himself does indeed believe his heroine is striking a blow for all women, everywhere, when she garottes her lover, even though, by that time, he has turned the actress who plays her into a demented fiend with dishevelled hair and a crazy smile, robed in a kimono of the bloodiest, most ominous red.

Then he makes her stand over the corpse in an attitude strikingly reminiscent of Max Ernst's castratory painting, *The Robing of the Bride*, gloatingly stroking her exceptionally large knife. I know Kichi-san was asking for it; but that doesn't mean a girl has got to give it to him. Need female submission go so far?

Ai No Corrida is a pornographic film. I don't see why anybody should argue about whether it is or isn't, or should care. Films about people having sex are pornographic in the way that films about cowboys are western; it is a description, not a value judgement. (Now *Love Story* was obscene.) Most major film-makers (of whom Oshima is one) have made pornographic films during the seventies and I don't think this is to do solely with market pressures. Sexuality is a hitherto taboo area of human experience which it is now possible to explore for the benefit of large audiences. It always raises, in the most provocative fashion, the nature of the relation of the individual to society. Which is one of the reasons why pornography as a genre attracts radicals. However, pornography presents a number of artistic problems – not least because it has even more stringent intellectual limitations than the Western. It also necessarily involves a discussion of the nature of realism.

Since pornography, almost more than any other cinematic genre, must depend on its audience suspending disbelief, the audience must be persuaded through a suave and, as it were, invisible photographic technique, that they are watching a couple actually screwing. (Or whatever else they are getting up to.) But, at the same time, the audience must be persuaded by a variety of means – Oshima uses a heavy overlay of period Japonaiserie detail – from asking themselves whether the couple they are watching *are* actually screwing. Because, if you start wondering whether the actors personating, say, Sada and Kichi are indeed getting it on in the studio, then the illusion of reality is broken at once. And once this illusion is gone, then the whole thing flies out of the artistic control of the director.

Upon the beautiful image of the privacy of the lovers, the busy, populous, brightly-lit image of the film-studio superimposes itself. We are no longer eavesdropping on the activity of desire; we are watching, instead, an elaborate mimetic paraphrase of desire, the appearance of realism which is, *per se*, unreal. And even if they *are* doing it, we are not watching *them* do it. We are watching the people they are pretending to be do it; that is part of the bargain we made with the nature of reality when we entered the cinema. But now everything you see is false; it all means something other than the spectacle before us, but the genre itself denies you access to that meaning!

So the film-maker perforce plays a game with the audience's perception of his creation which the essential, and probably crippling, discipline of pornography – that it must look as real as he can make it – prevents him from acknowledging. Alienation is the essence of pornography. In *Casanova*, Fellini coped with the presentation of alienated sexuality with characteristic brio; Donald Sutherland never took his trousers off, all his diverse adventures, were conducted in a stylised mime, at high speed. The effect was harsh, satiric and anti-erotic – as if to say, repressive desublimation will get you nowhere fast. Yet *Casanova* is not a puritanical film, while *Ai No Corrida*, with its abundance of fictive copulations, *is* deeply puritanical. No movie with the central message that the price of gratified desire is madness and death could fail to be puritanical. That love should end in the death of the object of the other's desire is a refinement of a notion of sexual love as transgression, which is not unique to Judaeo-Christian culture. If the film is intended as a critique of the social basis of this notion, then I simply don't think pornographic realism can cope with this kind of input.

Near the beginning of the film, there is a sequence where a group of children poke open the robe of a sleeping tramp with Japanese flags; they reveal his senescent tool. This they then pelt with snowballs. Oshima's other films have made very free use of expressionist devices; and this extraordinary image of nationalism and impotence dominated the film, and made me wonder: what does he mean by all this screwing, what does he *mean*? The emblematic tramp cannot get it up at the sight of Sada's carelessly revealed nudity; perhaps *Ai No Corrida* is a film about a less specific kind of inadequacy than that which Kichi, and who can blame him, finally exhibits. Liberalism, perhaps? Or, what? About female sexuality it is not, although it exploits male fear.

It is, finally, bitterly ironic that Oshima, who has made some profoundly serious films about modern Japan, should achieve his breakthrough to critical acclaim in the West with a film that enshrines certain Western stereotypes of Japanese culture in the glossy context of a period piece. Oshima is himself, perhaps, aware of this irony.

New Society, 1978

'Spend, Spend, Spend'

Nice to see a play about ordinary people. The pity of it was, that Jack Rosenthal found it necessary to conclude his real-life drama about Yorkshire folk with its heroine in tears for the lost innocence of the very slums that she had spent all her life, with varying degrees of success, trying to get out of. More fitting if she'd been crying because she was still there. How much, one was tempted to ask, does Jack Rosenthal *know* about ordinary people?

Spend, Spend, Spend occupied that uneasy limbo between fiction and documentary beloved of TV drama. It is a sort of social-democratic perversion of social realism that assures you what you see is real while at the same time consoling you by saying it isn't *really* real, it is a show, a play, an invention. Certainly the overt moral of *Spend, Spend, Spend* was a splendidly comforting bow to the bourgeois version of reality – that the working class don't know the value of money and if, by a million to one chance like a big win on the football pools, they get their hands on it, they'll piss it against the wall.

So, you see, it is actually cruel to give them money, for if they have money, they will only destroy themselves. As if it isn't perfectly possible, indeed, much easier for the poor to destroy themselves, anyway. And it certainly looked as though the celebrated pools' winners hero and heroine of *Spend, Spend, Spend*, Keith Nicholson, and his wife, Viv, were hell-bent on self-destruction from the word go, a council-house version of Scottie and Zelda, who substituted light ale for Champagne before they struck lucky. Why, goodness me, Keith was planning to give up work to concentrate on his fucking when he hadn't even finished his apprenticeship, let alone filled in his winning coupon.

Furthermore, Jack Rosenthal seemed to be saying, it is *very* cruel to chuck a naïve young miner's wife into the glare of publicity for doing nothing but being lucky – even if she *is* a raging exhibitionist, who regards being famous for being famous as a far better thing than not being famous at all. In fact, her being a raging exhibitionist makes it the cruellest thing of all, because she will get above herself if given half the chance.

So, curiously enough, Jack Rosenthal, with the best and most sympathetic will in the world, managed to trap Vivian Nicholson in the same value-system as that of the factory girls down home, who used to shout 'Jammy pig' at her. Though abuse is often a mark of affection around Leeds, and at least the factory girls were not ashamed to display naked envy.

The confusion between art and life demonstrated in this play about the life and times of real people still alive meant that, after *Spend, Spend, Spend* was broadcast, Viv had a real-life set-to with her first husband on account of the play, in which he had been portrayed as a witless ninny. So now she has to live with an even more dubious reality than ever, like the Warhol superstar *manquée* she undoubtedly is, a quality the play celebrated but never came to terms with.

Of course, few people write plays about the poor as such. Viv did not become the subject of a TV play because of the extravert savagery of temperament she revealed in her autobiography on which the play was based. Nor because the passionate mores of the mining culture of Yorkshire would provide sufficient material in itself for a British demotic *Dallas*. No. It was the legendary pools win of a quarter of a million pounds that was the *real* subject of *Spend, Spend, Spend*.

The poor only emerge into the public arena when they do something dreadful, or if they become rich. For Vivian Nicholson, it was the same thing. 'What are you going to do with the money?' they asked her. 'Spend, spend, spend,' she replied. And isn't that reasonable enough? Isn't that what money is for – made round to go round?

Apparently not. Money must be for something other than spending because she instantly achieved notoriety as the 'Spend, spend, spend' girl that night in 1961 when Littlewoods gave the happy couple their cheque. Those guardians of public morality, the *Sunday People* and the *Sunday Mirror*, watched her like hawks to make quite sure that, whatever else her money did to her, it wasn't going to upset the moral apple-cart by making her happy.

It is a characteristic of the very poor to see money only in terms of what you can buy with it. Not as a thing in itself, an object of reverence, to be treated as a precious seed that, if tended, nurtured and loved, will bear blossom and fruit a hundredfold, a harvest that, in its turn, the reaper is duty-bound to plough back into the soil so that each new fruit seeds another hundredfold, and so on *ad infinitum*. Nothing like that. Like the very rich, they see money as valuable only in its exchange value – in terms of the things you can buy with it, as if it were not capital but cowrie shells.

Keith Nicholson was earning seven quid a week as a trainee miner when Littlewoods lobbed the fatal cheque into their lives. They were very young, in their early twenties, with four kids, one of them his, and a support order for another kid a judge had decided was his. Even in the early sixties, seven quid a week was an irrational sum to support seven people on; from being irrationally poor, they became irrationally rich.

Part of the irony of it all is, that in terms of inherited wealth, a quarter of a million is peanuts. Shortly before *Spend, Spend, Spend* was screened, a well-connected company director ran up gambling debts of well over the Nicholsons' winnings and I doubt if his story will be singled out for the delectation of those less fortunate. And he's not reduced to living in a back-to-back with an outside bog, as far as I know, because he knows how to make debts and survive. The Nicholsons knew how to make debts, all right, but took no thought for the morrow, just as Christ said they should.

As soon as they got their hands on the bread, they had the impudence to live like the very rich. In fact, they'd always lived like the very rich, except they had no money. Viv's dad would have heartily concurred with Wilde that work is the curse of the drinking classes. Everything came on credit — disaster struck when the grocer stopped giving it. There were maintenance orders and unwanted pregnancies galore, proof of a sexual profligacy only the very poor and the very rich can get away with, the poor because nobody knows but the social worker, the rich because they can afford hush money.

They'd always lived with an aristocratic disdain of the Protestant ethic, ironically enough, since Viv and her mum, at least, worked very hard indeed for twopence half-penny a week. Now they had a chance to flout the Protestant ethic in public and let everybody watch.

There's a picture of Viv on the front of her autobiography, larking it up with Cecil Moore, the Littlewoods king's bowler perched on her bright, blonde head, flourishing his brolly. That picture became very famous, she says — picture of a smashing, buxom young woman gleefully mocking the iconography of the city gent and his world full of money farms. *He* had to work for it; she got it all for nowt!

She's kicking her leg up and flourishing her tits with extravagant abandon; her flamboyant sexuality is in itself a grand defiance of the bowler hat. What she doesn't know is, she's not going to be allowed to get away with it. This little lamb frolicking in its first spring is ripe for slaughter; heedless, feckless, the light of piracy may be in her eyes but the Jolly Roger won't fly over Castleford for long. That now she has made a bob or two from the story of how she squandered her fortune is a small victory for the anarchic id, which never counts the pennies.

Rosenthal seemed to have some vague idea that the real fascination of the Nicholson drama is its fusion of sex and money but he's content to let Viv be a simple victim of circumstances, bad environment, bastard men, vulturish yellow press, vulgar honeypot beauty that always comes to a bad end. (And because her blokes tend to beat her up, he thinks she must be a masochist; I hate that. Agressive women get beaten up for the same reasons as do aggressive men, especially north of St. Albans.) The fascination of it is not that Viv was sexy but unfortunate, won a lot, lost a lot; it is that somehow she performs some emblematic function *vis à vis* the sexuality of money itself.

'Spend, spend, spend', she said. Spend, the Victorian euphemism for orgasm. The Nicholsons engaged in an orgy of spending. Actually, all this orgy amounted to was a house, a few cars, a cupboard-full of clothes, a fishing-rod or two and a lot of booze and then Keith crashed one of the cars and died; after a legal tussle with the estate, his widow ended up with a meagre twenty thousand, most of which went pathetically on business ventures that failed. She should have stuck to what she was good at, frittering.

But don't let us allow actuality to interfere with the legend; nobody else does. Orgiastic spending, and the resulting postspending *tristesse*, is part of the moral fable. The squandering was, in its promiscuity, its evidence of a gluttony for luxury, its uncontrollable quality, orgiastic. All kinds of sexual metaphors link money and sexuality – he always has his hand in his pocket, masturbation, generosity. If money is seed, it is the sin of Onan to scatter it on barren ground.

For a brief season, the Nicholsons indulged freely in the wanton sensuality of sheer spending; God knows, they were a sensual couple and, since booze was the first thing they thought of when they had an odd bob, the fluid of their orgasm was frequently spew. When drinking too much began to affect Keith's sexual performance, Viv tells us she began to look around for another partner, a kind of pragmatism that goes against the Protestant ethic also. That his death made this unnecessary does not detract one jot from her atrocious grief.

Not the win itself brought out the worst in the neighbours, but the enviable spectacle of all that profligacy. The Nicholsons did it in the streets and frightened the horses and Mrs Nicholson, in spite of straightened circumstances, has gone on doing so. And now here is this woman called Susan Littler impersonating a woman called Vivian Nicholson who is alive and kicking, on the production team in fact, so that Miss Littler has the unique opportunity of studying the original, though we cannot allow the original to be herself because this is a fiction, not a documentary.

This seems to me very odd. Does the bizarre exercise of turning Susan Littler into a carbon copy of Vivian Nicholson and letting her go through the basic motions of her life for our viewing pleasure somehow make this last and most extravagant exploitation of Vivian Nicholson less reprehensible? Neither art nor life wins.

Admittedly, the British are not good at making art out of real life. The Nicholson story would be better material for the stern rigour of Fassbinder. I think Fassbinder would have understood it instantly, casting one of his monolithic and irreducible cowwomen as Viv and avoiding, or transforming, the play's climax. Which I think Rosenthal understood, all right, but interpreted all wrong.

You win some, you lose some, she's lost one husband, then another, she's broke, again; she strips down to glitter bra and *cache-sexe* and sings in clubs. Viv/Susan in her amazing halo of hair clutching the mike, forced to sing the one song they all demand: 'Hey, Big Spender'. Viv/Susan has a breathy little voice, like a terrified Monroe; and this is her crucifixion, huffing and puffing her way through verse after verse, a poignant sight, the ghastliest of humiliations, the Big Spender in person expending her spirit in a waste of shame. She's in a fit state to weep, now, for the child she was, who thought five bob was a fortune. Rosenthal has made quite a striking image out of a verifiable fact of her life.

Now, according to her autobiography, she never *liked* singing that number, certainly, although she was often asked for it. But the only song she really liked, the one the audiences loved to hear, was 'My Way'.

Because, in all its kitsch excess, 'My Way' was *her* song; no, I have no regrets, declaimed a ravaged Piaf and similarly Nicholson vindicates herself by the same rhetoric. She did it her way; of course she did, and they thump their pint pots on the table and cheer. Perhaps they didn't use 'My Way' because Susan Littler can't sing; but they could have dubbed her, couldn't they?

Because, for once, the exploited was exploiting her exploiters, making an honest bob out of her piratical status, for once, an ambivalent but real triumph. After all, you don't become a folk-heroine in Yorkshire by sitting around on your arse feeling sorry for yourself. But maybe Jack Rosenthal doesn't know that.

New Society, 1977

The Belle as Businessperson

Look, if you can't see what's so irresistible about Clark 'Jug Ears' Gable of the Jack o' Lantern grin, then much of the appeal of *Gone With the Wind* goes out the window. Furthermore, if Vivien Leigh's anorexic, over-dressed Scarlett O'Hara seems to you one of the least credible of Hollywood *femmes fatales*, most of whose petulant squeaks are, to boot, audible only to bats . . .

And, finally, if you can't see anything romantic AT ALL about the more than feudal darkness of the Old South, then, oh, then, you are left alone with the naked sexual ideology of the most famous movie ever made in all its factitious simplicity. Macho violence versus female guile, bull v. bitch.

The first time I saw this meretricious epic, it was the fifties, on one of the many occasions when they dusted off the reels and sent it on the road again to warp the minds of a new generation. Though I was but a kid in short pants, then, with zilch consciousness, truly I thought it stank. But – I was of that generation whose sexual fantasies were moulded by Elvis Presley and James Dean.

Presley, white trash with black style, in his chubby, epicene and gyrating person himself the barbarian at the gates of Tara – talk about irresistible, how could even Scarlett have resisted had Elvis pleaded with her to let him be her teddy bear? As for Dean – impossible to imagine James Dean carrying a girl upstairs. I used to fantasise about doing that to *him*. Fifty-six was, perhaps, the best year in which to view *Gone With the Wind*.

But the big question. Why, oh, why did the BBC choose to empty out *Gone With The Wind*, that hoary sackful of compulsive trash at this point in time? More – why did the Corporation decide to play Santa with this thing at the fag-end of Christmas, when, softened up by grub and booze, the notion might be deemed to be uniquely vulnerable? Impossible not to smell a rat. Part of the Women's Lib backlash?

I still think it stinks, this movie famous for being famous: that reduces the American Civil War to the status of spectacle (the Hollywood attitude to war, which reaches its apogee in *Apocalypse Now*); that advertises the masochistic pleasures of tight lacing – did you notice how often Mammy is depicted brutally compressing Scarlett into her corset? What kind of an image is that?

But, goodness me, how enjoyable it is! I curled up in my armchair, giggling helplessly, weakly muttering: 'Break his kneecaps', about every five minutes, sometimes more often.

Whose kneecaps? Well, Ashley Wilkes', obviously! What a whingeing creep. *Not* those of Big Sam, patently the Best Man on the entire plantation even if touched with Uncle Tom, such an obvious father figure that I can't see why Scarlett, father-fixated as she is, doesn't marry *him*, thereby giving the plot a whole new dimension.

But it is, of course, Rhett Butler's kneecaps that seem ripest for the treatment. That Rhett Butler and his travelling salesman's lines: 'You need to be kissed often, by somebody who knows how to do it.' This is the authentic language of a sexually incompetent man whistling in the dark, but let me not continue with that train of thought or else I'll start feeling sorry for him. And who could feel sorry for a man who says, as he closes in for the clinch: 'This is what you were meant for'?

Since Scarlett is characterised as a Maggie Thatcher *manquée*, I would have thought she was meant for high office rather than low innuendo. And, give *GWTW* its due, implicit in the script is just how ill at ease Scarlett is with the role in which the plot has cast her. Given any other option than that of the Southern belle, even that of a poor white farmer, she grasps it with both hands. Her sexual manipulations seem to spring from sheer boredom rather than actual malice, from the frustrated ambition of a baulked entrepreneur of the kind who has given capitalism a bad name. A bitch, not from sexual frustration (that old chestnut!) but from existential frustration.

After all, as soon as she gets her hands on that lumber mill, she starts coming on like the Godmother and Rhett can't think of a way to stop her.

Yet all this is going on in the gaps of the overt ideology of the movie. Which is very simple – no more than *The Taming of the Shrew* in hooped skirts. But in a film so extravagantly long, the viewer has ample time to ponder the socially determined nature of the shrew, which is often that of a woman forced to live for love when she really isn't interested in love at all, and why should she be, dammit.

Not that Rhett Butler does manage to tame *this* shrew, in the end. He may give out with genuinely unforgivable things such as: 'I've always thought a good lashing with a buggy whip would benefit you immensely.' But he never does batter her. Since he is the sort of macho weakling who is off like a long dog at the whiff of a genuine emotional demand, the obvious strategy to be rid of him is to say you truly love him.

So Scarlett wins out; off goes Rhett, thank goodness, and tomorrow is another day. Now Scarlett can get on with amassing a great estate and bankrupting small businessmen, for which activity breaking hearts must always have been an inadequate substitute.

There is, of course, the one really disgusting scene, that of the famous marital rape, which, in the late thirties, was deemed the very stuff of girlish dream and is now grounds for divorce. As a teenager, I'm bound to admit I didn't find this scene as repellent as I do now. Since it occurs three-quarters of the way through the second half, it is high time for Scarlett's come-uppance and, God help us, the whole scene is set up so that the viewer *wants* Rhett Butler to rape his wife!

Not that there is any suggestion it *is* rape. Irresistible Rhett, his ears rampant as if ears were secondary sexual characteristics, is but asserting his rights over the body of the woman who has rejected him out of selfish, narcissistic reasons such as a disinclination for motherhood. 'This is one night you're not turning me out.' He scoops her up in his arms.

Cut to the morning after. Scarlett stretches luxuriously in bed, smiling, singing a happy little song to herself. See? That's just what the bitch needed all the time.

And if you believe that, you will believe anything.

But. Perhaps. Perhaps she had broken his kneecaps, at that! Surely that is the only thing that could make her smile, at this juncture! And that must be the real reason why he has to go off to Europe, to visit a good kneecap specialist. Of course, they can't say that in the script, but I am sure that is what happened, really.

Observer, 1982

6

BOOKS AND BOOKPERSONS

The following pieces are mainly book reviews.

Linda Lovelace later repented, married and composed another autobiography in which she claimed that her entire life as Linda Lovelace had been a lie, a fraud and a monstrous imposition on her by brutal entrepreneurs. I don't see that this revelation invalidates anything she or her ghost writer said in Inside Linda Lovelace.

Should the human race last so long, however, the porno-boom of the late twentieth century will no doubt appear to succeeding generations as odd as the vogue for hoop skirts in the nineteenth or footbinding in Ancient China. The reviews of the Linda Lovelace and Gay Talese books seem naturally to lead into the examination of Judith Krantz's celebration of consumer fetishism.

The review of Anthony Alpers' biography of Katherine Mansfield is for Carmen Callil, who has also 'come home'.

For this revised section I have now included 'Love in a Cold Climate' and 'Alison's Giggle'.

Love in a Cold Climate

Some Problems of Passion, Protestant Culture and Emily Brontë's *Wuthering Heights*.

One of the most successful plays of recent years in London's West End was a farce called: *No Sex, Please! We're British*. It ran to packed houses for something like a decade. The title conveniently sums up both the stereotypical European attitude to the passionate, erotic life of the British, (that is, given the reluctance with which the British exhibit any evidence of erotic initiative at all, it is a wonder the race has contrived to perpetuate itself); and also the attitude of the British bourgeoisie towards itself – its own furious reticence about the life of the senses and the life of the emotions. Here is Tusker Smalley, in Paul Scott's novel, *Staying On*, writing to his wife, Lucy, whom he loves but whom he's treated badly:

'Can't talk about these things face to face, you know. Difficult to write them . . . Don't want to discuss it.'

This is the familiar imaginative territory of Celia Johnson and Trevor Howard and *Brief Encounter*, where a woman's heart breaks silently under her pastel-coloured twin-set and, in moments of extreme emotion, a man might clench his strong, white teeth around the stem of his briar pipe. Repression, not ecstasy, is the goal towards which British lovers strive and which they applaud themselves upon achieving. The language of passion is extruded with extraordinary difficulty through the stiff upper lip. Georges Bataille opines that 'the essence of mankind lies in sexuality.' That may be true on the continent, perhaps. In Britain, no.

However, the British popular press has always recorded, in lip-smacking and salacious detail, a sexual culture and a sexual folklore of bizarre vitality. This is a phallic, aggressive culture, leering, comic, serving up naked women as dish of the day. If, for the bourgeoisie, sex is unspeakable and hence remains unspoken about, the proletariat has no such problems – the white, male, heterosexual proletariat, that is.

For many years *The News of the World* boasted the largest circulation of all British newspapers. It was published on Sundays, when its public had the leisure to enjoy its tradition of uninhibited court reporting, especially of juicy divorces, atrocious rapes and sexual crimes. (*The News of the World* used to advertise itself with the slogan, 'All human life is here', a sad reflection on our species.) It has lately moved into the area of sexual gossip, centred on pop music or television celebrities and, when it gets the chance, the royal family. The rich diet it offers has been recently augmented by the arrival of the nude sexploitation daily newspapers, *The Sun* and *The Star*.

The enormously popular bi-weekly, *The Sport*, is entirely devoted to the reporting of sexual news and scandal to the exclusion of virtually all else except a little sports coverage. *The Sport* also carries advertisements for telephone sex. 'Hanky Panky! White Panties, Red Cheeks.' They charge calls at thirty-pence-per-minute cheap rate, forty-four-pence-a-minute at all other times.

A recent lead story in *The Sport* was as follows:

Disc jockey Ernest Hughes sexually aroused his wife with a bizarre collection of fruit, vegetables and household items, a court heard yesterday. Candles, bananas, cucumbers . . .

('My vegetable love,' as Andrew Marvell said, 'shall grow Vaster than empires . . .')

The British bourgeoisie, however, prefers to represent itself as the embodiment of the superego, pure, clean, above reproach – even if the Conservative Party is periodically wracked by sex scandals, of which the Profumo case ('Cabinet minister shares mistress with Soviet spy') is the most famous and the Cecil Parkinson affair the most recent ('Cabinet minister reneges on promise to wed pregnant mistress.') On the other hand, perhaps it is only in Britain that these predictable goings-on would be scandals at all.

But, if the British bourgeoisie thinks of itself as superego, the working class is happy to identify itself with id, pure id, and nothing but id, and a positively gendered, masculine id, at that. Not only to identify itself with id, but also to approximate the most riotous manifestations of the id in its public behaviour – riotous, brutal, murderous, obscene, given to Dionysiac displays of public debauchery when it runs howling through the streets. At international football events, it destroys everything it can lay its hands on.

In fact, this orgiastic, working-class culture, culture of the Saturday night drunken spree, the fist-fight, the gang-bang, retains a profound resemblance to Tusker Smalley's culture of repression, even if it is more energetic. Both are based on a denial of the power of language to communicate feeling. This orgiastic riotousness is the *inversion* of the bourgeois culture of repression and is based on the same set of existential premises, on a sense of self with rigidly defined boundaries, on a fear of the expression of emotion as, perhaps, eroding those boundaries.

Of course, actual practice does not conform to its representation either in the mock-Tudor palaces of the stockbroker classes or in the tower blocks of subsidised housing. The couple in the farce, *No Sex, Please! We're British*, did not, it turns out, object to sex as such; they had become the unwilling targets of a massive publicity campaign on the part of a mail-order sex-aids firm and were rapidly being submerged in 'a rising tide of filth', that is, were being deluged with mail containing many copies of publications like *The Sport*. The representation, not the actuality, irked them.

And another story in *The Sport* suggests the sad reality of sexual mores among the British working-class, for whom, it would seem, energy might be eternal delight but foreplay is a waste of time. Listen, for once, to the voice of a British, working-class woman, asked, during the course of a court-case, if her husband would normally kiss her during sexual intercourse, she replied: 'Not really.' Georges Bataille once diagnosed the problem, here:

'Utilitarian sexual activity is in conflict with eroticism,' he opined, albeit in another context.

In short, ours is an orgiastic, not an ecstatic, culture. The morning after orgy comes a hangover; 'never again', we cry. But the morning after ecstasy comes enlightenment, and the desire to do it again as soon as possible. Passion is the metaphysics of ecstasy but we are a pragmatic nation. We invented empiricism. But although I am a good pragmatist, too, and am perfectly happy to ascribe the state of ecstasy to an explosion of body chemistry, that does not change the nature of the *feeling*. You can explain why ecstasy happens but you cannot explain it away.

The language of sexuality in Britain admits of no chink through which ecstasy might shine.

The Sport has been instrumental in popularising the verb currently in common use in English to signify the sexual act, that is, 'to bonk'. The verbal adjective, 'bonking', is used with a freedom that surprises me, even though I am a child of the permissive 1960s. For example, the tennis player, Boris Becker, became nationally known as 'Bonking Boris' during the Wimbledon championship a few years ago, evidently solely on the grounds that he was accompanied by his girl friend. (What would the papers have said, one wonders, if the girl friend had been a boy friend?) The explicit euphemism is tolerated everywhere; but the verb for which 'to bonk' is a transparent substitute still provokes a furore if it is used on television or in the newspapers.

'Bonking'. Onomatopoeiac, almost. The sound of clinking bodies. Bodies that are not animated by soul. If British bourgeois culture posits a sexual relation like that which Milton attributed to the angels, a kind of non-physical 'mingling', these are animal passions, the product of a culture of sexuality that has a pagan simplicity and excess.

If there is an abyss, the diabolic abyss of transcendance without mysticism, between sacred and profane love, the abyss over which Pier Paolo Pasolini teetered on a tightrope, the abyss into which Jean Genet plunged with joy, then my native culture is rich indeed in simple profanity.

Profane love is often expressed in a language continuously-subverted by innuendo, where tone of voice or body language are as important as the words themselves. The flicker of an eyebrow can convert a simple inquiry, 'How's the missus,' say, or, 'Keeping perky?' into something over which blows might be exchanged. Marie Lloyd, the turn-of-the-century music hall artiste, used to reduce her audience to tears of mirth when she announced her arrival: 'Sorry I'm late . . . I was *blocked* in the Strand.'

When it is *not* expressed in innuendo, the language of profane love is not suitable for public consumption because it is not the language of love at all but the language of vulgar abuse.

When D.H. Lawrence single-handedly attempted to put the profane language of proletarian sexuality in English at the service of a higher vision of class mobility in *Lady Chatterley's Lover*, something went badly wrong. It proved impossible to cleanse the words of the delirious violence that a millenia of use as the basic weapons of non-physical brutality had given them. Whatever else Anglo-Saxon might have been in its time, it turned out that it was *not* the language of passion. Lawrence did not manage to resanctify a system of sexual signifiers that had been transformed over the centuries into the cruellest kind of verbal abuse. Instead, he repeated them as farce.

However, by restoring the ancient nouns and verbs to their dictionary meaning, Lawrence did succeed in doing something very odd. He reminded us that things, words, concepts, the pig, women, the organs of generation, blood, the verbal adjective, 'fucking', only become prohibited, taboo, unclean, 'filthy', if, once upon a time, they have been sacred. The profane language of proletarian sexuality in English is a kind of blasphemy – indeed, it has a far more profound effect as swearing than blasphemy does itself. 'Fuck', like 'shit', is a far stronger exclamation than 'damn', 'For fuck's sake!' is stronger usage by far than 'For God's sake'. The sacred is absent even when its very name is taken in vain.

In fact, we British do not have a very clear notion of the 'sacred' as a special sort of category at all. The rending, sadomasochistic savagery of the idea of 'passion' – passion as a litany of exemplary suffering, illumination, transcendance, as an access of desire, not necessarily gratified desire, in which 'opposites vanish, in which life and death, time and eternity, are mixed,' – in Octavio Paz's phrase, well! . . . 'Don't want to discuss it,' as Tusker Smalley would say.

The very word, 'passion' in English has lost almost all trace of its Latin root; it no longer has any relation to suffering. We think it is about rough sex. I wrote a novel some years ago with the title, 'The Passion of New Eve'. The 'passion' of the title refers not only to the erotic attraction between the two principal characters – a man who has been changed into a woman, Eve, and a man who has elected to become a woman in appearance, Tristressa – but also to the process of physical pain and degredation that Eve undergoes in her apprenticeship as a woman. This led to some confusion in Britain. In its first English paperback edition, the novel was issued with a cover depicting a woman in tight jodhpurs and transparent blouse, flourishing a riding crop. 'Hanky-Panky'.

There is no visual tradition in Britain to correspond to the Renaissance one of the representations of 'sacred and profane love' – the Reformation and the English Civil War effectively terminated the possibility of that kind of theological speculation in paint: the Protestant faith, like Islam, does not approve of painted idols. You cannot get away with the idea that a naked lady represents a higher form of spiritual truth. In Britain, a naked lady is implicitly lewd. We are essentially a Northern peasant culture, of the earth, earthy.

It is therefore very difficult, in English, for profane love to collide with any version of the sacred kind in order to create that explosion of transcendance the surrealists called 'amour fou'. Indeed, there is no adequate translation of 'amour fou' in English. 'Mad love' isn't quite right; the translation already contains an implied value judgement. There is also very little space in the national sensibility in which that grand confusion of the senses might take place. 'I want you to be madly loved', wrote André Breton to his infant daughter. We would not want that for *our* children. A.A. Milne wrote *Winnie-the-Pooh* for *his* infant son, with a very class-and-culture-specific vision of eternity at the end of what turned into a series of much-loved children's books, a boy and his teddy bear playing together endlessly in a sunlit wood, a prepubescence without end, unless, perhaps, boy and bear might finally 'mingle' like Miltonic angels.

Milton, having allowed himself to believe in the physical integrity of angels, since to believe in them solely as spiritual emanations went against the grain of his intellect, was then forced to construct their theoretical reproductive and digestive systems so that he could go on believing in them. He was a good empiricist, in his way. He could not allow angels to exist purely as sacred beings, sufficient to themselves according to some metaphysical law we do not understand.

Milton is the greatest of all Protestant poets and the culture of the English language is essentially a Protestant culture. The language itself as we know it today was standardised out of a welter of dialects in the sixteenth century by the widespread dissemination of a single book – the book whose existence was itself predicated by the Reformation – the Bible in English, in which the Old Testament had equal importance with the New Testament. The theological imagination was kept in check by the presence of the text, which also restricted metaphysical speculation about the events described in the Bible to a marked degree. The doctrine of the Virgin Birth is certainly not something that Tusker Smalley would care to discuss and is certainly not something that the average reader of *The Sport*, with his 'hands-on' approach to human reproduction, would entertain for one moment. In the Protestant communions service, the bread stays bread, the wine stays wine – the drama of the Christian liturgy passes us by. The majestic tragedy of Good Friday passes us by – Easter has never been an important popular festival in Britain since the Reformation. But the festival of Christmas – in England a thoroughly orgiastic festival – grafted as it was originally onto celebrations of an impressively orgiastic and pagan nature, has always had more hold on the popular imagination. A number of intellectually influential Protestant sects – in particular, the Unitarians – posit a Holy Family that is not, in itself, divine. The Scots inherited

Calvinism and Original Sin; The English constructed a form of Protestant humanism out of Lutheranism and then rarely gave it another thought.

And if the Old Testament urged us to contemplate the Fall of Man rather than the Passion of Our Lord, nevertheless, the vicissitudes of our later history as Great Britain have more or less wiped out a sense of sin from our consciousness. A sense of sin is a gross impediment to an empire-builder. Graham Greene deplores this lack of a sense of sin; of my immediate contemporaries, Ian McEwan enjoys it and Martin Amis, without quite knowing what it is he is missing, seems as though he would rather like to have a sense of sin all to himself. But it is gone for good, especially where sex is concerned, and with it, the glorious transgressive impulse the surrealists valued most of all about passion. I cannot imagine that André Breton would identify the 'Hanky-Panky' girl with her white panties and red cheeks with a practitioner of one of the 'mysterious perversions' with which he believed 'amour fou' surrounded itself.

Yet we cannot blame our lack of passion and our conspicuous profanity on the Reformation alone. Geoffrey Chaucer predates the Reformation by some two hundred years and some of the stories in *The Canterbury Tales* wouldn't seem out of place in this week's *The Sport*. Some of the others he borrowed from Boccaccio, who was not a Protestant, either.

Furthermore, it was the twenty-five-year-old daughter of a Protestant clergyman living in the most unaccommodatingly rugged and dissenting part of England, the Yorkshire moors, who wrote *Wuthering Heights*, an impossible novel that ought not to exist, a novel that makes us believe the world can crack apart like an egg when its shell is blown apart by the irrepressible force of human desire.

Wuthering Heights is one of the greatest, if not the greatest, love story ever written but it is not in the least like *Anna Karenina*, because it is a ferocious celebration of exactly those imperious qualities of desire for which *Anna Karenina* is a lament. It is a love story that takes for granted, that takes a perverse pleasure, an insane joy, in fact, in the way desire rips through the fabric of

172

society and demands the sacrifice of status, family, honour. And finally of life, probably.

Ivan Karamazov, in one of the three or four nineteenth-century novels that may be compared with *Wuthering Heights*, was thrust into existential terror at the thought that, if God were dead, then anything might be possible. In the story of this phosphorescent man and woman, Heathcliff, and Catherine Earnshaw, Emily Brontë seems to be saying: God *is* dead. Anything *is* possible. If . . . you have the will. This violent and extraordinary romance is about a desire that is stronger by far than death, that does not acknowledge death as in any way an impediment to passion. If the price of the lovers' desire is damnation – and there is a strong suggestion that this is so, for, if God is dead, then surely the Devil has been left in charge – then Heathcliff and Catherine will delight in being damned.

It is a mistake to think that *Wuthering Heights* is about Heathcliff, about the charisma of that fatal, demon lover. This is not so. There is no denying that Heathcliff has sold his soul, probably to the Devil, quite early in the narrative, but Catherine it is who emulates Lucifer. She dreamed, once, that she went to heaven, and:

> '. . . heaven did not seem to be my home; and I broke my heart with weeping to come back to earth; and the angels were so angry that they flung me out into the middle of the heath on the top of Wuthering Heights; where I woke sobbing for joy.'

Milton's Lucifer fell from 'dawn to dew eve . . .' but even he did not weep for joy when he found himself exiled from God forever. Catherine's is the authentic voice of the rebel angel and it is easy to forget, because of her gender, that, if Heathcliff is a demon lover cast in the same mould of diabolic grandeur as the romantic poets revisionist reworkings of Satan, then so is Catherine Earnshaw, too. Perhaps more so, a Lady Lucifer.

She, like Heathcliff, effortlessly devastates tranquillity, domesticity, honest affect. When she falls ill with fever, Mrs Linton, mother of the unfortunate man she eventually marries, takes her off with her to convalesce. 'But the poor dame had reason to repent of her kindness; she and her husband both took the fever and died within a few days of each other.' Cathy is, literally, a 'femme fatale'.

Heathcliff's problematic humanity is constantly discussed throughout the novel: 'Is Mr Heathcliff a man? If so, is he mad? And if not, is he a devil?' 'Is he a ghoul, or a vampire?' And so on. Catherine herself is quite explicit that, if something is wrong with him, then the same thing is wrong with her. 'Whatever our souls are made of, his and mine are the same . . .' She, too, is daemonic. Nelly Dean, the housekeeper, who knows her very well, does not believe that heaven can hold her but neither Nelly nor anybody else think of Catherine as resembling a vampire or a ghoul herself, even though we first meet her in the novel when she is manifesting herself as a phantom, and one should not think that Emily Brontë composed the passage about Catherine's dream in ignorance of Milton. (We are the first generation of readers of English Literature who haven't read Milton with the same closeness and concentration with which we read Shakespeare.)

Nelly Dean, always the voice of normative repression, speaks disapprovingly of Cathy's 'fits of passion', meaning, in that curious Victorian usage, bad temper. (Passion is perceived as irritability.) By passion, Nelly means Cathy's wilfullness. Her uncontrollability. Her deep *unfemininity*. But Catherine Earnshaw's passion is – passion. She and Heathcliff are locked in the mutual incandescence of 'amour fou'.

The author of this novel wrote it when she was almost as young as that other rebel angel, Arthur Rimbaud, when he wrote *Les Illuminations*. She belongs more fittingly with him than with those who died young because the gods loved them, like Keats. Emily Brontë died at the age of thirty, but not from some tragic accident or chance infection. She appears to have died as the result of an exercise of will, to have deliberately starved herself to death a few months after the death from consumption of her brother, Branwell. In the period shortly before she died, she destroyed all her personal papers, which probably included another novel. She covered her tracks almost completely before she concluded this last, most ambitious project, her own death.

It is one of the strangest and, in a way, least tragic deaths one can imagine, and all of a piece with the stray images of Emily Brontë it is possible to glean from her sisters' accounts. We know she kept a pet hawk, called Hero; that once, shopping with Charlotte and Anne, she bought a dress length of white fabric printed with a design of purple thunder bolts and lightning flashes. They were horrified; they preferred the subfusc, wanting to go unnoticed in the crowd, but Emily the recluse never went out in crowds and wanted to be attired in the tempest. Once she was bitten by a mad dog, took up a red-hot iron and cauterised the wound herself. *Wuthering Heights* is the work of a woman capable of all these things.

Heathcliff's death, also the result of self-starvation, may have suggested to her her own passionately wilful suicide – but his death is not an act of will, rather, the result of a giant *absence of mind*. He forgets to eat in his eagerness for union, or reunion, with the dead beloved. He forgets, you could say, to live . . . but then, Catherine is both dead, yet not dead, a restless phantom maintained in the limbo between heaven and hell by her passionate will. And Heathcliff does not so much die as abandon his body.

Let me quote those wonderful lines of Joseph Glanvill, that Poe used as a motto for *his* story of the passion that transcends death, *Ligeia*. Remember, Ligeia and Catherine Earnshaw are both Protestant revenants, that is, not supernatural beings so much as beings with a passionate excess of will to live.

'And the will therein lieth, which dieth not. Who knoweth the mysteries of the will, with its vigour? For God is but a great will pervading all things by nature of its intentness. Man doth not yield himself to the angels, nor unto death utterly, save only through the weakness of his feeble will.'

But Emily Brontë *died* by willpower, unless death appeared to her as a form of escape from a world which denied the existence of the elemental passions in which her fiction delights like the albatross delights in the storm. Octavio Paz: 'Women are imprisoned in the image masculine society has imposed on them; therefore if they attempt a free choice it must be a kind of jail-break.'

Emily Brontë seems to have been singularly unconcerned with the image masculine society imposed on her. Nevertheless, the only free choice she appears to have entertained was that between life and death and perhaps her death was in itself a kind of jail-break.

Catherine Earnshaw *is* imprisoned in an image of femininity. The process is described in no uncertain terms. She is socialised as a woman by the Lockwood family. They take her off the moors, a savage child as fierce, violent and impetuous as her adopted brother, and transform her. When she comes back home again to 'Wuthering Heights', she is utterly changed. 'Instead of a wild, hatless little savage jumping into the house, and rushing to squeeze us all breathless, there alighted from a handsome black pony a very dignified person with brown ringlets falling from the cover of a feathered beaver, and a long cloth habit which she was obliged to hold up with both hands that she might sail in.'

Together with her new clothes and her new feminity, she has put on repression. ('Today put on repression and a woman's name.') She can't play with the dogs any more for fear of messing her new clothes. She can't hug Nelly Dean because Nelly is covered with flour from cake-making – now Catherine can't even associate herself with the unclean activities of lower-class images of femininity. She has become not only a woman but a bourgeois woman, an object of conspicuous display, something to be looked at, not touched. She can't forebear to rush towards Heathcliff when she sees him, to hug him – the Earnshaw children are physically exceedingly free and demonstrative. But she draws back when she sees he is dirty – covered with farm-boy muck. He is *filthy*. Cathy retreats with a prim shudder from what she suddenly perceives as a 'rising tide of filth'. (I do not apologise for the *double entendre*, here.)

She has already made her choice between the dirty and the clean. She will make the *sensible* choice, the asexual choice, the clean and passionless choice. She is going to marry into heaven – to marry the good angel, the clean, blond, rich, squirearchical Edgar Linton. She is going to ascend, on the ladder of social mobility, into the paradise of the lower reaches of the upper-classes.

All post-sixteenth-century English art contains a subtext concerning class and *Wuthering Heights* is no exception to this. All the same, such is the furious endorsement of transgression in the incandescent personages of Heathcliff and Cathy that it comes almost as a shock of anticlimax to realise that all they are transgressing is the barrier of social class. One feels that at least they ought to be brother and sister, to make the transgression really worthwhile.

'Why did you betray your own heart, Cathy?' asks Heathcliff in that extraordinary love scene that culminates in Cathy's death, a scene of great emotional and physical violence given an added dimension of horror by the fact that Catherine is seven months' pregnant. She 'betrayed her own heart' – she betrayed the pure imperative of 'amour fou' – because she did what was expected of her. She reneged on free choice. She failed to make the jail-break in life – although her death has also a suspiciously willed quality about it. (Her last words are: 'Heathcliff, I shall die.' More of a promise than a threat.)

But Cathy certainly makes her jail-break posthumously. She comes back for Heathcliff. She returns and she *takes* him, as if, now all that remains of her is passion. The novel is a triumphant celebration of that 'amour fou' of which there is no adequate translation in English.

Wuthering Heights – together with *Alice In Wonderland* – was a favourite book of the surrealists. Luis Buñuel prepared a script in the 1930s but was unable to make a film until he was living in Mexico in 1953. Then he found himself saddled by the producers with a cast who had been hired for a musical, including a rhumba dancer named Lilia Prado who played Isabella Linton. In spite of the surreal aspect of all this, the random juxtaposition of Mexican song and dance team with this blazing text did not produce one of those accidental miracles so beloved by André Breton. The film creaks; so does the chocolate-box conjunction of Laurence Olivier and Merle Oberon in the William Wyler Hollywood version. But Buñuel at least knew he was dealing with some kind of blasphemy; William Wyler was content to film a romance.

There is a profound impropriety in *Wuthering Heights* that seems to touch some even more sensitive subject than that of the female libido, although certainly the novel states categorically that Cathy's mortal being, though not her ravenous immaterial part, is destroyed by her betrayal of her own desire. The relation between Cathy and Heathcliff seems almost too intense to be normal, to be transgressive *in itself*.

It should be said that, in the novel, incest occurs in every respect except the actual. Heathcliff marries Cathy's sister-in-law; their son marries Catherine's daughter, also named Catherine; after his death, the second Catherine marries the son of her mother's brother, a boy whom Heathcliff has reared according to his own deplorable methods and for whom he feels the closest possible affinity. (He seems, says Heathcliff, 'a personification of my youth, not a human being.') The intricate matings demanded by the plot, a series of permutations on the marital possibilities of two nuclear families, skirt around potentially incestuous relationships in every case and, though Catherine and Heathcliff are *not* biologically brother and sister, they grow up together as brother and sister – closer than most siblings, in fact.

But, then, again, *Wuthering Heights* is in no sense about physical consummation. The question of whether Heathcliff and Catherine ever had sex is beside the point. Their's is a pure passion, pure transgression, an eroticism so violent it does not need to name itself. Virginia Woolf said about the book: 'There is love, but it is not the love of men and women.' Well, not perhaps as the love of men and women manifested itself in the Bloomsbury group. The US critic, Camille Paglia, puts it more clinically: 'Heathcliff and Catherine seek sadomasochistic annihilation of their separate identities.'

At one point, Catherine tells Nelly Dean, who is her servant and confidante, that she would certainly have married Heathcliff – she could have envisaged no other partner but Heathcliff – had not her brother, Hindley, set out to humiliate and degrade Heathcliff, to return him to the condition of savagery in which he first came to them.

But it is impossible to imagine these beings of sulphur and

lightning as Mr and Mrs Heathcliff. If they touched, we feel, they would explode. That final, terrible love scene is a battle. She pulls out a handful of his hair, he leaves blue bruises on her arms. Their final embrace is like the inexorable mingling of two drops of mercury. 'An instant they held asunder and then how they met I hardly saw, but Catherine made a spring, and he caught her, and they were locked in an embrace from which I thought my mistress would never be released alive,' says Nelly Dean.

She *is* released alive – just. Heathcliff gives her back to her husband in a coma which is the prelude to her death. Flesh is too fragile a receptacle for this amount of feeling. They suffer a fire which burns and is not consumed; they burn in a mutual flame; they transcend the unique individuality of the body; they distill from physicality a pure spirit . . . and so on.

They aspire to the language of mysticism in their relationship, although Emily Brontë does not allow herself to use the language of mysticism.

What could they possibly want from one another. They want what Octavio Paz wanted – 'an instant of that full life in which opposites vanish, in which life and death, time and eternity, are united.' It is the high, romantic vision of passion. And, in the end, what Catherine Earnshaw and Heathcliff want is precisely what they get. In no other novel in English is passion permitted to triumph. Emily Brontë even permits passion to triumph over death.

The ending of the novel is ambiguous. Emily Brontë gives the last words to the fatuous, town-dwelling, stranger, Lockwood. He pays a visit to the three graves, Catherine, her husband, her lover. The graves seem quiet enough, to him. 'I lingered round them under that benign sky; watched the moths fluttering among the heath and harebells, listened to the soft wind breathing through the grass, and wondered how anyone could ever imagine unquiet slumbers for the sleepers in that quiet earth.'

But don't forget that Lockwood is a fool, and a fool without imagination. A shepherd boy has just told us he saw a couple on the moors: 'They's Heathcliff and a woman, yonder, under t'nab!' The ghosts have even been seen at the windows of unused rooms in Wuthering Heights itself, as if waiting until the house is empty enough for them to move downstairs. Even Nelly Dean doesn't like to be out late, on the moors, these days.

Catherine Earnshaw dreamed the angels threw her out of heaven and she sobbed with joy to find herself back on the moors again. Perhaps her dream came true. Listen to the sound of the tears of joy of the rebel angels; it is the authentic sound of passion and we do not hear it often in England.

A paper given at a Conference on the Language of Passion,
University of Pisa, Italy, 1990

Lovely Linda

(*Inside Linda Lovelace:* by Linda Lovelace, star of *Deep Throat,* Heinrich Hanau Publications, Ltd.)

'Some people,' our Lady of Hard-Core Porn reflectively begins her memoirs, 'are born to greatness, others have greatness thrust upon them.' Her own fame devolves partly upon her own sexual virtuosity but, more, upon the demands of a society that utilises limited libidinal gratification as a soporific in a time of potential social disruption. She, the archetypal swinger, is the product of the 'permissive' society she eulogises; but the notion of 'permissiveness' can only arise in a society in which authoritarianism is deeply implicit. Now I am permitted as much libidinal gratification as I want. Yippee! But who is it who permits me? Why, the self same institutions that hitherto forbade me! So, I am still in the same boat, though it has been painted a different colour. I am still denied authentic sexual autonomy, perhaps even more cruelly than before, since now I have received permission to perform hitherto forbidden acts and so I have acquired an illusory sense of freedom that blinds me more than ever to the true nature of freedom itself.

With no surprise, one learns from the preface that Ms Lovelace is 'no adherent of Women's Lib'. She preaches sexual freedom divorced from social or spiritual emancipation: 'the only place she wants to be equal is in bed.' Nevertheless, she exemplifies what could be called 'porn pride' when she states: 'I have learned to do things with my mouth and vagina that few women anywhere can hope to achieve.' However, she gives credit for her training to Chuck, the 'sexual engineer', a libidinal Svengali who launched her in blue movies; she didn't even invent it for herself, or learn it from her mother (which, I suppose, would be the natural way in a less repressed society). In an interview published in the afterword, she claims always to achieve orgasm herself in the act of fellatio which is physiologically impossible. Therefore I suggest her relation to men and to her own sexuality is ambiguous, and, coloured by either a degree of self-deceit, or the desire to deceive.

Nevertheless, she can ingest an entire foot inside her vagina; we know not only because she tells us so (which wouldn't be the strongest evidence of veracity) but because she has been filmed doing it. Fame, however, came with *Deep Throat*, since when her name has become synonymous with a fellatory technique that looks, to the cold eye, uncommonly like a sublimation of a suppressed castratory urge of immense proportions. If my sexuality had been as systematically exploited by men as Ms Lovelace's has been, no doubt I, too, would want to swallow men's cocks whole; it is a happy irony she should have found fame and fortune by doing so.

Now, in spite of the respect she has for her achievements as a unique phoenix of fuckery, Ms Lovelace does only what any accomplished whore is expected to do in a society where the profession of prostitution demands specific sexual virtuosities. Any Bangkok prostitute can blow smoke rings through her labia minor and be certain of applause and thanks. Her own fellatory technique is derived from that of a Japanese geisha (via, of course, Chuck. You wouldn't find Ms Lovelace in a Japanese whorehouse, learning her trade the hard way.)

Not every girl can insert a foot inside her vagina and those with this talent are surely entitled to public recognition; but our society generally denies the prostitute both appreciation of and the opportunity to exercise particular sexual virtuosity and, besides, Ms Lovelace is no prostitute. Perish the thought. All is done for love. The pay in porno movies is 'lousy' until she hits the big time — that is, until the porno movies become respectable. Sometimes, in her movies, she plays the role of a whore, but she is not a whore herself. Her attitude to sex is not commercial. It is sacramental.

'My God is now sex. Without sex. I'd die. Sex is everything.'

In the service of the god, she has taken the repertoire of sexual display from the commerce and intimacy of the brothel and allowed her performance to be frozen upon celluloid, condemned to a sequence of endless repetitions. In doing so, she has removed any element of tactile immediacy from her exposition of the potentialities of the body and therefore completely defused the sexual menace implicit in her own person and her polymorphously perverse talents. And that menace is enormous. If she can engulf a foot, what else could she not engulf? The owner of the foot in his entirely? The world itself?

But, though the cinema has become an imaginary brothel, it is not one in which the flesh on display is for sale. Hence it can never be handled. On the screen, she is safe from real contact with the impulses she arouses. (She constantly reiterates her own sexual exclusivity; she does not fuck with *anybody*. They must be special. They must be 'swingers'.)

These defunct images of her sexual virtuosity do not involve nor implicitly challenge the potency of the spectator.

And, in the eternity of the celluloid, the cock exists as a thing in itself. The exigencies of porno-movie making means that: 'Many of the cocks seen in the nitty-gritty close-ups don't belong to the guys that are seen leading up to the action.' Because those who can act can't fuck, and vice versa. Indeed, she reveals, many of the actors are homosexual; and the faces of the owners of the most active organs never appear on the screen. Dispossessed, then, of all human attributes but the anonymity of the genital organs, nothing is generated. Nothing will come of nothing.

Like a postulant, Ms Lovelace shaves herself before she engages in these primal yet abstract confrontations. She has removed all traces of the animal from her body, so that it has the cool sheen, not of flesh, but of a mineral substance. She is not an embodiment but a crystallisation, even a reification, of libido; her art or craft, the public exposition of sexual activity reduced to a geometric intersection of parts, her queasily kitsch prose style, her leer, her simper, her naivety, her schoolgirl humour, effectively anti-septises all the danger from that most subversive and ambivalent aspect of our selves.

No more terror, no more magic. Sex utterly divorced from its reproductive function, its function as language and its function as warfare.

She is a shaven prisoner in a cage whose bars are composed of cocks. And she has been so thoroughly duped she seems quite happy there.

Each age gets the heroines it deserves and, by God, we deserve Linda Lovelace.

New Society, 1974

The Sweet Sell of Romance

(*Princess Daisy* by Judith Krantz, Sidgwick & Jackson)

Glamour has returned to the White House, according to the magazine headlines, and *Princess Daisy* has at last joined its stable-mate, *Scruples*, in the US paperback outlets, twinned in self-adver-tisement: '*Princess Daisy*, a novel by the author of *Scruples*'; '*Scruples*, a novel by the author of *Princess Daisy*.' Judith Krantz is the author in question. Glamour has also returned to the best-seller lists. And how.

Though you couldn't quite say that Judith Krantz is to these troubled times what Scott Fitzgerald was to the Jazz Age, her two novels so far – she's reportedly working on a third – certainly offer some insights into the mood of the United States in these regrettable, even implausible days of disquiet, when the century trembles on the cusp of *fin de siècle*, and there is even an unstable undercurrent of *fin du monde* about it all. The manner in which her books have been sold to the public is certainly indicative of a new role for the novel.

According to an exhaustive blow-by-blow account of this entire marketing process, in a recent *New Yorker* article, a certain Morton L. Janklow, after first reading the manuscript of *Scruples* a year or two ago, told Judith Krantz: 'If you want to see that book covering the faces of every woman on the beach in America next summer, let me be your agent.' This statement lets the cat out of the bag. You are not reading a book if it is covering your face. Any fool can see that. Selling the book is more important than having people read it.

Presented with this notion of fiction as pure commodity, Mrs Krantz enthusiastically concurred. And is it any wonder! Because both *Scruples* and *Princess Daisy* are romances of high consumerism.

In *Scruples*, the incredibly rich Billie Ikehorn Irsini, after a period as a compulsive shopper, finds true fulfilment by opening a shop herself (the 'Scruples' of the title), and selling luxury items of personal adornment. In this novel, some tacky nostalgic stuff about the movie industry is thrown in towards the end as a glamour makeweight, but in *Princess Daisy*, consumption is allowed its own complete integrity. Princess Daisy, the eponymous heroine, achieves a more radical apotheosis. She herself becomes a brand name. Indeed, she is transformed into a perfume when a matching fragrance and line of cosmetics are named after her.

The final effect of both novels is of being sealed inside a luxury shopping mall whilst being softly pelted with scented sex technique manuals. It is a uniquely late twentieth-century experience and not without a certain preposterous charm, as of a champagne picnic on the crust of an active volcano.

I don't think that Mrs Krantz's novels offer a richly informative guide to the fantasy lives of Middle American women. Rather, they are indications of what a lot of people think a lot of other people's fantasy lives *ought* to be like. They are prescriptive rather than descriptive. But I think this is unconscious. No doubt Judith Krantz believes she has merely tapped one or two veins of wish-fulfilment fantasy that have existed since time immemorial. The one about being a rich widow. The one about being a beautiful princess.

A *beautiful princess*? Yes! That one! In this day and age? Never, it seems, more potent. In republican America? You bet.

Krantz knows better than to repeat successful formulae. There are fascinating differences between the two novels. *Scruples* (1978) is a West Coast novel. The meat of the action takes place in and around Los Angeles. Billie's shop is on Rodeo Drive, where luxury boutiques create 'the most staggering display of luxury in the western world', *Princess Daisy* (1980) is basically a Manhattan novel. (Presumably the work in progress will be a sagebrush rebel novel, centred on Houston or Dallas, where the action is now said to be.)

Billie is an Amazon-tall, sexually voracious brunette whose wealth is her problem. Daisy is a fragile, sexually reticent blonde, a White Russian heiress who loses her family fortune because her father invests it in Rolls-Royce, which the British government then heartlessly nationalise. She becomes poor; that is *her* problem. She works hard, and practises elegant economies like dressing in old Schiaparelli suits bought at jumble sales.

Though Daisy's period of poverty (in New York's new bohemia, SoHo) has elements of Marie-Antoinette playing milk-maid, her full-time job still gives her more quiddity as a character than Billie. In spite of her ludicrous pedigree, Daisy is more believable within the terms of the fictional convention. It is always difficult to empathise fully with somebody whose relation to the world is blunted at the edges by an excess of the green stuff.

Krantz makes a valiant attempt to promote Billie as a 'poor little rich widow', imprisoned in the magic castle of her wealth. But there's a lack of conviction about it because, in her heart, Krantz obviously believes (as I do myself) that if the rich are not seen to be happy, then there is no validity to the concept of personal wealth. It goes without saying that, in the Krantz world, money means gratification. More, it is a primary requisite of existence. After all, it takes a million dollars to make Daisy solvent – which is rather more than it would take, for example, me.

The difference in the treatment of sex between the two novels is the most startling single contrast. *Scruples* contains anatomically precise descriptions of the parts of the greater part of the male principals. Those of the hero of the sub-plot, 'Spider' Elliot, are constantly visible, in a state of excitation, beneath his jeans. Billie's own well-developed clitoris 'pouts' through her labia major in a manner which, in the real world, usually belongs only to the female orang-utang. Men and women fall to it in soft porn sequences at cannily spaced intervals. There is an interlude of men-only sex. Oral sex is high on the menu and Billie ('got something to show you . . . you'll like it') is herself a *vade mecum* to sexual expertise.

But sex in *Princess Daisy* is soft focus rather than soft porn. It rises to infrequent peaks of the explicit only on special occasions – Daisy's father's boyhood initiation by an older woman; Daisy's rape at fifteen by her half-brother, a difficult boy; a lesbian episode which does *not* involve Daisy . . . big erotic set-pieces like that.

Krantz may have perceived that, even in the two short years between the books, the sexual hard sell is already *déjà vu*. The women's lib backlash supervened. Daisy's best friend, the 'ribald' automobile heiress, profligate as she is, must now descend to playing hard to get to stir the interest of the man for whom she really cares. Femininity is back in fashion.

If Billie is always fumbling in men's trousers, Daisy's sex life, somewhat inhibited by that rape, is done with a rose-tinted delicacy. Men part her thighs and whisper, 'May I?' proving that she is a real lady.

Krantz herself acknowledges that Billie, with her 'huntress's stride' and 'almost virile beauty', is an out-of-date model, when the cosmetics executive in *Princess Daisy* says: 'I think the time has come to return to a romantic sell in fragrance, a classy, feminine sell.' That romantic sell in fragrance is the one to which Princess Daisy lends (or, rather, sells, for a million bucks) her name. And the book is a 'romantic sell', too.

The novel's title suggests a fancy conflation of Henry James' *The Princess Casamassima* and *Daisy Miller*. It hints at sophisticated, cosmopolitan goings-on, and the novel spends time in London, Venice and other romantic European places, besides SoHo. To a certain extent, pure snobbery – an awed gasp at the divinity that still hedges White Russian royals, at least for Krantz – supplies the charge in *Princess Daisy* which sex has supplied in *Scruples*. Such good, old-fashioned snobbery is making a big come-back these days.

Scruples, however, has the more startling vision. It offers a total eroticisation of the idea of the shop, the shop as magic brothel. In Billie's boutique, not only do you pick 'clothes that are right for you, but you had to be hot for them, dizzy with a desire that can't be forced, any more than a faked orgasm can be enjoyed'.

Buying a dress is, or ought to be like a good fuck (*sic*). Customers are described as 'gratification junkies'. They spend freely, recalling the Victorian use of the verb, 'to spend', as a euphemism for ejaculation. Cash has an intimate relation to libido. Never, you might say, has it been so hard.

A shop like 'Scruples', we are told, will succeed in any city 'full of very rich, very bored, very elegant women'. All it needs is a large leisure class. It is an emporium that expresses the values of imperialism in a late Roman sense. Profit has no relation at all to productive labour. The shop could only have been conceived in a period of sharp inflation, where there has been a loss of faith in money as a medium of exchange. The wealth that the customers of 'Scruples' expend within it is real, but meaningless. Like fairy gold.

And Billie deeply needs her shop to be a financial smash, just because she herself doesn't need the money. Similarly, it is central to the mystique of Krantz as author that she herself is not short of a bob or two. She is, apparently, a well-to-do woman, married to a Hollywood film producer, and a graduate of classy Wellesley.

No rags-to-riches story, hers. The story of Judith Krantz, like that of her heroines, has as its motto the fiscal policy of the Reagan administration: 'Unto every one that hath shall be given.' The *real* poor exist in an unimaginable limbo.

That Krantz is rich and worldly-wise to start with is what gives authenticity to her account of the high life. Even if Kenneth Clark himself told you how lunch at the Connaught Hotel was 'one of the première experiences of western civilisation, the Uffizi gallery of dining', you might well think he was having you on. The serene self-confidence with which Krantz imparts this information puts it beyond question.

Throughout both novels, Krantz is always comfortingly *there*, not in person, but as an utterly authoritative authorial voice, imparting what purports to be solid information about the world, often in almost aphoristic cadences. From *Scruples*: 'Going into research is the only way a doctor can positively insure himself against making a decent living'; 'The [Cannes film festival] audience is the most purely vicious since Christians were thrown to the lions.' From *Princess Daisy*: 'There is no team so committed to their joint and individual successes as the homosexual husband happily married to a lesbian wife.' And so on, and on.

Her novels offer, at a modest price, what purports to be an insider's comprehensive knowledge of the inside workings of the tiny, glamorous world of the gossip columns and media fame. They are handbooks of a certain kind of social mobility, masquerading as good reads. The information about what to eat, how to dress, where to buy (she is hot on real restaurants, real brand names, and real shops as well as imaginary ones) is guilelessly presented in terms of fantasy.

This is fiction as service industry to an emergent class of media aristocrats; or, at least, would-be media aristocrats. Her initial success came with just such a class: with the people who bought the paperback rights, and the television rights, and God knows what other rights, and ensured that both novels would be bestsellers long before the books ever got to the wire racks in the paperback outlets, and thence to the person in the shopping market.

Towards the end of *Princess Daisy*, Judith Krantz starts playing a dangerous game, under the circumstances. Virgil to the reader's Dante in the inferno of the advertising industry, she invites us to inspect at close hand the very confidence trick which lures the cash out of the pocket in the first place. 'When cosmetics and perfumes start selling for anything *near* the price they cost to produce,' ruminates an executive, 'it'd be like fucking Russia.'

Here, in her desire to identify the reader/consumer with the men at the control boards of power, she forgets that the reader *is* consumer. She comes perilously close to labelling her or him as a credulous gull, and so disclosing, in all its luminous purity, the value system underlying her novels.

This is the value system of capitalism in its great rock candy mountain phase, where only money makes more money. Which is precisely where it's at in the United States now.

New Society, 1981

Alison's Giggle

In the Miller's Tale of *The Canterbury Tales* by Geoffrey Chaucer, a young woman, who has just played a sexual practical joke on a young man whom she does not want, emits a satisfied giggle. We know Alison giggles rather than bursts out laughing, because Chaucer tells us that she does so: 'Tehee! quod she.' She giggles; and returns to bed with a more attractive partner. Her husband, meanwhile, has strung himself up in a tub under the rafters, awaiting the arrival of the Flood, which his wife and her lover has convinced him is imminent so that he will vacate his bed and leave it to them. (Alison's husband believes the tub will make an excellent improvised boat and proposes to launch it at the first sign of the inundation by cutting the ropes which attach it to the roof.)

Alison's giggle is not a sound which is heard very often in literature, although, in life, it can be heard every time a young girl successfully humiliates a would-be admirer. (My mother taught me to say this to young men in dance halls who wanted to buy me gin and orange even though they had spots: 'Does you mother know you're out?' Off they would squelch, abashed, on their two-inch thick crêpe soles. And we girls would giggle.) Perhaps, given the traditional male narrator in literature, the sound is so rarely heard just because it expresses the innocent glee with which women humiliate men in the only way available to them, through a frontal attack on male pride. To reproduce this giggle, a man must identify with a woman rather than with another man and perceive some aspects of male desire as foolish. Indeed, in a sense, perceive the idea of the supremacy of male desire as foolish.

Admittedly, Chaucer, through the mouth of the Miller whom he has invented to tell this tale, is careful to present Alison's failed suitor, Absolon, the parish clerk, as a ninny; that makes it easier for them both to take Alison's point of view. All the same, Absolon, looked at objectively, is no more of a ninny than Don José in *Carmen*, who also attempts to thrust his attentions on a woman who is no longer interested. But Prosper Merimée saw nothing foolish about *his* hero. And even if he *is* a ninny, Absolon is so roundly humiliated – Alison tricks him into kissing her backside, rather than her mouth – most men would think she'd gone too far. But, in the tale, Absolon's vengeance goes badly wrong and misses Alison altogether; and, more significantly, Alison is not censured by her creator for asserting a woman's right to humiliate in however light-hearted and girlish a fashion.

Alison's giggle sets up a series of echoes disturbing our preconceptions whilst echoing our experience. If male narrators, in general, cannot bear to hear it, the female narrator, increasingly frequent over the last two hundred years, especially in those forms of the novel that purport to give an exact transcription of everyday life and so ought to tally better with our experience than medieval poetry does, have also tended to omit both the giggle and the kind of sexual circumstance that best provokes it.

Hard to imagine Jane Austen's Elizabeth Bennett playing a sexual practical joke on the curate in *Pride and Prejudice* who so richly deserved it, and not only because Jane Austen's genteel scenario, centuries away from that of the 'fabliau' of the middle ages, does not allow to take place the kind of events in the course of which Mr Collins might, literally, kiss Elizabeth's arse. (Indeed, linguistically, Elizabeth is not in possession of an arse.) And, apart from these limitations, Jane Austen arrives in history at that curious time when women, as a fiction reading as well as a fiction writing class, were supposed to affect ignorance of just exactly what it was Alison was up to in bed with her Nicholas when she was interrupted by the unwelcome serenade of the parish clerk.

Whether a *female* narrator of Chaucer's period would have felt the Chaucerian freedom of diction and situation is moot. The female narrators whom Chaucer invents himself are perfectly decorous in diction, although the Wyf of Bath's tale is not particularly decorous in content and her soliloquies on life, love and the management of husbands have badly upset centuries of male commentators. The Wyf of Bath is, however, a fictional invention, and her self-determined sexual appetites ('I folwed ay myn inclinacioun,' she says) and her robust speech belong to the sexual stereotype of the middle-aged woman, who may speak as she pleases since the sexual threat she poses has been removed by the menopause. She is the same kind of fictional person as the nurse in Shakespeare's *Romeo and Juliet*; and as Mae West. Situation complicated, here, by the fact that Mae West was both a fictional invention, a woman who re-invented herself in terms of the movies she wrote and starred in, and also a perfectly real woman who, it would seem, often behaved and spoke like the fictional Mae West. Stereotypes only become stereotypes, after all, because they correspond to certain kinds of real behaviour. It is possible to surmise, therefore, that there were sufficient middle-aged women rich enough and tough enough to behave not unlike the Wyf of Bath in England in the fourteenth century, which is, in many ways, a daunting thought.

Such a woman, with a perfectly good trade of her own (the Wyf of Bath was a famous weaver of cloth) and a very active sexual and emotional life, would scarcely have had the time to write poetry, nor, one imagines, would she have seen the point of the activity. And she may not have known how to read and write too well (although she could certainly count). Marie de France, the twelfth-century poetess (called 'De France' because she was a Frenchwoman who lives in England) composed infinitely elegant poetic tales of impeccably courtly love, befitting a person with a nice mind and, presumably, a private income. However, since women certainly contributed to the anonymous body of traditional lyric which survives in manuscript from the medieval period, and survives in other forms in folk songs collected in the nineteenth century, and which is often very rude indeed, it is possible that *illiterate* women may have had a freedom of creative expression, and the opportunity to do so, denied to those of higher rank and accomplishment.

Whether women could, if the possibility had been widely available, have written in a 'Chaucerian' manner in Chaucer's time is an unanswerable question; but we know that medieval women, of whatever class, were not supposed to be shocked by Chaucer because *The Canterbury Tales* was intended for a mixed sex audience. There are two women on the pilgrimage itself, one the Wyf of Bath and the other a nun, who listen and comment upon a collection of stories many of which, by Jane Austen's time, were not considered suitable for women at all, at all. When the Miller sums up his tale in the phrase, 'Thus swyved was the carpenterys wife' ('That's how the carpenter's wife got herself fucked'), it may be assumed that not only the male pilgrims and the Wyf of Bath but also the nun knew what 'to swyve' meant and did not think it reprehensible or unusual activity between consenting adults.

The representations of women in English literature by male narrators (and we can assume a dominant male narrator until the mid eighteenth century) are, however much determined by contemporary notions of the position of women, based on the assumption that men and women share an equal knowledge of the basic facts of sexual experience up until, curiously enough, that very time in the eighteenth century when women in significant numbers take up their pens and write. The poet, the writer of fiction and the dramatist always write in the context of the assumed knowledge of the listener, the reader, the spectator; when, for whatever reasons, there comes about a time when rather more than half the audience for any given literary production is presumed to be in ignorance of the basic facts of the continuation of the human race. Then a whole group of literary productions becomes 'unsuitable for women', especially those in which women *are* shown as knowledgable and active sexual beings. (Witness the wrath the nineteenth century inflicted on Restoration comedy and the way the female dramatist, Mrs Aphra Behn, became unmentionable, due to her 'indecent' wit.)

It is not a naive question, that of whether Jane Austen, a provincial maiden lady, was herself precisely aware of the actual mechanics of sexual intercourse. It is reasonable to assume, from the degree of sexual tension between her female and male characters, that, even if she were unfamiliar with the practice, she was conversant with the theory, to some degree. The twanging eroticism of Austen's novels may even owe some of its power to the taboo upon pre-marital or extra-marital sexual intercourse and upon discussion of these things in any but the broadest terms. Yet the conventions of her time and class, conventions of both fiction and of actual behaviour, force her to deny to her heroines the practical use of the sexual allure with which she so abundantly equips them – assuming, that is, she did indeed know just what such use would mean.

The sexuality of Austen's heroines exists as a potential; as a potential, it is fully utilised as lure and bait. But her narratives ceased abruptly with the marriages of the heroines, although this is the point at which, for the British bourgeoisie of the late eighteenth century, a woman's life actually begins. That is, her *real* life, as mistress of a house and as a being-in-the-world; all this is symbolised by marriage as the beginning of a woman's sexual life.

Austen shares this cut-off point in her heroine's stories both with the nameless authors of fairy tales and with most writers of fiction primarily intended for a female market in her own day and in ours. Her heroines remain electric virgins, charged with a power of which they know the value – indeed, perhaps they over-value it – just as long as it remains within their own control. But, as regards that power in the context of a marriage, when the woman herself is no longer in complete control of it – for Austen, and, perhaps, for many women, this remains unquantifiable, and not only if they remain unmarried. Austen ends her heroines' stories at the moment when the virgin is about to die as a virgin, and be born again as – and, you see, there is no word for it. No word for a 'respectable' woman as a heterosexual being except 'wife,' that is, by definition, a contingent being.

If both words, 'virgin' and 'wife', define a woman by her sexual status, 'virgin' describes a condition-in-itself, while the word 'wife' implies the existence of a husband, just as the word 'prostitute' implies the existence of a client.

Even so, the conventionalised 'happy ending' of the wedding in fiction by and for women may signify not so much the woman's resignation of her status as autonomous individual, a status that might be at best problematic in a society with little available space for anybody's autonomy, but the woman's acquisition of a licence to legitimately explore her own sexuality in relation to a man, as well as acquiring part shares in her husband's public status and wealth, and inheriting all the folklore of sex and reproduction that is passed from generation to generation of married women. For a woman, to marry, in fiction, is to grow up; all the same, there is something rather honourable about the simple reluctance of fiction by and for women to accommodate itself to that kind of maturity. The narratives stop short at the altar, as if they cannot bear to go on. As if to travel hopefully, the chase, the courtship, the acceptance or rejection of suitors, were better than to arrive at this ambivalent destination. All such fictional narratives of women that end in marriage could just as well end with a death, because marriage means the death of the virgin, that is, the termination of her narrative as an individual, however hedged about with prohibitions that individualism might be.

Alison, the carpenter's wife, is brusquely defined by her sexual status in a perfectly straightforward way. Since she is a wife, we know she is not a virgin and also that her sexuality belongs to somebody else. Further, she carries her husband's social status around with her like a badge. Artisan class. (The Wyf of Bath, by the way, is simply a woman from the city of that name; she's had too many husbands to be easily defined by the status of one of them and has, besides, a perfectly good status of her own.) Alison's story does not end with marriage; she is married before her story begins and the plot quickens when she becomes the focus of male extra-marital desire. Alison is a contingent being in every way. We are not even given a hint of her former history as a virgin; whether or not she, like the Wyf of Bath, had 'other company in youth' is a mystery. But marriage has not robbed her of the ability to keep her hands on the reins of her own life; she can grab back control of her sexuality and compensate herself thereby for some, at least, of the more unpleasant consequences of marriage to a silly old man.

George Eliot's *Middlemarch*, unlike the novels of Jane Austen, begins with the marriage of its heroine, a marriage the success of which is indicated by the scene in which we find Dorothea Casaubon, on her honeymoon, weeping in a cemetery. The tears of Dorothea come from a different world, a different kind of experience and an utterly different narrator than the giggle of Alison. Eliot is a woman. Chaucer is a man. The two fictional women demonstrate the change in fiction in the intervening five hundred years: Dorothea, clever, sensitive, middle-class, aspiring towards she knows not what, is an inhabitant of the fully three-dimensional Victorian novel with its project of transmitting the whole of human life irradiated by a vision of a transcendent morality. If that, too, was Chaucer's project in *The Canterbury Tales*, he went about it in a different way, and his Alison is an inhabitant of the shadowless, two-dimensional world of medieval fabliau, the eighteen-year-old wife of an artisan whose class has disappeared from bourgeois fiction by George Eliot's day, except as picturesque extras mumbling proverbs and old saws in dialect. Alison is coltish and wild, slim as a weasel, with a 'likerous ye,' (a lecherous eye). She is described as an object of desire, not from the inside. She is compared to a young pear tree, a colt, a calf, a flower; all in all, the typical young girl of male imagination. Yet, when she giggles, that 'Tehee! quod she' comes rippling across the centuries, giving that entirely spurious sense which only the greatest art gives us, that the past, in all its unimaginable difference from our lives, can nevertheless shiver, fall apart and reveal human beings who, for all they believe the sun went round the earth, lived on the same terms with themselves that we do and made the same kind of compromises with circumstances.

Dorothea's dilemma, marriage to a man she finds sexually odious and from which there is no way out except his death, is presented by George Eliot as a paradigmatic moral dilemma which has nothing to do with Dorothea's sexuality, nor with desire nor with pleasure – least of all, with pleasure. It is just possible to imagine Jane Austen, had she been born, not a vicar's daughter in the Home Counties but into that world of the amoral Regency aristocracy which scared her so much (see her treatment of the Crawfords in *Mansfield Park*) thoroughly endorsing Alison's strategy for the perpetuation of pleasure after marriage – that is, infidelity and the use of her sex as a weapon. Jane Austen's heroines have a glittering confidence in their own allure, even if it is always allure and never the lineaments of gratified desire. Fifty years later, Eliot, a writer of infinitely greater intellectual resources than Austen, effectively begged the entire question of the sexual nature of the heroine of her finest novel by presenting it in such an oblique way that Dorothea seems almost asexual and is constantly assimilated to unsexed female images of saints.

Yet Dorothea weeps on her honeymoon; and it is her husband Casaubon's attempt to regulate her actual sexual behaviour – according to his will, her inheritance depends on her *not* marrying the young, toothsome Will Ladislaw – that finally causes her to rebel. Casaubon, in his senile jealousy, noticed something that F.R. Leavis, in his commentary on the novel, did not, something Eliot veiled in sentimentality but did not entirely obscure – that Dorothea, even if she does look like a cinquecento madonna, is subject to the ancient sexual law of 'like unto like' upon which the Miller's tale is based. Dorothea wants to sleep with Ladislaw because he is young and handsome, and so is she. In their social context, to 'sleep with' means to marry. So marry they must and, in order tactfully to indicate that there are no tears on *this* honeymoon, Dorothea's story ends, not with the marriage, but with the birth of her child.

What is odd about all this discretion is that George Eliot herself led a sexual and emotional life that would have been considered unusually rich and full even by liberal late-twentieth-century standards, and was perfectly well aware that marriage, in reality, is neither an end nor a beginning but only a legislative change, and also that one does not need to marry men in order to sleep with them. Within the bounds of the conventions of her time, Eliot succeeds in writing about sexual relationships as they are, not as they should be, to a quite remarkable degree; her grasp of emotional logic is as straightforward as Chaucer's was. All the same, those tears of Dorothea in the Italian cemetery are a kind of code, a code which, at that period, only married women, ie non-virgins, were supposed to understand, although those tears tell us more, perhaps, than we might wish to know about Casaubon as a husband, and fill in many of the gaps in the idealised characterisation of Dorothea herself. Those tears, in fact, prepare the reader for her eventual remarriage; they tell us that Dorothea is a sexual being and her protracted intellectual disillusionment with her husband has started off from an equally unforgiveable sexual disappointment.

I suspect George Eliot would have been glad to have been able to describe the nature of that disappointment in more detail, if not in the self-same language used by Chaucer's Miller. However, it was not permissible for her to do more than hint; and, unsatisfactory and destructive as her marriage is, once Dorothea is married she is condemned to weep over her frustration without her inventor being able to tell us, in so many words, that this is what ails her. Both Dorothea and her inventor must present this aspect of the failure of the marriage between Dorothea and Casaubon as if it were of peripheral significance to Dorothea.

However, such is Eliot's respect for, and partial idealisation of the beautiful and saintly woman she has invented that, as well as convention and acceptability, a resistance to acknowledging Dorothea's sexuality in a more explicit way on Eliot's own part prevents *this* plot quickening at the notion of extra-marital inter-course. Small town gossip would have singled out the friendship between Dorothea and the handsome Dr Lydgate as almost certain to blossom into the right, true end of two unsatisfactory marriages. Eliot hints at this as a might-have-been; a union that would have redeemed Lydgate from the besetting sin of his own vulgarity, if – even without the complicating factor of their two spouses – Dorothea had shown the least sign of being attracted to a 'manly' Englishman of Lydgate's type. Since Dorothea gladly throws up her inheritance in order to marry an effete, curly-headed Slav, it would seem that Lydgate was the last kind of man she'd find attractive. By the end of the novel, marriage has taught Dorothea one important lesson – now she knows just what and whom she wants, and takes it the moment it is offered her. She wants, in fact, the kind of pretty, malleable man strong women very often want. (It is odd how many people find this aspect of the novel unsatisfactory, or unlikely.)

But all this is dealt with in such a discreet way that Eliot seems almost to be censoring herself. Eliot is certainly capable of presenting women who *are* deeply aware of their sexual being; in the same novel, Lydgate's wife, Rosamund, is perfectly aware, and is presented by Eliot as a poisonous, manipulative bitch.

The sexual relations between the Lydgates are left, of course, unstressed, although they produce children in due order so we know the marriage has been consummated. If there is a suggestion Rosamund is frigid, this is depicted as no more than an aspect of her selfishness; Lydgate can't possibly have anything to do with it.

Eliot castigates Lydgate for his foolishness in thoughtlessly marrying a pretty girl in the same way as he might have acquired an attractive piece of bric-à-brac, but the piece of bric-à-brac in question is condemned for no more than – being a piece of bric-à-brac. (Which is just how Rosamund tends to think of herself; as a precious ornament for a home, a fine possession for a man. This is a bad way for a woman to be in, but Eliot spares her no pity.) George Eliot neither likes nor approves of Rosamund and treats her touching provincial aspirations to material comfort, to social position, to respect, with contempt. But the relish with which she describes Rosamund's long-term corrosion of Lydgate's self-satisfaction has something self-contradictory about it. Reprehensible as Rosamund might be, her campaign of attrition against her husband may be read as the prototype of the revenge of any disappointed wife. She does to Lydgate what Dorothea, were Dorothea not such a saintly human being, might have felt perfectly justified in doing to Casaubon. (And, of course, we know with hindsight that Lydgate's medical research into the origins of typhoid will, on the evidence the novel gives us of its nature, lead him up just the same blind alley as Casaubon's theological research has led *him* – not that Eliot could have known that, of course.)

But Eliot – and this is a recurring phenomenon with the female narrator – simply can't bear to put her beloved Dorothea in a bad light. Dorothea is not allowed to exhibit the least resentment. She must be the type of the 'Patient Griselda', who suffers in silence the tyranny of an appalling husband, gaining treasure in heaven thereby. 'Patient Griselda' is the idealisation of one type of medieval wife as Alison is the crystallisation of a more down-to-earth variety. Rosamund Lydgate, with far more of the Alison in her make-up than the Griselda, is offered to us as a 'bad woman', in contrast to Dorothea's 'good woman'. Rosamund is judged in the text by her narrator for her embittered attitude to her husband and found wanting; Dorothea is celebrated for concealing her bitterness. Yet both suffer the same affliction, which was Alison's affliction, too; all are married to men whom they do not, to use a shorthand phrase, love.

The nineteenth-century bourgeois novel is in the business of making judgements. The medieval fabliau was not. Chaucer, and the Miller, suspend judgement on everyone. Yet it's noticeable that Absolon, Nicholas and even the carpenter – all the men in the story, in fact, suffer some kind of hurt, either of the feelings or the body. Absolon is tricked into kissing Alison's backside; intent on revenge, he returns with a red hot iron bar and asks for another kiss. However, Alison's lover, Nicholas, decides it would be fun if *he* were to stick his backside out of the window, this time, and so it is Nicholas, not Alison, who is branded on the buttock. When Nicholas cries out for water to cool his smart, the carpenter believes the Flood must have at last arrived, cuts the rope keeping his tub hanging in the rafters, and falls to the floor, breaking an arm. Only Alison, the adulterous wife and heartless humiliator of men, ends the story in as fresh, lively and 'likerous' a way as she began it.

Unjudged, perhaps, because not deemed responsible for her

own actions, being so young, so coltish, so female? When the Miller concludes: 'Thus swyved was this carpenterys wife' the use of the passive mood is striking. But at least Alison managed to get herself fucked by the man of her choice, to her own satisfaction and with no loss of either her own self-respect or the respect of her male creator, which is more than a girl like her will be able to do again, in fiction, for almost more than half a millenium.

Very well. Alison is a character in an extended joke, not in a three-decker novel, even if that extended joke forms part of a long novel in the form of a poem that describes Chaucer's world and preoccupations as fully as *Middlemarch* does George Eliot's. But when she giggles, after Absolon has kissed her bum in error, she turns into a person who is literally uncontainable within the limitations of the kind of novel Eliot wrote and even, perhaps, uncontainable within Eliot's ability to imagine.

Alison will have one or two naughty sisters in other medieval fabliaus, a handful of rather more vicious great-great-granddaughters in Restoration comedy, but nobody in literature quite like her, with her light heart and her guiltlessness, until Colette summoned up her own girlhood in order to invent Claudine, nearly six hundred years later. And even Colette would have been unable to express, with such limpid simplicity, what it is that Nicholas does to Alison, could not have written down the Burgundian dialect equivalent of 'to swyve' and assumed all her readers would know what she meant without a gloss, would have been able to count on her readers not needing to have the activity spelled out blow by blow or euphemistically mystified.

In fact, Chaucer *does* expand a little on the swyving. He tacitly assumes his audience is perfectly familiar with the organs involved and so on, an assumption it might be gross to make even today, so he has no need to describe thrusting pistons or yielding walls or anything like that. He sums up the encounter thus:

And thus lith Alison and Nicholas
In bisynesse of myrthe and of solas.

Laughter and consolation. Nothing Lawrentian or metaphysical about *this* coupling; simply, it is as much as any sane person can hope for from sex and more, perhaps, than Alison deserves.

Then the serenader interrupts them. Alison humiliates him and giggles. If Colette could have entertained the possibility of that giggle, the female narrators who followed her in the latter part of the twentieth century would find it difficult to let their heroines get away with it. Anna, in *The Golden Notebook*; the lugubrious heroine of Marilyn French's *The Women's Room*; the moonstruck demi-vierges of Jean Rhys – to none of them, is adultery less than an existential challenge, while sexuality, either male or female, is no laughing matter and good women do not behave badly to men but gain treasure in heaven by letting men behave badly to them.

These heroines must be blameless, or else they cannot be heroines. They are recycled Patient Griseldas, tyrannised, not by one man as Griselda was, but by the entire sex, and now idealised by women themselves, rather than by men. The very question of sexual pleasure is hedged around with ambiguities and the desire to please is often mistaken for the desire for pleasure. When these heroines go to bed with their men, 'myrthe and solas' are the last things on their minds, which is just as well, since these things are rarely on offer.

There is a moving passage by Theodor Adorno, in *Minima Moralia*:

> Society constantly casts woman's self-abandon back into the sacrificial situation from which it freed her. No man, cajoling some poor girl to go with him, can mistake, unless he be wholly insensitive, the faint moment of rightness in her resistance, the only prerogative left by patriarchal society to woman, who, once persuaded, after the brief triumph of refusal, must immediately pay the bill.

Well, yes. Frigidity in the Victorian married woman, the headaches, the neurasthenia, the fabled vague ill-health that drove her husband into the arms of whores, may be seen as no more than a strategy of self-preservation, in the light of the maternal mortality statistics. (In the light of the ravages childbirth often inflicted upon women before the introduction of antisepsis and modern surgery, the lingering malaise of the married woman may, of course, have been genuine, protracted ill-health.) The nature of sexual repression in a society where heterosexual activity usually results in pregnancy and pregnancy may result in death is quite different from that of sexual repression in a society where birth control is freely available and childbirth is not feared, although, as Adorno implies, the ghosts of the old pain may not be so easily exorcised as all that.

Alison, unrepressed, giggles in the medieval fabliau, creation – however sympathetic – of a male narrator (and Chaucer is as sympathetic a male narrator as one will find in English literature, himself.) She and Chaucer live in a pre-bourgeois world, where women, as women, have somewhat more autonomy as workers and as beings-in-the-world than they will have by the time the novel, the bourgeois form of literature *par excellence*, is established. When this form becomes established, it becomes largely dominated by women themselves, as both readers and writers of fiction, and there seems to arise a conspiracy to deny women access through fiction to certain aspects of real life which are deemed unsuitable for them largely because they are concerned with sexual practice. There is some logic at work, here, a logic of repression related to the price of experience which is to do not with submission to the notion of the supremacy of male desire but an evasion of that presumed supremacy.

It should be noted that Alison seems untroubled by the idea of fertility. Perhaps, like the Wyf of Bath, she is fully aware of the 'remedies of love' (by which Chaucer presumably means abortificants); or, more likely, Chaucer temporarily forgot that sex often leads to babies. This is the characteristic sign of the male narrator everywhere in fiction. Either their mothers never told them, or the connection slipped their minds.

At the end of Colette's novel, *Ripening Seed*, the boy looks up at the window in which the girl whom he has just deflowered greets the morning with a song.

> From the window came a faint, happy little tune that passed over his head. Nor did the thought strike him that in a few weeks' time the child who was singing might well be standing in tears, doomed and frantic, at the same window.

The thought strikes Colette, of course; but it rarely strikes the male narrator. Phil continues meditating on how little the encounter has meant to his Vinca:

> A little pain, a little pleasure . . . That's all I shall have given her, that and nothing else . . . nothing . . .

So the novel ends, on a note of the bitterest irony; it is obvious from this that Colette intends the reader to understand that Vinca *has* conceived, and the seaside idyll of the teenage lovers is going to end very badly indeed. The connection between sex and reproduction does not slip a woman's mind so easily.

It is almost a cliché of orally transmitted poetry, that is, folk song, that one unprotected act of intercourse will lead inevitably to pregnancy; the pleasure principle remains undivorced from the reproductive function. Since performance of traditional song is fairly evenly divided between women and men, and the anonymous material is kept alive and often considerably altered in performance, it is fair to assume that women not only shape the songs they sing but invented some of them, long ago, in the first place.

> When I wore my apron low
> He followed me through frost and snow.
> Now I wear it to my chin
> He passes by and says nothing.

Although always found in the song called *Died for Love*, this is a 'floating' verse, that may be used at appropriate moments in all manner of different versions of different songs. Sex; pregnancy; desertion. That is a woman's life.

> I wish my baby little were born
> And smiling on its nurse's knee,
> And I myself were dead and gone
> For a maid again I'll never be.

Such songs were, no doubt, intended to help proscribe extramarital sexual activity on the part of young village girls. Whether they had any effect on illegitimacy rates is now unguessable.

However, the study of the representations of women in unofficial culture, in orally transmitted songs and stories, even in bar-room anecdotes, may prove a fruitful method of entry into the lived reality of the past. So may research into those forms of fiction that pre-date the bourgeois novel, in which the giggle of Alison, however disingenuous, suggests the possibility that, at some time in the past, a male narrator has been able to laugh at the pretensions of his own sex and therefore it is possible this may happen, again, in the future.

The Left and the Erotic, edited by Eileen Philips,
Lawrence and Wishart, 1983

The Life of Katherine Mansfield

(Anthony Alpers, *The Life of Katherine Mansfield*, Jonathan Cape)

There is the heroic myth of colonialism, the setting out across the sea to domesticate the unknown. It has its no less heroic reverse; the colonial's return, 'coming home', as they say, an unfledged arrival at a known yet unknown motherland that prefers to acknowledge no other reality than itself. Katherine Mansfield liked to present herself as a prodigal daughter in letters from England to her father in New Zealand, where he had prospered, becoming, unforgivably in terms of motherland snobbism, *nouveau riche*. But her own relation as unforgiven prodigal daughter to Britain, a culture of which she was subtly never a part, is something Anthony Alpers does not explore in this otherwise exhaustive, especially gynaecologically exhaustive, biography, which he intends to replace one first published in 1953, when many of Mansfield's contemporaries, including her husband, John Middleton Murry, were still alive and some capable of addressing writs.

Though Katherine Mansfield was one of the greatest of expatriate writers, she may never have fully realised that, in London, she *was* an expatriate, though her biographer, perhaps unconsciously, often stresses the point by referring to her as 'the Colonial' from time to time. Born in Wellington, she 'came home' first to school, in 1903, at fourteen; sailed back across the world to endure the rigours of a Wellington débutante ('violet teas' where sandwiches with violets in them were served); came home, again, at nearly twenty, to sow her wild oats. Tremendous youthful follies leading to cohabitation with and eventual marriage to Murry and a hectic shared life of little magazines and *literati*. Garsington and the Bloomsburies, a battery of hypocrisy and snobbery, she colonially innocent and unprepared. Death of tuberculosis at thirty-four. She left behind short stories, letters and, most traditional of all women's literary forms, a journal. All her written remains are capable of being construed as a fabulous – and I use the word advisedly – autobiography of the soul; one of the great traps for the woman writer is the desire to be loved for oneself as well as admired for one's work, to be a Beautiful Person as well as a Great Artist, and Katherine Mansfield was only saved from narcissic self-regard by the tough bitchery under her parade of sensitive vulnerability. She also seems to have been ravaged by sexual guilt, which probably helped.

Inevitably, the best of her short stories, including 'Prelude', 'At the Bay', 'The Garden Party', are set in New Zealand, in everyday domesticity, and have a shimmering tenderness, as of memories of a happy land far away to which return would have been death. But she died, anyway, in famously bizarre circumstances at Gurdjieff's fancy-dress commune outside Paris.

Mansfield's life, with its inherently tragic quality, a youth spent slowly dying, a sexual freedom for which she paid such a price in mental and physical pain, considerable artistic achievement and the early close clouded by the occult, is bound to make her something of a heroine for our times, not least because the period in which she lived here, 1903-23, now looks as though it was England's last artistically vital one. Indeed, everyone who was anyone put her down – Wyndham Lewis, Bertrand Russell, Gaudier-Brzeska – the list is endless. Virginia Woolf was 'shocked by her commonness'. One wonders, at the end of Alpers' loving, even besotted biography, why someone so gifted, so charming should have been so universally detested. It is good to get a hint of the reason in a crisp note to a girlfriend of her husband's: 'I am afraid you must stop writing these little love letters to my husband while he and I live together. It is one of the things which is not done in our world.' She must have been formidable.

If magnificent Gudrun in *Women in Love*, the *castratrix triumphans*, is partly about her, then the cutesy-poo way she snuggled up to Murry and, indeed, the world, must have seemed to Lawrence a shocking betrayal of her true nature. Which does not excuse the unforgivably cruel letters Lawrence wrote to her in her last illness. But Alpers somewhat underplays the full complexity of the *ménage-à-quatre* of Lawrences and Murrys in Cornwall in 1916. It is surely not enough to say that Lawrence took against Mansfield because he was in love with Murry; wasn't Murry already sniffing after Frieda? And 'Tig' and 'Wig', the Murrys called one another. They used to sit together writing poems about their happiness. Enough to turn a stronger stomach than Lawrence's, especially if you smelled the power in her.

Alpers, to some degree, attempts to whitewash Murry, but the outlines of a truly nauseating creep still show through and Mansfield's relation to him seems less true love than a painfully sustained romantic illusion. Since she called her lifelong champion, Ida Baker, her 'wife' and treated her with a truly marital contemptuous affection, perhaps Mansfield had more sense of emotional self-preservation than meets the eye.

And, after all, Alpers doesn't give much impression of his heroine's true nature. Not because he doesn't try, almost too hard, sifting and resifting contradictory evidence about a deeply ambiguous personality. But, then she *was* mysterious and, in the manner of the colonialised, rather than the Colonial, she used her charm to deflect attention from a core of mystery she wished to keep to herself; perhaps the mystery was her very creativity. It is right she should retain it.

The biography, impeccable in every other respect, suffers from a prurient intimacy of tone. For example, once Alpers has worked out the code Mansfield used in her journals to indicate her periods, she is allowed no outburst of temper or fit of depression without a reference to pre- or post-menstrual tension. He is so protective of 'Katherine', as he always calls her, that he appears to be conducting a posthumous affair with her. Presumably this is the fate of any attractive, mysterious and sexually experimental woman at the hands of a gallant male biographer.

Guardian, 1978

The piece about D.H. Lawrence combines two great loves of mine; his novels, and the sociology of clothes. It is impossible for any English writer in this century to evade the great fact of D.H. Lawrence, but taking him seriously as a novelist is one thing, and taking him seriously as a moralist is quite another.

Lorenzo the Closet-Queen

A piece of comment I once read about that monstrous book, *The Story of C.*, suggested that only a woman could have written it because of some curious metaphor about, I think, curlers, somewhere in the book. The commentators, a French intellectual, probably a member of the Académie Française and God knows what else besides, said this sartorial detail could only have been documented 'by a woman', because it was uniquely revelatory of a woman's eye.

Such, then, was the opinion of this Frenchman, whose name I forget; but it seemed to me that *The Story of O.* bore all the stigmata of male consciousness, not least in that details about clothes are just the sort of thing a man would put into a book if he wanted the book to read as though it had been written by a woman. Cleland uses much the same device in *Fanny Hill*. All the same, many women writers do themselves pretend to be female impersonators; look at Jean Rhys and Edna O'Brien, whose scars glorify the sex that wounded them. But the nature of female impersonation in art is a complex business and the man who sets out to do it must be careful not to let his own transvestite slip show, especially if he does not like women much.

The greatest drag artistes, of whom the most magnificent examples are the *onnagata*, the male actors who play the female roles in the kabuki theatre of Japan, betray their authentic gender only by too great a perfection of performance, so that a real woman looks butch beside them. Which brings me to the strange case of D.H. Lawrence, and the truism that those who preach phallic superiority usually have an enormous dildo tucked away somewhere in their psychic impedimenta.

I should like to make a brief, sartorial critique of *Women in Love*, Lawrence's most exuberantly clothed novel, a novel which, furthermore, is supposed to be an exegesis on my sex, trusting, not the teller but the tale, to show to what extent D.H. Lawrence personated women through simple externalities of dress; by doing so, managed to pull off one of the greatest con tricks in the history of modern fiction; and revealed a more than womanly, indeed, pathologically fetishistic, obsession with female apparel. *Women in Love* is as full of clothes as Brown's, and clothes of the same kind. D.H. Lawrence catalogues his heroine's wardrobes with the loving care of a ladies' maid. It is not a simple case of needing to convince the reader the book has been written by a woman; that is far from his intention. It is a device by which D.H. Lawrence attempts to convince the reader that he, D.H.L., has a hot line to a woman's heart by the extraordinary sympathy he has for her deepest needs, that is, nice stockings, pretty dresses and submission.

Yet Lawrence clearly enjoys being a girl. If we do not trust the teller but the tale, then the tale positively revels in lace and feathers, bags, beads, blouses and hats. It is always touching to see a man quite as seduced by the cultural apparatus of femininity as Lawrence was, the whole gamut, from feathers to self-abnegation. Even if, as Kate Millett suggests, he only wanted to be a woman so that he could achieve the supreme if schizophrenic pleasure of fucking himself, since nobody else was good enough for him. (The fantasy-achievement of this ambition is probably what lends *Lady Chatterley's Lover* such an air of repletion.)

Lawrence is seduced and bemused by the narcissistic apparatus of femininity. It dazzles him. He is like a child with a dressing-up box. Gudrun, witch and whore, is introduced in a fanfare of finery: 'She wore a dress of dark-green, silky stuff, with ruches of blue and green linen lace in the necks and sleeves.' The Brangwen girls habitually come onto the page dragging *Vogue* captions behind them, until you start looking for the price tag. (How could they have afforded to dress like that on teachers' salaries in those days?) It is the detail of the 'linen lace' that gives Lawrence away, of course. He is a true *aficionado* of furbelows. What the hell is linen lace? I'm sure I don't know. It is a delicious feminine secret between Gudrun and her dressmaker.

Gudrun completes her ensemble with emerald-green stockings. Gudrun's stockings run through the book like a *leitmotiv*. Very gaudy stockings. She will keep on drawing attention to the pedestals which support her, her legs, though these legs are rarely mentioned by name. Her stockings become almost a symbol of her contrariness. When she arrives at the Crich mansion wearing thick, yellow woollen ones, Gerald Crich is a little taken aback. 'Her stockings always disconcerted him,' notes Lawrence, to underline just what a bourgeois cow Gerald is, that he can't take a pair of Bohemian stockings with equanimity.

But Lawrence himself is so deeply disturbed by the notion of Gudrun's legs he cannot bear to see them uncovered; they must be conspicuously concealed. That will negate their discomforting, unmodified legginess. Stockings as censorship.

Stockings, stockings, stockings everywhere. Hermione Roddice sports coral-coloured ones, Ursula canary ones. Defiant, brilliant, emphatic stockings. But never the suggestion the fabric masks, upholsters, disguises living, subversive flesh. Lawrence is a stocking man, not a leg man. Stockings have supplanted legs; clothes have supplanted flesh. Fetishism.

The apotheosis of the stockings comes right at the end of the novel, where they acquire at last an acknowledged, positive, sexual significance. 'Gudrun came to Ursula's bedroom with three pairs of the coloured stockings for which she was notorious and she threw them on the bed. But these were thick, silk stockings, vermillion, cornflower blue and grey, bought in Paris.' With sure, feminine intuition, Ursula knows 'Gudrun must be feeling *very* loving, to give away such treasures'.

The excited girls call the stockings 'jewels', or 'lambs', as if the inert silky things were lovers, or children. Indeed, the stockings appear to precipitate a condition of extreme erotic arousal in Gudrun; she touches them with 'trembling, excited hands'. The orgasmic nature of the stocking exchange is underlined by a very curious piece of dialogue.

'One gets the greatest joy of all out of really lovely stockings,' said Ursula.

'One does,' replies Gudrun. 'The greatest joy of all.'

What *is* Lawrence playing at? Or, rather, what does he think he's playing at? This sort of camp ecstasy more properly belongs in Firbank, who understood about dandyism in women, dandyism and irony, the most extreme defences of the victim. But Firbank, as plucky a little bantam-weight as ever bounced off the ropes, had *real* moral strength.

I think what Lawrence is doing is attempting to put down the women he has created in his own image for their excessive reaction to the stockings to which he himself has a very excessive reaction indeed, the deep-down queenly, monstrous old hypocrite that he is.

Of course, at this point in the novel, Lawrence must be feeling very full of Woman since Birkin has just ingested Ursula, swallowed her whole in the manner of a boa constrictor. So he can really deceive himself with his own drag-queen act, and it doesn't seem to him in the least incongruous that his heroines, who were initially scrupulously established as very heavy ladies indeed, are now jabbering away to one another like the worst kind of school girl.

The girls have just met again in Switzerland, after Ursula's marriage and Gudrun's dirty weekend in Paris with the atrocious Gerald. They scuttle off immediately to Gudrun's bedroom to talk 'clothes and experiences', in that order. Curled up with a box of Swiss chox, I dare say. My God, what an insult. Lawrence's prose gets progressively sloppier and sloppier towards the end of the book, but weariness and laziness is no excuse for this kind of patronising dismissal.

But cunning old Lawrence can have his cake and eat it, too. Earlier on, in Derbyshire the miners' children call names after Gudrun. 'What price the stockings!' they cry. This is realism, of course. The penalty of sartorial eccentricity is always mockery, some kinds of clothes are a self-inflicted martyrdom. But D.H. Lawrence can put all these lovely garments he himself desires so much on the girls he has invented and yet cunningly evade the moral responsibility of having to go out in them himself and face the rude music of the mob.

And he luxuriously allows himself the licence to mock the girls for parading about in the grotesque finery he has forced them to don. He judiciously allots Gudrun a sartorial crucifixion by the miners. Never, they allow, have they seen night-soil in such a lovely bag but, with Pauline resolution, they never lose sight of the fact that night-soil, nevertheless, she remains. She has committed the solecism of wearing 'bright rose stockings' for a walk in the village.

'What price, eh? She'll do, won't she?' See the emphasis on the cash nexus. Her dandyism, her sartorial defiance, is only an invitation to humiliation. The miners look, not for the price-tag on the stockings as did the relatively innocent children, but they are brute enough to perceive the flesh beneath the stockings and speculate about the price-tag on *that*.

The old miner thinks she'd be worth a week's wages. Indeed, he would put them down straight away. But the younger 'shook his head with fatal misgiving'.

'No,' he said. 'It's not worth that to me.'

Lawrence hates the miners with the lacerated, guilty passion of the true class-traitor. All the same, he is delighted to use the frank speech proper to the degraded status he gives them to put Gudrun, sashaying out in her Lunnon clothes with her high-falutin ways, firmly in her place. 'Not worth a week's wages', eh? So much for your subtle little carvings of water-wagtails, girlie. Get down on your back for free.

All the same, Lawrence has given Gudrun a particularly shocking kind of beauty, for God knows what masochistic reasons of his own. And it is a perpetual affront to him. Not 'Beauty's self is she when all her clothes are gone', by any means; never that. There is no sense of the tactile immediacy of undressing in Lawrence's relation with his unruly heroine. Rather, it is like strip-tease in reverse; the more clothes he piles on her, the more desirable she becomes, because the less real.

At the Swiss hotel, in her evening dress of green silk and gold tissue (and where *does* she get the cash to pay for all this glamour? not on the streets, he's made *that* plain), 'she was really brilliantly beautiful and everybody noticed her'. Which is an astonishingly mean and bald description of the effect of an erotically disturbing woman on a party. He has already had a stab at describing the effect of an erotically disturbing man on a party. (Gudrun's description of Gerald at the studio party in Paris.) But he can't get much above the cock-of-the-midden scenario. Perhaps he wants to say that Gudrun exerts the dominance of desire; but he is too mean to admit a woman can do that, and too hypocritical to let his heroes do it seriously. Birkin is described somewhere as extraordinarily desirable, but his dominance is not an erotic one; he is really what the Brangwen girls call him in one of their more lucid moments, an intellectual bully.

Hermione Roddice, inevitably, gets the full weight of the sartorial stick. She disappears under layer upon layer of cloth. Cloth of gold, fur, antique brocade, enormous flat hats of pale yellow velvet 'on which were streaks of ostrich feathers, natural and grey'. What an asset Lawrence would have been to those fashion writers who report the Paris collections where photographers are not allowed, so they have to remember everything.

Hermione's clothes are visible alienation. They verge on fancy dress, which is dress as pure decoration, unmodified by function or environment. 'Hermione came down to dinner strange and sepulchral, her eyes heavy and full of sepulchral darkness, strength. She had put on a dress of stiff, old, greenish brocade, that fitted tight and made her look tall and rather terrible, ghastly.' Lawrence is plainly terrified of her and full of an awed respect. Her exoticism, for Lawrence primarily an exoticism of class, is expressed in a self-conscious strangeness of apparel. Her dress defines the area of abstract power she inhabits.

Hermione is a portrait from life, and Ottoline Morell did indeed get herself up like that, but she arouses Lawrence to such a heightened awareness of lace and trimming he might almost have spent lots of furtive, happy hours at Garsington, rummaging through her wardrobe.

The house-party at Breadalby sees them all going for a swim together. Gerald looks 'white but natural in his nakedness', with a scarlet silk kerchief about his loins. The ladies decorously expose their flesh, for once, but not much; Hermione approaches the water in a 'great mantle of purple silk', ornate, disguised, shrouded in baroque finery. Indeed, her appearance has the gilded formality of an icon. This is probably because she is an aristocrat and therefore holy.

If Lawrence is making some pseudo-philosophical point about these heavily over-dressed women, that they themselves retreat behind their clothes, he never makes it overtly, which is odd, for him. But it is almost as if he is inverting the Baudelairean paradox, 'woman is natural, therefore abominable', and saying: 'Woman, when unnatural, is abdominable', and making a platitude out of Baudelaire's thrust at the notion of 'natural man'. For most of the women he dislikes in *Women in Love* end up as apparatuses constructed out of fabric, stalking clothes' horses which suggest only the appearance of women. Lawrence approaches these women via their apparel. Their clothes are the only thing he can hold onto. Like a drag-queen, but without the tragic heroism that enables a transvestite to test the magic himself, he believes women's clothes are themselves magical objects which define and confine women.

And his heroines cannot get out of the sartorial trap Lawrence has laid for them, though there is a connection between the amount of clothes he piles on them and their own erotic quality. Erotically-disturbing women get bundled up more. Ursula starts off just as ostentatiously clothed as Gudrun but descriptions of her apparel tail off after Birkin castrates her. But Gudrun, the Pussum (poor Carrington, again, getting hers), Hermione – always, always subsumed to their appearance, since that defuses their sexuality, their challenge. Unless, for Lawrence, their appearance alone constitutes their sexuality.

Yes, Hermione. She plainly functions as the most erotically disturbing of all the women in the novel, not because Lawrence apprehends her in a sensual mode – far be it – but because she is spiced with what, for him, is the only potent aphrodisiac, that of class.

Clothes acquire such an elaborate significance as the armour of womanhood it is striking that, when Ursula and Hermione meet for their *tête à tête* (chapter 22, 'Woman to Woman'), when they are tussling for possession of Birkin, there is no mention at all of what either of them have on. They are stripped for battle, you understand.

Most of the time in *Women in Love*, Lawrence is like a little boy dressing up in his mother's clothes and thinking, that way, he has become his mother. The con trick, the brilliant, the wonderful con trick, the real miracle, is that his version of drag has been widely accepted as the real thing, even by young women who ought to know better. In fact, Lawrence probes as deeply into a woman's heart as the bottom of a hat-box.

He is too female by half. His surreptitious, loved and envied slip is always dipping a good two inches below his intellectual hemline. The stocking covers a hairy, muscular leg.

Next to this *onnagata*, Colette looks like Cassius Clay.

New Society, 1975

Colette

(*Colette: a biography*, by Michèle Sarde, Michael Joseph)

Colette is one of the few, possibly the only, well-known woman writer of modern times who is universally referred to simply by her surname, *tout court*. Woolf hasn't made it, even after all these years; Rhys without the Jean is incognito, Nin without the Anaïs looks like a typo. Colette, Madame Colette, remains, in this as much else, unique.

However, Colette did not acquire this distinction because she terrorised respect language out of her peers, alas; by a happy accident, her family name also doubles as a girlish handle and a very ducky one, too. One could posit 'Bonny' or 'Rosie' as some kind of English equivalent. It was by a probably perfectly unconscious sleight of hand that Colette appropriated for herself the form of address of both masculine respect and masculine intimacy of her period, a fact that, in a small way, reflects the whole message of her career. This is: if you can't win, change the rules of the game.

Her career was a profoundly strange one and necessarily full of contradictions, of which her uncompromising zeal for self-exploitation is one. Madame Colette, though never quite Madame Colette de l'Académie Française – one game she couldn't crack – was accorded a state funeral by the French government; this was the woman whose second husband's aristocratic family dismissed as a cunning little strip-tease artist over-eager for the title of Baroness. As Madame Colette, she first appeared on pin-up pictures of 'Our pretty actresses: Madame Colette of the Olympia'. And, in these pictures, taken in her late thirties, she is very beautiful and sexy indeed; she looks out at you with all the invitation of the stripper, '*you* can call me Colette', a familiar show-biz trick, the relationship of artificial intimacy the showgirl creates between her named self and the anonymous punter, with its intention to disarm.

This artificial creation of a sense of intimacy with Colette herself is one of the qualities that gives her writing its seductiveness; Colette certainly wasn't on the halls all those years for nothing, although the extent to which a wilful exhibitionism kept her on the boards against the advice of the majority of her critics well into her fifties may be connected with a certain capacity to embarrass that often frays the edges of her writing.

Because '*you* can call me Colette' isn't a statement of the same order as: 'Call me Ishmael.' The social limitations to experience in a woman's life still preclude the kind of unselfconscious picaresque adventuring that formed the artistic apprenticeships of Melville, Lowry, Conrad, while other socio-economic factors mean that those women who see most of the beastly backside of the world, that is, prostitutes, are least in a position to utilise this invaluable experience as art. Somewhere, Norman Mailer says there won't be a *really* great woman writer, one, you understand, *con cojones* and everything, until the first call-girl tells her story. Though it's reasonable to assume that, when she does, Mailer won't like it at all, at all, the unpleasant truth in this put-down is, that most women don't have exposure to the kind of breadth of experience that, when digested, produces great fiction. (Okay, so what about the Brontës? Well, as vicar's daughters in a rural slum parish, peripatetic international governesses and terminal consumptives, they *did* have such a variety of experience. So.) But the life of Colette was as picaresque as a woman's may be without putting herself in a state of hazard.

Her first novel, *Claudine at School*, and its sequels, appeared with the name of her husband on the title page. This man, the peculiar Willy, one of the best-publicised Bohemians of the Belle Époque, ensured that the little Burgundian village girl, Colette's favourite disguise, encountered not only numerous whores of both sexes at an impressionable age but also *everybody*, Proust, Debussy, Ravel, you name them. When Willy left her, his wife found herself in the unusual position of having written a number of best-sellers whilst being unable to take any financial or artistic credit for them. To earn a living in the years before the First World War, she felt she had no alternative but to go on the halls. Since she could neither sing nor dance she performed as a sex-object and subject of scandal, and not a particularly up-market sex object, either. Since Willy had enjoyed sexually humiliating her, no doubt there was a special pleasure in exploiting her sexuality whilst herself secure and unavailable; after Willy, she took refuge in the bosom of the lesbian Establishment of the period. Our pretty actress had an aristocratic protector, the Marquise de Mornay; nothing unusual, not even the sex of the Marquise, about this in those permissive times.

Then came a Cinderellaesque marriage to (Baron) Henry de Jouvenal, editor of *Le Matin*, later a politician of considerable distinction. One thing about Colette interests me; when did she stop lying about her age? The voluptuous dancer was pushing forty when she married de Jouvenal; 'But the registry office has to know your age!' she complained to a friend. There comes a time when a woman freely publicises her age so people can say: 'How young you look!' It seems to have come later than most to Colette, but when it did, she gloried in it, as in all else.

In tandem with this characteristically if rather Hollywood Edwardian career, not one but two writers are growing within Colette. One writes *La Vagabonde* in 1910, a novel which is still one of the most truthful expositions of the dilemma of a free woman in a male-dominated society. Perhaps because Colette, having the triumphant myopia of a vain woman, refused to acknowledge her society as male-dominated, she sees no dilemma; there is no real choice. One *is* free. In the same year, the other writer, the one more nearly related to our pretty actress, began work as a journalist for *Le Matin*, which is how she met its editor. Renée Néré, music-hall artiste, prefers to go it alone in *La Vagabonde*, but Colette, Colette married and married well. Her marriage also sealed her fate as a journalist, which in turn sealed her fate as a novelist, because the professions are mutually exclusive, even if simultaneously conducted.

Colette became literary editor of *Le Matin* in 1919 and thereafter was to work almost continuously in newspapers and magazines in one way and another, whilst continuing to write fiction and, from time to time, to act. In 1924, after her divorce from de Jouvenal, she started signing her work, for the first time, neither Colette Willy nor Colette de Jouvenal but simply 'Colette'. Her third marriage, some ten years later, would never make her dwindle into Colette Goudeket, even if Colette was not her own but her father's name. You can't subvert patriarchy *that* easily, after all, even if your father's name might be roughly analogous to 'Darling', and he so weak and feckless you have only acquired the very haziest grasp of the power of patriarchy. However, now 'Colette' she was, for all seasons.

As a writer, of both journalism and of some of her fiction, Colette exploits this intimacy of the stripper with her reader quite remorselessly. She trades on the assumption that you are going to care about Maman because this is the unique Colette's unique Maman. The details of her Burgundian childhood, endlessly recapitulated and, one suspects, endlessly elaborated over the years, are purveyed with a child-like sense of self importance, such a naïve expectation that the smallest details of the Colette family diet and customs are worth recounting that it seems churlish to ask: 'What is the point of all this?'

She puts herself into much of her actual fiction. Not so much that all her fiction tends to draw on childhood, on the music-hall, on the sad truths distilled from unhappy marriages as that whole short novels – *Chance Acquaintances*, *Break of Day* – and many short stories are recounted in the first person of a Colette very precisely realised as subject and object at the same time. In the collection Penguin publish under the title, *The Rainy Moon*, most of the stories feature Colette herself, if not as a major character then never as passive narrator. She always gives herself a part, as though she could not bear to leave herself out, must always be on stage.

She stopped writing fiction altogether after *Gigi*, in 1942, a Belle Époque fable of the apparent triumph of innocence that would be nauseating were it not so cynical. Her later work, until her death in 1954, is mostly a series of extended autobiographical reveries, among them *The Blue Lantern*, *The Evening Star*. These, and the volumes of autobiographical journalism that preceded them, *My Mother's House* (given this curious biblical title in English – in French, *La Maison de Claudine*), *Sido*, *My Apprentice-ships*, *Music-Hall Sidelights*, etc. are a peculiar kind of literary strip-tease in themselves, a self-exploitation that greedily utilises every scrap of past experience in an almost unmediated form.

Yet there is no sense of the confessional about this endless flow of memory. Colette never tells you about herself. Instead, she describes herself. Few writers have described their own physicality so often; 'savage' child, with the long, blond plaits; bride with the 'splash of red carnations on the bodice of her white wedding gown'; in dinner jacket and monacle; pregnant, looking like 'a rat dragging a stolen egg'. And so on.

But she gives the impression of telling all, in a literary form unclassifiable except as a version of what television has accustomed us to call 'fictionalised documentary'. Robert Phelps was able to construct a perfectly coherent autobiography from Colette's scattered reminiscences, and present *The Earthly Paradise* as if it were, not an imaginative parallel to her real life, but the real thing. All Colette's biographers rely heavily on the sources she herself provides, even Michèle Sarde's recent, exhaustive, lengthy life, as if Colette could be trusted not to keep her fingers crossed when she was talking about herself, even when remembering events across a great gulf of years. Also, as if her sincerity was in itself important. Such is the sense of intimacy Colette creates; you feel you know her, because she has said '*you* can call me Colette', although she says this to everybody who pays.

And yet these memories, this experience, are organised with such conscious art, such lack of spontaneity! She must have acquired from Balzac her taste for presenting those she loved best and admired most, including herself, as actors in *tableaux vivants*, as beings complete in themselves, as if unmodified by the eyes of an observer who is herself part of the tableau; she describes finished objects in a perfect perspective, almost *trompe l'oeil*, stuck fast in the lucid amber of her prose. Her portrait of her friend, the poet, Renée Vivian, in *The Pure and the Impure*, has the finite quality of nineteenth-century fiction. 'I remember Renée's gay laughter, her liveliness, the faint halo of light trembling in her golden hair all combined to sadden me, as does the happiness of blind children who laugh and play without the help of light.' All that Colette has left out of this portrait is the possibility of some kind of inner life beyond Colette's imagining which belongs to Renée Vivian alone. This holds true for all the dazzling galaxy of heterogeneous humanity in Colette's fictionalised documentaries. The apparent objectivity of her prose is a device to seal these people in her own narrative subjectivity.

The portraits, of Renée Vivian, of actresses like La Belle Otéro and Polaire, even of Willy and, later of her own daughter, are exemplary because of their precision and troubling because of their detachment. Even in the accounts of her beloved mother, Colette's actual prose implicitly invites the reader to admire both the quality of the observation and the skill with which a different time and place are recreated; then, with a shock, you realise you have been seduced into applauding, not so much a remarkable woman, as the quality of Colette's love for her. Colette's actual prose is itself narcissistic.

So her apparently total lack of reticence tells us, in the end, nothing about her real relationships and her self-absorption becomes a come-on, a device like a mask behind which an absolute privacy might be maintained. Her obsessive love of make-up, of the stage, of disguises, suggests a desire, if not to conceal, then to mystify. The daughter of Captain Jules-Joseph Colette of the Zouaves could die happy in the notion she had never been on first-name terms with anyone outside her immediate family, not even, least of all, with any of her three husbands.

Since she appears to have been a profoundly disingenuous person, there seems no reason to think she did *not* die happy in this respect. The best lie is the truth, after all. Colette was indeed her name. Her childhood *was* a Burgundian idyll, even if one sister later killed herself, while a brother burned all of Colette's two thousand letters to her mother, as if to ensure that some things, at least, would remain sacrosanct from the daughter's guzzling, inordinate rapacity for material. Because the demands of journalism made Colette desperate for material; once a journalist has established the power-base of a cult of personality, he or she is positively encouraged to trot out their own opinions and anecdotes over and over again.

Colette's novels are of a different order of reality than her autobiographical pieces, because her novels are fiction and hence the truth; the rest is journalism and so may bear only the most peripheral relation to truth, even if a journalist tells you every single thing that actually happened.

In Colette's first novel, *Claudine at School*, she kills off Claudine's mother before the action begins. Claudine, her first *alter ego*. This is a far more interesting fact than all the obsessive gush about her own real mother, that spills out later in *La Maison de Claudine*, *Sido* and *Break of Day*. In this last novel, in fact a transparently fictionalised documentary using real Provençale locations and some real persons, Colette virtually apotheosises her dead mother, but leaves out altogether her third husband, Maurice Goudeket, who was happily ensconced by her side as she scribbled: 'I have paid for my folly, shut away the heady young wine that intoxicated me, and folded up my big, floating heart.'

The extent to which Colette came to believe her own mythology of herself is, of course, another question. Goudeket himself entered into the spirit of the thing wholeheartedly. His memoir of her last twenty years with him, *Close to Colette*, celebrates her peasant wisdom, her child-like enthusiasm. To him we owe the anecdote of her encounter with the cat in New York: 'At last someone who speaks French!' Michèle Sarde repeats this unblushingly, as if it told us something about the wit and wisdom of Colette. Michèle Sarde has swallowed the mythology whole; but the anecdote *does* tell us a good deal about Colette. It shows how wisely she picked her last companion, her Boswell, her PRO faithful beyond the grave.

Goudeket rhapsodises: 'There were so many arts which she had not lost. With her the art of living came before the art of writing. She knew a receipt for everything, whether it was for furniture polish, vinegar, orange-wine or quince-water, for cooking truffles or preserving linen and materials.' French, he says – she was French to her fingertips, and provincial to boot, even after sixty years total immersion in the heady whirlpool of Parisian artistic life. French and provincial as Elizabeth David's *French Country Cooking*, and just as much intended for publication.

I must say, now, that this ineradicable quality of the fraud, the fake, of the unrepentant self-publicist, is one of the things about

Colette I respect most; indeed, revere. Michèle Sarde's biography, however besotted, however uncritical, however willing to draw illegimate parallels between art and life, nevertheless demonstrates how it was the passionate integrity of Colette's narcissism that rendered her indestructible.

It's possible to see her entire career as a writer, instigated as it was by Willy, who robbed her of the first fruits of her labours, as an act of vengeance on him. A certain kind of woman, a vain woman, that is to say, a woman with self-respect, is spurred on by spite. Had the Rev. Brontë supported and encouraged his daughters' ambitions, what would the poor things have done then? I don't think Leonard Woolf did his wife a favour by mothering her. After Colette met kind, sweet, intelligent, loving Goudeket, she wrote very little major fiction.

In Simone de Beauvoir's memoirs, there's a description of a dinner party de Beauvoir attended with Sartre, at which Colette, already the frizzed and painted sacred cow of French letters, babbling away to *les gars*, as was her wont, about dogs, cats, knitting, *le bon vin, les bons fromages* and so on, offered de Beauvoir only the meagre attention of an occasional, piercing stare. De Beauvoir thought Colette disliked women. Possibly Colette, never a one to be *bouleversée* by a great mind, and, perhaps, privately relishing boring a great mind into the ground with nuggets of earthy Burgundian wisdom, was no more than contemplating the question every thinking woman in the western world must have posed herself one time or other: why is a nice girl like Simone wasting her time sucking up to a boring old fart like J.-P.? Her memoirs will be mostly about him; he will scarcely speak of her. Colette would have *known* so, intuitively.

Of course, Colette could no more have written *The Second Sex* than de Beauvoir could have danced naked on a public stage, which precisely defines the limitations of both these great ladies and it is this very self-exploitative, stripper quality that earths most of Colette's later writing. However, it is hard to imagine Colette, had she attended the Sorbonne, getting any kind of buzz out of coming second to Sartre in her final examinations, or, indeed, out of coming second to anybody. She had to be number one, even if she had to reinvent a whole genre of literature, and herself included, to do so.

Even after all these years, de Beauvoir still appears to be proud that only Sartre achieved higher marks in those first exams than she. What would have happened, one wonders, if she had come top? What would it have done to Sartre? Merely to think of it makes the mind reel. Only love can make you proud to be an also-ran. Would love have made J.-P. proud like that?

But Colette simply did not believe that women *were* the second sex. One of Goudeket's anecdotes from her declining years is very revealing. He carried her in her wheelchair into a holiday hotel; the lobby filled with applauding, cheering fans; she was a national institution in France, after all. Colette seemed touched: 'They've remembered me from last year.' This isn't modesty, though Goudeket pretends to think so; it's irony, I hope, because, if it isn't irony, then what is it? What monstrous vanity would think it was perfectly natural for a little old lady to receive a tumultuous welcome from her hotel staff? Of course she didn't believe she was really famous, towards the end. She knew she wasn't famous enough to gratify her unappeasable ego. Magnificently she did not know her place.

But to believe women are not the second sex is to deny a whole area of social reality, however inspiriting the toughness and resilience of Colette and most of her heroines may be, especially after the revival of the wet and spineless woman-as-hero which graced the seventies. (The zomboid creatures in Joan Didion's novels, for example; the resurrected dippy dames of Jean Rhys, so many of whom might have had pathetic walk-on parts in Colette's own stories of Paris in the twenties.) Colette celebrated the status quo of femininity, not only its physical glamour but its capacity to subvert and withstand the boredom of patriarchy. This makes her an ambivalent ally to the Women's Movement. She is like certain shop-stewards who devote so much time to getting up manage-ment's nose that they lose sight of the great goals of socialism.

Her fiction, as opposed to her journalism, is dedicated to the proposition of the battle of the sexes – 'love, the bread and butter of my pen', she observes in a revealing phrase. But, in Colette's battles, the results are fixed, men can never win, unless, as in the short story, 'The Képi', the woman is foolish enough to believe a declaration of love is tantamount to a cessation of hostilities.

In the brief, fragile, ironic novels that are Colette's claim to artistic seriousness, *Ripening Seed*, *The Vagabond*, *Chéri* and *The Last of Chéri*, the men are decorative but useless. The delicious adolescent Phil, in *Ripening Seed*, lolls at ease on the beach while little Vinca arranges their picnic, her role is to serve, but this role makes him a parasite. The beautiful (and economically self-sufficient, as so many of Colette's heroines) lady who seduces him, whom he calls his 'master', is not really Vinca's rival at all, but her fellow conspirator in the ugly plot to 'make a man' of Phil with all that implies of futility and arrogance and complacency.

Renée Néré, the vagabond, tenderly consigns her rich suitor to the condition of a fragrant, unfulfilled memory since that is the only way she can continue to think kindly of him; she knows quite well the truth of the fairy tale is, kiss Prince Charming and he instantly turns into a frog. Léa simply grows out of Chéri, which is tough on Chéri.

The two Chéri novellas probably form Colette's masterpieces, although they are now so 'period' in atmosphere that the luxurious Edwardian décor blurs their hard core of emotional truth. As they recede into history, the décor will disappear; we will be left with something not unlike *Les Liaisons Dangereuses*. They are her masterpieces because they transcend the notion of the battle between the sexes by concentrating on an exceptionally rigorous analysis of the rules of war. Léa's financial independence is, of course, taken for granted; otherwise, in Colette's terms, there would be no possibility of a real relationship.

Julie de Carneilhan, published in 1941, a brief novel about upperclass alimony, is interesting in this respect because it deals specifically with a woman as an economically contingent being. I suspect this is what Colette meant when she said it was as close a reckoning with the elements of her second marriage as she ever allowed herself, since de Jouvenal was theoretically in control of their joint finances for the duration of their relationship. Without financial resources of her own, Julie is duped and stripped of self-respect by her husband, finally taking refuge with her brother and father, an obvious fantasy ending to which the shadow of approaching war promises an appropriately patriarchal resolution. Curiously enough, another war, the First World War, provides the watershed between the two *Chéri* novellas; released from the maternal embrace of Léa, anyone but Colette would have thought the trenches would make a *real* man of Chéri. But she knew it wasn't as simple as that.

The Chéri novels are about the power politics of love, and Léa and Chéri could be almost any permutation of ages or sexes. It is not in the least like *Der Rosenkavalier*, although we first meet Léa in her graceful late forties, some twenty-five years older than her boy lover. But they could both as well be men; or both women. Psychologically, Chéri could just as well be Chérie and Léa, Léo, except that we are socially acclimatised to the sexual vanity of middle-aged men; a handsome, successful, rich, fifty-year-old Léo might well feel that Chéri, at twenty-five, after an affair of six years, was getting a touch long in the tooth for his tastes. But even the age difference is not the point of the stories; the point is, that Léa holds the reins. The only person who could film these novels with a sufficiently cold and dialectical eye is Fassbinder and he is the contemporary artist whom Colette most resembles. Not that she was a political person at all, in the Fassbinder sense, but she watched with a beady eye and drew the correct conclusions.

Given the thrust towards an idealised past of the major part of Colette's work, it is disconcerting to find that the moral of the *Chéri* novellas is: memory kills. When Chéri goes to see his ageing mistress, after the war and an absence of seven years, he finds, not the faded, touching ghost of love and beauty – no Miss Haversham, she – but a fat, jolly, altogether unrecognisable old lady quite unprepared to forgive him for once having flinched from her wrinkles. No tender scene of a visit to Juliet's tomb ensues, but a brisk invitation to grow up and forget which Chéri is temperamentally incapable of accepting. A bullet in the brain is the only way out for Chéri. Léa was forced to reconstruct herself as a human being in order to survive the pain of Chéri's first rejection of her; the reconstructed Léa inevitably destroys Chéri by her very existence.

Colette's 'personal' voice is altogether absent from this parable. All the leading characters are either whores or the children of whores. They are all rich. If Colette set in motion the entire Colette industy in order to create for herself the artistic freedom and privacy to construct this chilling account of libido and false consciousness, then it was all abundantly worthwhile.

Penguin continue to reissue translations of most of Colette by a variety of hands, some of them, especially Antonia White's (the *Claudine* books) conspicuously handier than others. These slim volumes are currently dressed up in melting pinks, tones of pink, mauve and almond green not unlike the colour of Léa's knickers drawer. The exquisitely period photographs on the covers often turn out to depict Colette's own foxy mask, done up in a variety of disguises – a sailor suit for *Gigi*; full drag for *The Pure and the Impure*. The Women's Press put a charcoal drawing of the geriatric Colette, foxier than ever, on their edition of *Break of Day*. The cult of the personality of Colette, to which Michèle Sarde's biography, *Colette*, is a votive tribute, continues apace although it detracts attention from the artist in her, turns her more and more into a figure of historic significance, the woman who *did*, who occupied a key position in a transitional period of social history, from 1873 to 1954, and noted down most of what happened to her.

Apart from the *Chéri* novels and one or two others, her achievement as a whole *was* extraordinary though not in a literary sense; she forged a career out of the kind of self-obsession which is supposed, in a woman, to lead only to tears before bed-time, in a man to lead to the peaks. Good for her. I've got a god-daughter named after her. Or rather, such are the contradictions inherent in all this, named after Captain Jules-Joseph Colette, one-legged tax-gatherer and bankrupt.

London Review of Books, 1980

Also by Angela Carter

THE SADEIAN WOMAN

**'Neither ordinary nor timid, the tone is one of
intellectual relish . . . rational . . . refined . . . witty'
– *Hermione Lee, New Statesman***

'The boldest of English women writers' – *Lorna Sage*

'Sexuality is power' – so says the Marquis de Sade, philosopher
and pornographer extraordinaire. His virtuous Justine keeps to
the rules laid down by men, her reward rape and humiliation;
his Juliette, Justine's triumphantly monstrous antithesis,
viciously exploits her sexuality.

But now Sade has met his match. With invention and genius,
Angela Carter takes on these outrageous figments of his
extreme imagination, and transforms them into symbols of our
time – the Hollywood sex goddesses, mothers and daughters,
pornography, even the sacred shrines of sex and marriage lie
devastatingly exposed before our eyes.

Angela Carter delves in the viscera of our distorted sexuality
and reveals a dazzling vision of love which admits neither of
conqueror nor of conquered.

FIREWORKS

'Fizzing with allegory, symbolism and surprises'
– *The Times*

'Angela Carter is the Salvador Dali of English letters'
– *Daily Telegraph*

Quintessential Angela Carter, *Fireworks* is a dazzling collection of nine short stories.

Here is the ritualism of Tokyo where lovers ponder intangible reflections of themselves, 'reflections of nothing but appearances, in a city dedicated to seeming', and 'the velvet nights spiked with menace' of a wasted London, poised on the brink of destruction. Here also is the marionette Lady Purple, the height of eroticism, whose electric energy is unleashed by a kiss, and the executioner's daughter whose pastel beauty shines incongruously amidst the chronic malevolence of a mountain community fit for Wagnerian cycles. In these extraordinary tales Angela Carter pinpoints the symbolism of city streets and weaves allegories around forests and jungles of strange and erotic landscapes of the imagination.

THE MAGIC TOYSHOP

'Angela Carter has the eye of a trompe d'oeil painter, bringing quite ordinary objects and scenes to vivid, sensuous, disturbing life. This works marvellously in *The Magic Toyshop*' – *Evening Standard*

Melanie walks in the midnight garden wearing her mother's wedding dress; naked she climbs the apple tree in the black of the moon. Disaster swiftly follows, transporting Melanie from rural comfort to London, to the Magic Toyshop; to the red-haired, dancing Finn who kisses her in the ruins of the pleasure gardens; the gentle Francie, who plays curious night music; dumb Aunt Margaret and, brooding over all, the sour and dangerous Uncle Philip whose love is reserved only for his life-sized puppets . . .

Original, visionary, and winner of the 1967 John Llewellyn Rhys Prize, *The Magic Toyshop* was made into a major British film in 1987.

THE PASSION OF NEW EVE

'If you can imagine Baudelaire, Blake and Kafka getting together to describe America, you are well on the way to Carter's visionary and lurid world' – *The Times*

New York has become the City of Dreadful Night where dissolute Leilah performs a dance of chaos for Evelyn. But this young Englishman's fate lies in the arid desert where a many-breasted fertility goddess will wield her scalpel to transform him into the new Eve. This is the story of how Evelyn learns to be a woman – first in the brutal hands of Zero, the one-eyed, one-legged monomaniac poet; then through the gentle touch of the ancient Tristessa, the beautiful ghost of Hollywood past; and, finally, in a deserted Californian cave by the sea.

The Passion of New Eve is an extraordinary journey into the dazzling imagination and apocalyptic vision of one of our most brilliant contemporary writers.

THE VIRAGO BOOK OF FAIRY TALES

'Angela Carter's imagination was one of the most
dazzling this century . . . For her, fantasy always turns
back its eyes to stare hard at reality, never losing sight of
material conditions. She once remarked, "A fairytale is a
story where one king goes to another king to borrow a
cup of sugar."' – *Marina Warner*

Fairy tales are a shorthand way of describing the marvellous
narratives that have been passed down through the generations
by word of mouth. We don't know the names of the people
who made up the stories, but there's a mythical figure, 'Mother
Goose', who knows *all* the stories. *The Virago Book of Fairy
Tales* contains the pick of Mother Goose's feathers. Lyrical
tales, bloody tales, hilariously funny, ripely bawdy, stories that
show the dark and the light side of life – from Europe, the
Arctic, the USA, Africa, the Middle East and Asia.

With a deft and magical touch, Angela Carter has put together
a collection of wonderful, little-known stories, featuring
startling heroines. Be they brave, good, silly, cruel, awesomely
clever or unfortunate, they are always centre stage, as large as
life, even larger.

Once upon a time fairy tales weren't meant just for children,
and neither is *The Virago Book of Fairy Tales*. It's a grown-up
book decorated with equally grown-up pictures – and teenagers
will love it too.

THE SECOND VIRAGO BOOK OF FAIRY TALES

'Trumps Grimm' claimed the *Observer* on the publication of the first volume of *The Virago Book of Fairy Tales*. Such was the delight in Angela Carter's pick of Mother Goose's feathers that she compiled a second volume, once again embracing the wicked, the funny and the bizarre from the Arctic to Asia.

This treasure trove, perfectly complemented by the bewitching drawings of Corinna Sargood, brims with pretty maids and old crones, crafty women and bad girls, enchantresses and midwives, rascal aunts and odd sisters.

The Second Virago Book of Fairy Tales is a fabulous celebration of strong minds, low cunning, black arts and dirty tricks – and a wonderful gift to us all, as could only have been collected by the unique Angela Carter.